REACH FOR ME

ALSO BY ELIZABETH COLE

Keep Me Close

Honor & Roses

Choose the Sky

Raven's Rise

Peregrine's Call

A Heartless Design

A Reckless Soul

A Shameless Angel

The Lady Dauntless

Beneath Sleepless Stars

A Mad and Mindless Night

A Most Relentless Gentleman

Regency Rhapsody:

The Complete Collection

REACH FOR ME

ELIZABETH COLE

SKYSPARK BOOKS

PHILADELPHIA, PENNSYLVANIA

SkySpark Books
Philadelphia, Pennsylvania
skysparkbooks.com
inquiry@skysparkbooks.com

Publisher's Note: This is a work of fiction. Names, characters, places, and incidents are a product of the author's imagination. Locales and public names are sometimes used for atmospheric purposes. Any resemblance to actual people, living or dead, or to businesses, companies, events, institutions, or locales is completely coincidental.

Ordering Information:
Quantity sales. Special discounts are available on quantity purchases by corporations, associations, and others. For details, contact the "Special Sales Department" at the address above.

REACH FOR ME / Cole, Elizabeth. – 1st ed.
ISBN-13: 978-1-942316-38-1

I

In the middle of the country, there was a midwestern state.

And in the middle of the midwestern state, there was a county.

And in the middle of the county, there was a town.

And way the hell on the edge of town, there was a hill.

And on that hill, there was a house.

And in that house was a…GHOST.

OR SOMETHING LIKE A GHOST. Cara had to admit the house looked haunted.

But she wasn't here to de-haunt the place. She was here to restore it.

Maybe that amounted to the same thing.

The house glowered down from the top of the hill. Cara peered through the windshield, craning her neck to catch the whole thing. She'd never seen it in person before, and none of the pictures did justice to the situation.

Built by an oil baron back when American oil barons were a thing, the house was a legitimate masterpiece: three stories of red brick, with a legit turret in the front corner, and lots of once-fancy details that were now rusting and rotting. Parts of the iron fence surrounding the yard had been stolen over the decades. The main part of the house and one wing still stood, but nearly all the windows were broken. Their shutters hung crazily or were missing altogether.

3

Not much survived the fire.

The fire happened in the late 1920s, and it destroyed a whole wing of the house, disrupting the symmetry of the design, and leaving the rest of the structure permanently damaged. Daniel Egan, the oil baron, apparently tried to repair it. But the Great Depression erased the Egan family fortune, and then World War II erased the Egan family bloodline, since both the sons died on the front. A trust maintained the property—barely—since then.

And then someone got the idea to restore it. And that was why Cara was here.

Cara Michaels knew the building industry inside and out, since she'd practically been raised on construction sites. She also had a genuine talent for woodworking. With that combination, her fledging business promised authentic historic home restoration no matter how unique the house.

Cara was excited beyond belief to get the job of restoring Egan House, undoubtedly the most unique and challenging site she'd ever heard of. If she succeeded here, she could bid for any job in the country. National landmarks, famous homes…anything.

"I got this," she told herself, turning into the drive and plowing up the hill.

Up close, Egan House looked even more ramshackle and broken. Shrubbery and overgrowth obscured much of the first floor, but the parts she could see looked rough. Rotten door frames, worm-eaten wood, crumbling brick…

"This is going to be great!" Cara whispered, her nerdy historical restoration tendencies fully engaged.

She stopped the car behind the house and got out. The growing light was filling the sky, the sun itself about to rise over the eastern tree line. Cara stepped up onto the wide back porch, which creaked alarmingly.

The back door was open. Cold clamminess hit her the moment she crossed the threshold. The air here was still and almost icy, decades of solitude undisturbed. The past was almost palpable, pushing right up against the present, unwilling to be put aside.

"I'm going to make you shine," Cara told the house. "We're going to clean you up and make you just like you used to be. You're going to be a home again."

The house, of course, did not respond. Houses never did, because they were houses. Cara didn't believe in much, and her house-whispering was just a quirk. But some old houses had personality, and she was getting a standoffish vibe from this one.

Oh, well. She'd bring it around. Cara was better with buildings than she was with people.

Her happy anticipation was cut short when she heard a sharp creak up above. Was someone in the house? No one was allowed to be here other than the work crew, and Cara was the first person to arrive on site. So why were there sounds?

Maybe it was just the house settling.

The distinctive patter of running footsteps quashed that theory.

She retreated to the car and pulled out a powerful flashlight from the toolbox in the back, the long one with the metal housing. It worked great as a flashlight, but it would also work great as a club, if it came to that. Cara marched back to the house, switched the flashlight on, and turned toward the sounds.

"Hello?" Cara called. "Who's up there?"

There was no answer, but Cara smelled smoke.

Without thinking twice, she ran up the central staircase. If some homeless person was squatting here and started a fire, her job could go up in flames before she even got a chance to pick up a hammer.

"Hey!" she yelled as she reached the second-floor landing. "Who's here? If you started a fire, you gotta put it out *now*. I won't call the cops on you, but it's not safe here!"

No answer.

Cara sniffed, and again caught the smell of smoke. She moved to the left-hand side of the hallway, where it seemed to be coming from.

The first room was empty, but a connecting door led to another room, and the smoke was stronger there.

"Hello?" she called again, nervous that the unseen person might get violent. "Is someone up here?"

She heard a scraping sound, like a door opening over a gritty surface. Cara rushed into the next room, hoping to catch whoever it was.

But this room was empty too. Cara looked around in frustration. There was a closed door on the far wall, and a faint sound from beyond. The person was hiding from her.

Her anger growing stronger than her fear, Cara stalked over to the door and wrenched it open, remembering too late that if you suspected a fire, you weren't supposed to open doors, and you should check if the doorknobs felt hot.

All she saw was yet another empty room. Empty of people, that was. A few wooden chairs lay on their sides, one smashed to bits, as if someone hurled it across the room. No trace of fire. No charred wood. No ashes.

In fact, the room was cold as ice. Cara shivered and wrapped her arms around herself, the flashlight's beam bouncing around the room as she did.

Just as the beam careened across the wall, Cara spied a figure in the brief spot of light.

She screamed before she could stop herself. Just a tiny yelp, but embarrassing even in her terror. Cara fumbled the light back to the right spot. No one was there.

"What the hell?" Cara's voice sounded weak in the empty room, the sound ricocheting off the walls. "Who's here?"

She spun around with her light, circling the room to catch the other person. But there was nothing to see. Cara's skin prickled and she winced as a wave of dizziness hit her after the sudden spin.

GO AWAY.

It wasn't a voice in the air, but in her heart.

Cara backed up, startled and ready to run.

GO AWAY.

The order came at her with the force of a battering ram, and Cara's knees wobbled.

Ok. Leaving. Leaving now, she told herself.

She raced through the rooms in reverse order. She knew the blueprints of this house, but at the moment, her mind was a total blank. She couldn't say which doors went where. Was she too far to the south? How big was this wing?

At last she reached the central landing with the staircase. Cara stepped gingerly as she realized just how shaky the stairs were. She reached the bottom, and then heard what could only be described as a *shriek* from up above.

Cara didn't wait. She hurled herself toward the doorway she'd entered from, panic rising. She had to GO outside, AWAY from this awful house.

She didn't see or hear anything else as she crossed the threshold.

Until she ran smack into a body.

And what a body.

The man who stood there was…hot. He wore nothing but gym shorts that came to his knees. Which left the rest of him fully on display.

He stood over six feet, making him almost a foot taller than Cara. He was big too, with broad shoulders and a chest that might have its own zip code. But none of that bulk was fat. It was all muscle. Big biceps, sinewy tough arms. His legs looked even more cut, if that were possible. Even his feet and hands looked like they could crush steel.

Cara always figured that six-pack abs were something faked with Photoshop. Nope. This guy had them.

He looked like a fighter, one of those guys who fought in matches in Vegas.

Cara took a breath to steady herself, and simultaneously remembered the reason she smacked right into this guy. She asked, "Do you smell smoke?"

"What?"

"Do you smell smoke?" she repeated. "I thought I did. That's why I went inside."

He went still, as if his whole being was trying to identify any smoke in the air. He looked tense, but then shook his head slowly. "No. No smoke."

Cara sniffed the air again. Damp, musty, mildewy. But not smoky. "Maybe it was just something in the wind?" she asked, more to herself than him.

"I would have seen smoke or flames coming up the drive."

"Why are you here, by the way? This is a work site, and only workers can have access."

He nodded as if she were an idiot. "Yeah. I'm a worker. My name's Malachy. Malachy East."

"Workers wear shirts," she said, rather tartly. "And pants."

"I'm going to change. Shift doesn't start for a half hour. I was just making this the end point of my morning workout."

He must work out full-time to achieve that physique. Cara wished her own decidedly not buff body would melt into a puddle and flow right into the nearest ditch.

After way too awkward a silence, he said, "I'm a worker. What's your excuse?"

She pulled herself to her full five feet two inches. "I'm Cara Michaels. I'm the foreman."

"Wouldn't it be forewoman?"

She raised her chin. "I'm de-gendering the term."

"How woke of you."

Ok, enough chitchat. "I'm pretty conservative actually, Mr. East. Like with my insistence that workers be dressed."

"Call me Mal." He said his name just slow enough that the sound had substance to it. *Maaaaalll*, like slow moving honey.

Annoyingly, he was not just ripped, he had great features too. Strong cheekbones and jaw, not to mention big brown eyes and very dark hair that hung long, almost to the base of his neck.

The kind of guy who never looked twice at Cara.

Except that he was looking at her hard now. "Why are you the foreman? Did you buy the property?"

"Like I could afford it," she said, far more bitterly than she intended. "I'm a licensed carpenter, and I specialize in historic restorations. This place is going to look amazing when it's done." Cara was unable to restrain herself from boasting a bit.

"Better post a bunch of before shots on Instagram, or no one will believe you."

"No photos! You can't post anything. No one can," Cara snapped back. It was one of the injunctions Mr. Morningside, the attorney, had laid down when she took the job. She wasn't allowed to let anyone on the property other than the hired workers and any inspectors who might be needed. She could take photos to chronicle her work, but she wasn't allowed to publish anything until the project was completed. "My client is very concerned about privacy."

Mal's lip curled into a sneer. "I bet."

Cara couldn't parse that response, and didn't want to. "Get changed into work gear, East. And next time I see you, you'd better be wearing a hard hat."

"You're not local."

Cara blinked at the non sequitur. "No. Why?"

Mal gave her a smile that made her body go all warm and buzzy. "Maybe you need someone to show you around."

"From what I can tell, there's not that much *around* to show."

"Oh, there's a few places. How about dinner tomorrow?"

The warm feeling spiked into an unpleasant heat as embarrassment washed over her. Cara just met this smoking-hot guy she was going to work with, and he was asking her to dinner? What kind of nasty trick was he planning? Hauling Cara to an all-you-can-eat buffet and leaving her there?

"How about no."

His forehead wrinkled a bit, like he didn't understand the words she spoke. "No?" he echoed.

"No. Not tomorrow, not ever."

Mal said nothing, still looking confused. He blinked, and then said once more, "No?"

"It means the opposite of yes," Cara explained as she maneuvered around him, intent on walking to her car and then to the prefab office trailer that had been delivered to the site. "If you're actually here at the beginning of the shift, you'll hear the spiel. Later, Malachy East."

II

MAL WATCHED THE WOMAN SWEEP past him on her way to her car. When she first ran into him, he caught only an impression of lushness, the smell of coffee and sawdust, and then a vivid sight when the morning sun hit her hair. Bright red like a fire engine, long and heavy. He could practically feel it against his fingers.

Her personality didn't match the soft look, to judge by how no-nonsense she was. She quizzed him and basically doubted he was really a worker. And then slammed down a simple invitation to dinner. Mal saw the way she'd looked at him before she got all salty about his wardrobe. Definitely interested.

But Cara went cold fast, ignoring him as she went to her car. She leaned into the back seat, putting one knee on the upholstery, and treated Mal to another look at her very full backside as she pawed through the stuff on the seat. A perfect ass. Big, beautiful, grabbable.

For a moment, she was just a leg, encased in tight jeans, revealed inch by inch as she crawled back out. Shapely calf, downright plump thigh. Then she wiggled back into open air, her hands hooked into a bankers box that must have weighed a ton, with yet more rolled papers stacked on the top.

He almost offered to help carry the box, except that she locked eyes with him and gave him a death glare. Ok, no chivalry this morning.

She huffed out a breath, kicked the door closed, and made her way to the boxy, prefab office trailer that all construction sites seemed to require. She didn't appear again, and Mal realized that he really did need to get dressed, or he'd get fired before he even picked up a hammer.

A half hour later, Mal was back on site, dressed and ready for work, exchanging small talk with the other guys who showed up. None of them knew each other, and all applied for the job online, just like Mal. However, he doubted any of the other guys knew the history of Egan House. To them, it was just a paycheck.

Mal was hoping to save the world.

Unknown to Cara Michaels, Mal lived right across the street from Egan House, and he was familiar with its features. Specifically, it sat on an interdimensional portal.

The fire that destroyed the house back in the day apparently also blocked the portal to the otherworlds—colloquially known as a hellhole.

The Salem family had known about the hellhole for years. That was why Aunt Josephine originally got the house across the street. It was a good assignment for a mostly retired demon-hunter. And Aunt Jo had been quite a hunter in her day.

But age caught up with her, and mounting health problems meant that she couldn't keep watch on the hellhole if it did become active again. The Salem family convened, as it did regularly, and discussed the matter of Aunt Jo's assignment. It was decided that "the boys" would be the best choice to take over. They were young, without attachments to anyone but each other, and none of them owned any place. Aunt Jo grumbled about it, but she acceded to the family's decision.

For the better part of a year, Dominic, Mal, and Lex lived at the old house. Their job was to continue Jo's work. Mal quickly got sick of watching the house because nothing evil seemed to be happening. But watching the house was his job. More than his job. His duty.

Salems fought evil. Hellholes were evil.

Or rather, hellholes allowed evil into the world. So Mal had to watch it, and whenever the evil started to emerge, he could go and kick evil's ass.

Still, nothing seemed to be happening.

But then things changed. A permit to improve the property was posted at the front gate, along with a sign advertising job positions on the site. Mal wanted one of those positions, and he lied about his identity a little, just in case someone would recognize the name Salem and get curious. He also lied about his address. And his work history.

Ok, he lied a lot to get the job.

But sometimes you had to do bad things for good reasons.

Still chatting idly with the other guys, Mal was distracted at the sight of Cara emerging from the office trailer. The sun hit her like a spotlight.

"Who's that?" one of the guys muttered.

She pulled her long, lovely hair into a ponytail and tucked it away under a hard hat she pulled from nowhere, then walked over to them. The workers all stood in a semicircle, waiting to see what was going to happen. No one had seen her before, and Mal doubted that any of them had heard the foreman was actually a forechick.

She pulled out her clipboard. "Ok. Quick roll call. Dan."

"Uh, that's me." A guy half raised his hand, like he was in school and she was a teacher. Dan was rail-thin and wiry, with shaggy hair and a seventies mustache. He was the oldest of the crew.

"Reyes."

"*Si*. Yes, ma'am." Reyes was short and stocky. He had one of those open, friendly faces, with brilliantly white teeth in a wide smile.

"Barry."

"How you doin'," Barry drawled. Everything about him, from his shoulders to his Steelers cap, said that he was once the star of his high school football team and still thought he was God's gift to the whole town.

"Jalen."

"Yeah." That was the black man who spoke. He barely looked at her, and Mal privately marked him down as one of those perennially surly types. Didn't matter, as long he got the job done.

"Malachy," she said, looking at him like she'd never seen him before.

"Call me Mal," he responded, more for the guys' benefit, since Cara already knew that and seemed determined to ignore it.

"And that makes you Kevin," she said to the final person.

"Yep." Kevin was a compact dude, not much taller than Reyes. Mal guessed he was the brainiest of the bunch.

She nodded, satisfied that her paperwork was in order. "Morning, gentlemen. You were hired for this job by Morningside Law Offices. My name is Cara Michaels. Mr. Morningside selected me to head up this project because I have a background in historical preservation and restoration. As you've undoubtedly realized, I'm a woman."

"Yeah, we got that," Barry said, grinning at her.

Cara didn't return his smile. She looked them all over. Her icy gaze lingered on Mal for a split second longer. "Here's the rules about that. As far as you're concerned, all of you, I'm your boss. You do not flirt with me. You do not hit on me. You do not ask me out. You do not assume I'm an idiot who wandered onto this site by mistake. When I tell you to do something, you do it. Other than that, all the usual rules of grown-up jobs apply. Show up on time, follow directions, and keep to the schedule. Am I really fucking clear?"

There was a moment of startled silence.

Finally, Dan spoke. "Really fucking clear…boss."

"Good." Now she smiled, and Mal wished she'd smile more, because when she did, she was less scary. "This house looks like a wreck now, but we are going to bring it back to its glory days. Mr. Morningside has given the go-ahead for a full restoration, and that means we'll have the budget to do right by this place."

"Where do we start?" Kevin asked. They all looked a little overwhelmed by the scope of the project.

"Clean up," Cara responded promptly. "I want half the team to work on the interior of the house. Pull out any debris, get it in the dumpsters, and note any unsafe areas with spray paint. The other half of you will clear the surrounding yard and make sure we can move equipment around and access the storage areas where supplies will be organized. I'm going to get the office in shape and review the blueprints before I tour the house. Knock on the office door if you have questions. Lunch is one hour, eleven to noon, and we knock off at four unless we get behind schedule. Ok? Get to work!"

Cara nodded to them and turned to walk back up the steps to the trailer.

"Wow," Reyes said after the office door closed. That statement could have a dozen meanings, and Mal thought that probably all of them applied. Cara had a…forceful personality.

"We're going to take orders from a damn girl?" Barry asked. "How do we know she knows anything?"

"Probably wouldn't have got the job if she didn't," Dan countered.

"Or she slept with the real boss," Barry said with a dirty grin, obviously picturing the scenario. "Some guys like 'em big."

"Not cool, man," Jalen said shortly.

Barry grinned wider, responding, "Bet you like 'em big, huh? That's, like, part of your culture."

Mal took a breath. *Do not punch someone your first hour on the job.*

Jalen, who must have had a side gig as a Zen master, simply took a few steps into the yard, as if deciding where he was going to plunk down a lawn chair.

Mal relaxed. If Jalen could handle it, so could he. "We should split up and get started," he said, hoping to get into the house and see if the existence of the hellhole was evident to ordinary people.

But Barry had different ideas. And Mal knew that by the time this job was over, he was going to make Barry very sorry he'd ever joined the crew.

III

AT THE END OF A backbreaking day, Mal hauled himself home. He had to wait until the others left, because he didn't want to explain that he lived literally across the street. Cara's vehicle remained, and the lights blazed in the office trailer. Everything about her said workaholic, but at least it meant her attention was not on Mal.

He reached his front porch, and the door opened before he could even take out his key. His younger brother, Lex, beamed at him. "You smell terrible and look worse. How was your first day?"

"Interesting." Mal was in no mood to talk about it, but he had to, because his brothers were relying on him to be the eyes and ears of this operation.

Operation Hellhole, Lex called it, only half joking. Once the brothers realized that the house was going to be worked on, it seemed like an inspired move to get one of them onto the actual construction crew. That way, they'd get firsthand knowledge of what was happening. The only downside was that Mal was the only plausible choice as the undercover Salem. Dominic was too important to the brothers' business to commit to a long-term job—he might have to leave town at any point if a paying client called. And Lex didn't exactly project the right image for the role. Mal did. Big and physical, Mal looked like he should be driving a bulldozer or just hauling lumber around. He was very aware that his strength was…his strength. He didn't resent it. But he was still damn tired at the end of the day.

"I thought you'd be hungry," Lex said. "I made a little extra for dinner."

Dom walked into the kitchen. "Oh, good. I can't wait to eat." He wrinkled his nose when he got within sniffing distance of Mal. "But shower first."

Agreed. That comment came from Behemoth, a big black cat who was curled up on an armchair. *I've been in charnel houses that smelled better.*

"Shut up." Mal didn't need the cats piling on too. He showered in record time, his growling stomach providing motivation. When he dried off and pulled on his clean but worn sweats, another cat sauntered up. The little calico sniffed at him, and then conveyed her opinion.

Much better. Now come feast.

"Thanks for the vote of confidence, Pie." Piewicket purred when Mal scooped her up and walked her downstairs. She was definitely the sweeter of the two cats.

Lex's *little extra* proved to be a huge lasagna casserole, garlic bread, a side of pork chops, and an apple pie for dessert.

Lex also said the Salem family's grace that night. "May this food feed us, bless us, and give us the strength to stand for those who cannot fight for themselves. Those we love who cannot be with us now, may your spirits always be welcome. Amen."

"How is pork a side?" Vinny asked after grace, regarding the platter of meat with suspicion in her eyes.

Mal smiled at Dom's very recent—and very decent— love interest. "Don't be normative, Vin. Pork is a side if we say it is."

Her real name was Lavinia, but she went by Vinny, which was basically all you needed to know about her as a person. Vinny was platinum blonde, tough as nails, and took shit from exactly nobody. Mal was actually a little intimidated by her. But since she was very likely going to be his sister-in-law at some point, he figured he'd better get over it.

Since moving in with the Salems a few months ago, Vinny unofficially took over as the office manager of their family business. She organized their financial system—ok, she made a system out of the piled up chaos from before. She spoke to potential clients, she arranged the brothers' schedules and jobs. She organized the pantry.

When Mal once commented on her weird ability to manage a demon-hunting business when she hadn't known demons existed three months ago, Vinny had said, 'Demons aside, it's not that much different from any other business. You got income, you got expenses. If I can manage tours for bands composed entirely of drunken punk rockers, I can do this.'

Now Vinny made a face as she passed Mal the plate of pork chops. "Enjoy your meat orgy. I'll stick to the salad."

Lex just laughed. "Mal's a growing boy and needs his strength to rebuild the hellhole house."

"Speaking of that," Dom said. "What does the hellhole look like? What state is it in?"

"I didn't see it directly," Mal explained. "I was stuck on outside duty today. Apparently, Mexicans excel at yardwork. That's what Barry said anyway, when he put me and Reyes out there. Never mind that Reyes is from El Salvador. And I'm only half-Mexican." The other half was Irish, but no one ever asked Mal about his thoughts on Guinness. His de Silva side was a lot more visible.

The mood at the table turned arctic. Dom, in the act of putting a giant square of lasagna on his plate, stopped and said, "Who did what now? How hard did you punch him?"

"Barry is a guy on the crew who fancies himself a manager. He took one look at Reyes and me and said we'd be perfect for landscaping. Oh, and Jalen too, though he's black. And I didn't punch anyone." Yet. Mal had plans to kick Barry's ass at some point. He had to admit the irony of the racist dude being correct in this instance. In the yard, Reyes explained that he actually did work in landscaping—his cousin's business—for ten years, and Jalen said he had five years' experience with a tree maintenance business down in Florida. They all laughed about it, and agreed that Barry was a tool.

"You are not getting paid enough for this," Lex muttered after swallowing his food.

Mal shrugged. "A day's delay won't matter. I didn't want to push things by complaining about being on outside duty. The foreman already doesn't like me."

"What'd you do?"

"Uh, nothing. But she seems like she doesn't really like anyone so far. Probably because she didn't personally choose us. She said all the hiring went through the law firm that controls the trust."

Vinny raised a hand. "She?"

He briefly told about Cara, and produced a business card he'd liberated from her car during lunch. "Michaels Historic Homes. There's a website. I'll check it out and see if it's legit."

Everyone had more questions about the house, and Mal answered them as best he could. Mostly, he promised that he'd get inside the next day.

"We need eyes on that hellhole," Dom said. "I have to know what it looks like. Take lots of pictures."

That would be difficult, especially since Cara warned him specifically against photos. But maybe he could get a moment alone and get some shots.

"Pie time," Vinny interrupted once the main dishes were demolished. "Lex, when did you make pie today?"

"I didn't. It was in the fridge," Lex confessed.

Mal said, "Yeah, Sheri made it. She wanted my help with something yesterday, and I wouldn't let her pay me. But you know her. She couldn't let me out of the house empty-handed."

"And she paid you in…pie?" Lex raised an eyebrow.

"Yes. *Just* pie."

"It's not fair," Dom said as he took a piece. "You've got like seventy exes and they're all basically nice. I had one ex and she turned into a literal vampire."

"She also didn't make pie like Sheri's," Lex added, wiping apple goo from his mouth.

Sheri did make a damn fine pie. Mal ate two pieces and thought about why things with her didn't work out. Sheri was super nice, not to mention hotter than a supermodel. Maybe he was freaked out by the fact she had a kid from a previous boyfriend. Mal didn't think he was old enough to be a decent father figure, and he was definitely not ready to settle down.

Meanwhile, Lex was eyeing the business card in the center of the table. He loved research. He read out,

Michaels Historic Homes

Restoration and Preservation

Cara Michaels, principal

Lex grabbed his laptop and went immediately to the website listed on the card.

They crowded around to see, and it sure looked legit.

There was a big photo gallery, which made sense. Lex skimmed dozens and dozens of photos of jobs—before and after shots that looked like something out of a magazine. The before shots looked like houses that had been condemned, and the after shots looked…amazing. Not just cleaned up rooms, but new walls and lots of custom touches that must cost a fortune. Carved wood panels and columns. Bookcases, fireplace mantels. Staircases that looked like some king was about to walk down them. Wooden sculptures.

"Wish we could hire her for our place," Lex joked.

"I doubt we could afford it." Dom pointed to a picture of a room with hand-carved columns with the appearance of vines growing all up and down them. "That's the kind of thing that millionaires do."

"What's that one?" Mal asked. Lex obligingly expanded one shot, which was of Cara bending over a wood carving on a table, tools in her hands as she did some detail work on it. It was one of the few photos with her in the picture. Maybe she was usually the person taking the pictures. Maybe she was camera shy. Maybe both.

"I think she's the one actually carving all this stuff," he said. One thing he could tell for sure was that she was the real deal. Whatever else she might be, Cara was a skilled professional.

"You got to get in there, Mal," his brother said seriously. "If this girl is so good, we need to know exactly what she's working on. And if she knows what she's doing—magically, I mean."

Mal chewed his lower lip. Maybe she was just a regular person, hired to do a job, with no awareness of the house's history or its supernatural qualities.

Of course, that didn't make her less of a threat.

"This girl, is she going to be a problem for you?" Dom asked.

"What do you mean?"

Lex interjected, "He means are you going to screw this up because you're going to try to screw her."

"Whoa. She's not my type."

Dom raised an eyebrow. "She sounds like your type. And by that I mean she has a pulse."

"Shut up," Mal said sulkily. He wasn't *that* bad.

"You are that bad," Lex said. Lex wasn't a mind reader, but he sometimes hit the mark way too well.

The last thing Mal should do after a long day's work and a huge dinner was work out, but he felt restless. He headed downstairs, having been excused from washing up by Vinny, who told him he was more likely to break all the dishes than clean them.

Mal's workout space occupied most of the basement. He had a heavy bag, a speed bag, and a few dummies with sensitive spots painted with targets on the surface.

He did his usual warm-up routine. Speed drills, forms, everything to keep him in condition to fight. Once warmed up, he moved into more complex sequences, testing his speed and reactions. And then he started adding his own, very particular practice.

After years of training, Mal knew how to dance right on the border of the otherworlds, slipping in and out, using the border both as cover and a tunnel. People on the outside, in the real world, only saw that Mal moved *fast*, faster than he ought to. They didn't know that he was basically cheating, taking a shortcut through another dimension, only to pop back into the real world in exactly the right place to land a perfect hit.

Mal was driven to excel at fighting, because fighting was the only thing he could excel at. He wasn't magically gifted like Dom, able to cast spells with such speed and confidence that it left observers astonished—or destroyed, in the case of demons and vampires. He didn't have Lex's incredible intelligence, his spongelike brain that soaked up every scrap of knowledge and somehow stored it like a supercomputer.

But Mal could kick ass. And he would keep doing it as long as his body held out. That was what his brothers needed him to do, and he'd never let them down.

Until I lose.

The thought popped up, as it often did when he was alone. It was not a good thought. Not a thought that helped him as a fighter. A few of his teachers explicitly addressed the issue of overthinking. A lot of times, a fighter's biggest enemy was his own doubt, not his opponent's physical strength.

He'd learned meditation to help deal with that, to stay in the moment, to put aside past regrets and future fears.

It worked most of the time.

But there was always this one thought, worse than a nightmare. At least he could wake up from nightmares.

The thought was simple, and logical, and chilling.

There was going to be a fight that he would lose. He'd be too weak, or too tired, or too old, or just unlucky. He'd lose and he'd get killed. And he would leave Dom or Lex open to the next attack. And their deaths would be his fault.

Mal tensed up, unable to shut down images of Lex or Dom dead because he failed to keep them safe. Or worse than dead. There were vampires in the world who wanted nothing more than to turn Dom into one of them, to make him into the thing he hated most.

Or Lex, sweet little Lex, trapped in some demon's pocket hell, to be a plaything for eternity.

"Breathe," he told himself. "Just breathe." He counted his breaths, like he'd been taught. He tried to let the thought go, just for a while. He tried to focus on the present. He reminded himself that he had a job to do.

The Salems did not have a safe occupation. But at least Dom and Lex had Mal at their backs.

After a few minutes, he felt a little calmer. He stretched his arms, rolled his head and neck to relax his muscles. It was all too much to think about.

What are you doing. The comment came into his mind at the same moment the massive black cat sauntered into the basement.

"I'm exercising."

You're exhausted, and you need to be awake tomorrow to keep your position. Or else what has all this been for? The years of your family watching and waiting? Just so you can squander the best shot you have at seeing the enemy?

"The construction crew is not the enemy."

You don't know what they are, Behemoth warned. *Now go to bed, and stop being a fool, Malachy Salem.*

He made a face at the cat, but went upstairs.

He'd insisted to his brothers that Cara was not his type, but when he went to bed that night, he couldn't shake off the thought of her. He could picture her face, her pouty lips opening when he got his hands in her hair and pulled her close. He could almost hear her moan when he kissed her, hard and deep, with their tongues sliding in and out, sparking more need in his groin. Damn, he could smell her, that combination of coffee and sawdust and varnish that shouldn't be remotely sexy, but if it wasn't, then why was the simple memory of that scent getting him hard right now? He'd just *met* her that morning.

Mal suppressed a groan, and hesitated only a second before letting his hand drop down, circling his cock. He envisioned Cara's red hair, but this time falling over bare shoulders and just grazing her nipples, hard and pink and totally exposed for him to see. He imagined how her tits would move during sex, and the resulting brain porn had him turning his head into the pillow so he wouldn't wake up the rest of the house with his pathetic panting.

He wanted to slow down, to enjoy this unexpected fantasy of curvy, sexy Cara, who hated him on sight. But she couldn't be all hate. He'd seen the way she looked him over when they met. Sure, she huffed and told him to put on a shirt, but not until she got a good eyeful.

It took half a second to rewrite that script. Now Cara didn't ask him to put anything on, and instead walked right up and ran her hands down his torso and told him to take his pants off. The idea of her touching him made him stiffen even more, and Mal worked himself shamelessly as he kept his mind on Cara.

The second he imagined her in a bed, underneath him, begging him for more, he knew he'd gone over the edge. He gasped once as his balls tightened before he came, hard, riding out the wave of pure pleasure, like a hit of something extremely illegal.

Mal exhaled, his body relaxing. He'd made a mess, leaving the sheets sticky, like he was a teenager still waking from wet dreams. But for this moment, it was worth it. His breathing smoothed out, the tension he'd been carrying now gone.

Why had Cara got him so worked up? She wasn't anything special. He'd dated way hotter girls, girl who knew just what to wear and how to smile to make the most of what they had.

But it wasn't any of those girls who just got him hard by the memory of her sawdust-laced hair.

"Oh, no," he groaned when he felt a stirring in his body. No way was he going to rub another one out, not tonight. He was tired. He was a grown man. He was not some hormone-fueled snot who'd just discovered the internet.

Think of her on top, that hair falling down... Mal's body was already reacting to that image, ramping up for another go. What was wrong with him?

His last hookup was only a week ago, and it had been great. Fun time, no commitment, no confusion. What was her name? Lindsey. Blonde. Leggy. Pool shark, super funny, hot. They both had a good time, and Lindsey told him to call her if he was up for a rematch. Pool or sex.

He could call. Mal bet that Lindsey would clear her schedule, even this late at night.

Or he could lie here and keep thinking of Cara. He didn't want a blonde in his bed. He wanted a redhead.

A redhead named Cara.

What if she's kinky? Mal's head rolled back a little at that thought. What kind of kink might Cara be into, and how hot would that be? Cara in restraints, maybe? Or Mal in restraints? He'd take either scenario.

He'd take whatever she offered, actually. Again and again and again, until he got her out of his system.

He fell asleep at last, but, like Mal, 5:00 a.m. came way too fast.

IV

Cara was back at work the next day at dawn. The project caught hold of her in a way no previous work had done.

She parked at the bottom of the hill, figuring that the walk up would do her good. As she got out, she got a much better look at the house right across the street. To call it a dump would be generous. It was an old Victorian, three stories tall and clearly once a beauty. Cara got angry on behalf of the house as she cataloged all the indignities it suffered over the years. Paint cracked and peeling. A bay window practically falling out of the wall. The roof sagging in parts. The front porch supported by a stack of concrete blocks in one corner. And all over, the wonderful original gingerbread detailing was rotten or entirely gone.

I could fix it up, she thought, feeling the familiar urge to make things beautiful. Then, *Hold up, sweetie. It's not like you're getting paid for that one.*

She glanced at the mailbox to her right. The name SALEM was stenciled in block letters onto the metal box, which was tilted at a crazy angle because the post it was attached to had been hit by a truck, or possibly a dozen trucks. She wrinkled her nose. She really hated it when people didn't take care of their homes.

But then, maybe the owner wasn't physically capable of maintenance. Cara tried to rein in her judginess. She'd hate to blame this wreckage on some frail old man who lived sad and alone here at the edge of town.

Something moved in the corner of her vision. A little calico rounded the side of the house and stopped as soon as it caught sight of Cara.

"Hey there," Cara said, feeling very awkward about talking to a cat almost too far away to hear. "This your place? I see you don't wait for Halloween to decorate."

The cat did not reply. It just regarded her with the sort of steady, unblinking stare that only cats could get away with.

Cara shifted her attention to the mailbox again. It annoyed her, and it also gave her an idea. She smiled at the cat. "Just you wait," she whispered.

Unaccountably cheerful, Cara turned and headed slowly up the drive to Egan House. Talk about getting a jump on Halloween. The place was a classic spook house from a 1950s horror film. If the owner wanted to skip the restoration and just operate the place as a haunted house tour, they'd make a killing.

But maybe that was one of the reasons Morningside's client was being secretive. Didn't want the bad press that came with stories of haunted houses and ghost tales.

Well, once Cara was done, all the news about this place would be positive.

That's what she silently told herself anyway. She had to keep her spirits up. It was difficult enough being the only woman on a construction site. It was way tougher when she was in the authority position. A lot of guys didn't react well to taking orders from a woman. Half the time, they didn't believe she knew what she was talking about. Until she slapped on a hard hat, pulled on work gloves, and proved it.

But damn, it was tiring to have to prove it over and over. Each new job was a new challenge, since she moved around the country and always had a new crew to work with.

This group seemed better than most. The first day had been a test to see how they worked together. She liked to see how the dynamic shook out among employees. Letting them figure out who was on what team told her a lot about them.

The crew had indeed split up, without any fuss or manly displays of hierarchy. The outside team appeared to be Reyes, Jalen, and Mal. Reyes had waved to her from the seat of the earthmover he was driving, using the gigantic blade as a shovel to push fallen branches and random trash out of the way. Jalen walked slowly across the property, head down, sticking flags into the ground to mark the old pipes and electrical. Hitting those by accident would be bad.

When she'd looked at Mal, he'd been carrying a literal tree trunk over his shoulder, a caveman display of strength that set her teeth on edge, and definitely had no effect on the lower part of her belly. At least Mal hadn't seen her watching. He seemed like the kind of guy who enjoyed making women all flustered. And it didn't help that he was the hottest man on the crew. Kevin was cute, but married. Dan was also married. Reyes was a little too old, and she didn't like the way Barry leered at her. Jalen was a dish, but he was also antisocial. He barely looked at Cara when she talked to him.

Nope. Cara was smart to keep to her ethical stance of never dating someone she worked with. It was too messy, and would ruin any respect she fought to earn. Mal would have to take his ridiculously ripped body and panty-melting, smoldery gaze elsewhere. Not that he was really interested. He probably just asked her to dinner out of habit, or with the aim to get a raise.

Ugh, stop thinking of him.

Cara unlocked the office trailer and hit the light on. Yesterday, she'd worked on making the temporary construction trailer into a proper work space. She set up a desk in one corner, with a couple chairs and a filing cabinet. A large table occupied the center, where she placed the blueprints to roll out later. She'd have to reference them every day, because the architecture and design of the house was unique. These prefab trailers were essential on job sites where the actual building was in no shape for habitation, like Egan House. But they were also plain and ugly, and Cara always wished there was a way to spruce them up. But what was the point? In a couple of months, she'd be on a different job site, in a different prefab trailer, and it would start all over again.

"Stay in the present moment, girl," she told herself.

She should be happy right here, right now. Finally, she had the perfect job to fit her skills. And even better, her client wanted the very best work, and was willing to pay for the right materials and the labor to do it well. Cara would still have taken the job—she had to eat—but it was awesome that she was going to be able to really do right by the house.

Armed with rolled-up blueprints and some old photographs, she put on her hard hat, tucking her hair up under the shell. Then she walked to the house, eager to get to work on a task she couldn't outsource to any of the crew.

Cara had set up her work table in a corner of the parlor. That was where her expensive tools stayed—the precision drills and blades and saws she needed to do the intricate detail work of the house's many decorative elements.

There was all the paneling in the front foyer and the staircase, and then the giant fireplace mantel in the dining room. But the real work would be in the parlor, which would require marquetry on a scale Cara had never seen before. It was a challenge and a threat to her skills.

At the moment, the floor of the parlor room was a wreck. An absolute wreck. Cara wanted to cry when she saw the condition of the floor with her own eyes. The inlaid wood was broken, cracked, curling up, or just plain dissolved. She picked up a pale piece of maple, and it disintegrated in her hands. A diamond shape of dark cherry lay warped, years of humidity having done its work.

She stood in the very middle of the cracked and broken surface of the parlor. Looking up at the ceiling—a horror show of water-stained and crumbling plaster—Cara smiled. She saw not the house as it was, but the house as it used to be and would be again.

Then without warning, a feeling of incredible sadness rolled over Cara. Pain. Sorrow. Years and years of loneliness, all at once. *How could they do this to me, my own parents? Hurting me like this, leaving me here, when all I ever wanted was to please them?*

She inhaled, not at all prepared for the onslaught of emotion. It didn't even feel like her own, but what else could it be?

Cara had dealt with some rough stuff over the past few years, but was it *that* bad? She wiped away the tears that had sprung into her eyes. She shuffled a few steps toward the wall, feeling dizzy.

Her dad let the family down, yes. He'd hurt Cara more than she ever admitted out loud. She'd looked up to him, and admired him and wanted to emulate him…and then she'd learned the truth, and it was like getting slapped in the face. *Daddy, why'd you do that?*

Cara shook her head once. The dizziness only increased. She was usually good about avoiding thoughts of her awful family dynamic. Don't talk about it, don't think about it, and eventually it will sort itself out in one way or another. She had to get herself together. There's no crying allowed in construction.

Cara reached for a tissue from her pack and was just wiping her eyes when she heard someone approach.

"Go away!" she snapped out. She didn't want anyone to see her, especially not Mal.

But it was Mal who stood in the doorway.

* * * *

Mal felt heat and violence in Cara's explosive words, but he stood his ground. "Cara? Are you ok?"

She turned her face to the wall. "I said go away." More muffled this time, without the power in the phrase before.

"Are you crying?" he asked.

"No!"

Mal moved over to her. "What happened?"

"Nothing! I'm not crying, because nothing happened."

"Something happened. What's going on?"

"Ugh, get off my case. We're not friends."

He tried to sound as inoffensive as possible. "Look, I guess I offended you the first day. Asking you out. I'm sorry. If I'd heard the rules first, I wouldn't have, ok?"

Cara looked at him, her eyes suspiciously puffy. "Fine. I didn't think you were serious anyway."

He picked up the scattered photographs and designs at her feet, giving them a once-over. "You like working with wood?"

She glared at him. "Yeah. And before you say one more word, I've heard every stupid joke about it already. Whatever clever, funny thing you were about to say, you can keep it to yourself."

"Actually, I was going to ask if you got into wood-working as a specialty in historical restoration or art school or what…" Mal trailed off, his attention captured by the image in the photographs.

Power. Mal looked at the floor in the old photograph and felt a sting of fear. The pattern was subtle, but it was there, concentric rings, with symbols inlaid in different colored wood all around the edges. It was hands down, no question, a summoning circle.

"Well, this is occult as fuck," he muttered.

Cara actually laughed, a warm sound that bubbled up out of her throat and hit Mal's ears and then slid right down his body to warm him in places he should not be focusing on right now.

"It does look that way, doesn't it?" she said brightly. Whatever made her cry was evidently forgotten. "It's an absolutely wonderful example of Deco Orientalism. There was a vogue for Egyptian revivalism at the time, and by all accounts, the Egans were wealthy, well-traveled people who had an obsession with archeology. This floor was specially designed by Egan to evoke the images people associated with ancient mysticism, but with a modern bent informed by Deco sensibilities. The detail is amazing. There will be over a dozen types of wood in the marquetry. I've never done a job with this many fiddly bits." She said the last part with unabashed joy.

He stared at the design, stunned by the complexity of it. "You'll make this? *All* this?"

"Yeah. I mean, I didn't design it. But I'll cut the new pieces and install them. Marquetry is really fun. It's not usually this big—a whole floor is incredibly unusual—but the method is the same."

"Oh." Mal got the sense that letting Cara create this design right over the hellhole would be a very, very bad idea. "You say the Egans designed it?"

"That's what the research suggests. This is a very personal thing, not a typical decoration at all. Probably it was Egan himself who chose how to make it. It's so intricate that I wanted to get here early and sort of…get the vibe of the area." She gestured to the place where the summoning circle was once laid out.

Evil. Mal got that vibe from across the street. "What's your verdict?"

"You interrupted me before I could figure it out." She shook her head. "Don't look at me like that. I'm not some new age crystal-toting nut. I don't mean I'm trying to see the house's aura. I just mean that I like to get a sense of what I'm working on. Pictures and newspaper clippings are all well and good. But it's nothing like really stepping into a place. That's how you know."

"You must have got some sense of the place."

She frowned. "Yeah. Well, yes and no. I want to love it. There's so much here—old craftsmanship, old materials. Clearly someone cared about this house and wanted it to be unique. But there's something off too."

Mal said nothing, hoping to encourage her. Cara went on, seemingly not even really talking to him. She was walking around, sorting out her own thoughts. "Maybe it's just the decades of neglect. But there's a sadness here. Really sad. More than sad. Depressed? No. Despairing? Despairing. It's like there's something despairing hiding in the corners of all the rooms. And you don't notice it all the time, but when you do, oy. It's like no amount of rehab or love or money is going to fix it. Might as well burn the place down."

Oh, no. She's walking counterclockwise. Around an old summoning circle. Mal realized that and moved to intercept her before she could complete a full circuit. "Here's your photos back."

She shook herself, focusing on Mal at last, but not taking the photos. She gave an obviously forced smile. "Wow. Where did all *that* come from? I don't mean what I said about burning, of course. I want to make it beautiful again. Everything should be made as beautiful as we can manage." Then she ducked her head, as if she hadn't meant to reveal that last part. As if it were too personal.

Well, Cara standing in the middle of a summoning circle was starting to feel personal to Mal. He was in over his head. He had to talk to his brothers. For now, he handed the photos back to Cara. "If you're making this whole place beautiful, you'll have your work cut out for you."

Cara put the photos and the designs in a corner, and Mal itched to "borrow" them one night so Dom and Lex could see the details. But Cara was already ushering him out of the parlor, back in her competent boss mode. "Come on, Mal East. Let's find the rest of the crew. We got a lot of work to do today."

Mal grinned, but hated the way she said his name, because it wasn't his real name. And the more time he spent with Cara, the more he hated lying to her about his real intentions.

The bad news was that Egan House was a deeply unsettling place to spend time, even for someone like Mal who didn't have a particularly sensitive attunement to magic. It suffered from the classic problems of unexplained cold spots, the creepy feeling of being watched, and even changing people's moods.

"This place, man," Reyes said at one point that morning. "Can't wait to make some progress. It gets me down."

And Dan said something similar later, when he'd been caught staring into space. "Sorry," he'd apologized. "I was just thinking about how sad this whole house feels. Like it knows all the bad stuff that happened here. That poor family and the fire and everything."

The good news was that Mal got himself onto the inside crew that day, and he kept an eye on Cara's movements so he could duck into the parlor over lunch and snap a few forbidden pics of the floor, as well as the old photos and blueprints.

That evening, he showed his initial intelligence to Lex.

Lex took his phone and studied the images. "Holy crap, that's a summoning circle."

"It's the original one," Mal said. "The hellhole must be centered right underneath that room, and now Cara is re-creating the circle, which might reactivate the hellhole."

"That's a terrible idea."

"She thinks it's a fancy Art Deco floor design. She doesn't know about summoning demons."

"The demons won't care if the creator knew what she was doing. In fact, they'll probably prefer to take advantage of an innocent person." Lex peered at one image, zooming in. "That's a symbol of…the lower hells? And there's the one to let the undead in. This is bad. I got to show this to Lily."

"Yeah, call her."

"No, I think we have to meet up. This is too much work for one person." Lex glanced at his own calendar. "I can head out this weekend. Her parents won't mind."

Lily's Chicago-based parents never minded Lex staying with them. They treated him as family, since he and Lily were basically best friends since kindergarten. Just as the Salems essentially thought of Lily as a non-blood relation.

"See what you can find out about the Egans too," Mal added. "Cara mentioned that they designed it, so it's likely they were magic users themselves. I know Aunt Jo put together a file, but maybe there's new info."

Lex nodded absently. "Will do. Take more pictures too. Not just the floor but whatever Cara works on. We don't know what could be relevant."

That would mean watching Cara pretty closely. Mal decided he'd be good at that.

V

OVER, THE NEXT FEW DAYS, Cara saw the guys making real progress on cleanup, and soon they'd be able to actually start repairs and installation of the pipes and electrical. Dan had emerged as a quiet second-in-command, able to deal with a lot of the work without needing to involve Cara for the details. Barry was a bit of a blowhard, but he did his work well. The crew, on the whole, made her breathe a sigh of relief. She'd been worried when she learned that the lawyer was going to hire them—some noise about "background checks," which gave Cara a few sleepless nights herself. But it worked out after all.

For her own part, she spent nearly all her time in the parlor room, cutting wood pieces for the marquetry design, and prepping the surface of the floor so she could begin assembling the most complex work within the whole house. Around her, she was dimly aware of the guys working at their assigned tasks. Through her industrial-strength earplugs, the sounds of drills and sledge-hammering filtered in.

Early on Friday, she looked over her week's work. She had cut hundreds of pieces of fine-grained, specialty woods to exact specifications. She'd spend the next week putting all those pieces into place, like a puzzle. The floor would be a whole intricate pattern of various shades of natural woods. She had cherry, ash, mahogany, ebony, naturally colored woods that ranged from palest grey to deep, grainy black. The cost was ridiculous, but the client didn't skimp. And now, with the materials in her hands, Cara could envision the gorgeous result. She'd make this room into a jewel box, an absolute piece of art. She followed the old plans exactly, by studying the old photographs and reading old accounts of the house to make sure she got it right.

She was smiling when Dan showed up, leaning in the doorway.

"Uh, boss? We got a problem."

"What is it?" She caught the worried look in his eye and knew she wasn't going to like what was coming.

"The copper piping for the kitchen…it's not in the shed."

"What? Of course it is. It got delivered Tuesday."

"Well, it's not there now."

"It must be," she insisted. Cara wanted to think it just got misplaced. Someone moved the shipment to a weird spot because they needed the space.

But after recruiting all the guys to help look for the copper, not a single pipe was found, even after an hour of searching.

She questioned each man, not accusingly, just asking if they'd remembered seeing anything, or if they might have covered the copper up and forgot. No one did.

"Next you're going to say one of us took the stuff, aren't you?" Barry asked, sounding wounded. "I need this job, ok? We all need the work. You can't fire us."

"All I'm asking for is a little help! That copper wasn't cheap, and none of the plumbing can get done until it's installed. What am I supposed to tell Morningside? He's going to be pissed, and if that copper doesn't turn up, maybe we'll all get fired."

Dan pointed to the shed, where the copper had originally been stored. "The padlock was real sticky to open this morning. I didn't think much of it then, but I bet someone pried it open last night, and jammed it closed after. That way no one would get suspicious."

"So it could have been anybody," Reyes said, sounding depressed rather than relieved.

Cara sighed. Apart from the fence and some basic locks, there wasn't any security around the site. It hadn't seemed to need it, in a small town like this.

She thought of Mal, who'd said very little during the whole search. Maybe he'd been more annoyed by her dinner refusal than he seemed. Or maybe he just saw an opportunity for a little profit.

"Boss?" Kevin asked. "What do you want us to do?"

Cara sighed. "I have to call the police and report it. Kevin, you and Dan got a new assignment. Take the credit card on my office desk and go buy new locks for the perimeter fence, and for the sheds. And the house. We'll need to be careful until we figure out exactly what happened."

"More lights would be good," Kevin said.

"Yeah. See what's available for security lighting."

"Budget?" Dan asked.

She frowned. The copper was going to be expensive to replace, but it was only a fraction of the value of all the tools and other materials. "Don't go over five hundred today. I'll talk to Morningside and see what he wants going forward."

"Sure thing, boss."

Cara was in a bad mood for the rest of the day. Morningside was unavailable until later, according to the snooty secretary who never remembered who Cara was.

For the next couple hours, she holed up in the office, bringing in each worker one at a time to ask if he'd seen anything. She hoped that by doing it in private, one of them might be more honest than he'd be if others were listening.

But no one saw anything.

When she at last called Mal in, she was full-on cranky. She toyed with the chisel on her desk, one of the vintage set of tools her father had given her for her sweet sixteen.

Other girls wanted cars. She was delighted with woodworking tools from the 1940s. Nerd.

Mal closed the door and took a seat across from her, his brown eyes decidedly not smoldery now.

"Ask away," he said.

Despite the late September afternoon, Cara was uncomfortably warm. "I got a problem. I've already asked everyone else, and they haven't seen or noticed anything."

Mal crossed his arms and raised one eyebrow, waiting. He wasn't going to make this easy on her. "And?"

"Well, I want to know if—"

"If I stole it?"

"Did you?"

"No. You can put that weapon down."

Cara sighed, relieved to hear such a simple, unequivocal denial. "Good." She took her hand off the chisel. It did have a pretty sharp edge.

"And I didn't see anything." Mal paused for a second. "But if you want, I could ask the neighbors."

"Maybe it was the neighbors who took it. From the look of that house, whoever lives there needs the dough. They can't even fix a stupid mailbox," Cara said glumly. "Think about it. A job site right across the street with no security."

He gave a snort. "Doubt it. But you can ask the cops to look if you want."

Cara only shook her head. She didn't want to involve the cops any more than she absolutely had to. "I was an idiot to not take steps. I just assumed it would be safe here."

"It's not your fault," said Mal.

"I'm the foreman. It's exactly my fault. Buck stops here and all that."

"Cara, whoever took the copper wasn't going to be stopped by a lock. Yeah, maybe it was easier than they expected, but it probably would have happened anyway.

And just because we're in a small town, it doesn't mean there aren't problems."

Cara wasn't really listening, too busy doing calculations in her head. There were ways to cut costs, to make back the loss of the copper. The last thing she wanted was for the client to think she was incompetent or worse, untrustworthy. "I'll make the numbers work," she muttered. Christ, that was probably what her dad said.

"Cara? You all right?"

"No, I'm not all right. I need to work on something." She stood up, eager to create, to make something with her hands. She needed to take the ugliness of the afternoon and fashion something beautiful out of it.

"What are you up to?" Mal asked, watching her a little warily.

"None of your business. Things are upsetting right now, and when things are upsetting, I need to take steps. Now go away. Your shift is over. See you on Monday."

"Yes, ma'am."

* * * *

The next morning, Mal was woken up by Lex prodding him in the shoulder. "Up, bro. Strange things are afoot at the Circle K."

He sat up, groaning. His job and his practice regimen were working together to make him exhausted. "It's Saturday and I want to sleep in. What happened?"

But Lex was already gone, his footsteps echoing on the stairs. Damn Lex and his morning energy.

Mal dressed and went downstairs. "What?"

"Look," Lex ordered, pointing out the front window. Dom was there too, arms crossed over his chest.

He looked up at Egan House, expecting to see something horrible, possibly a vortex of death or a cloud of demons or something.

"Lower down. Our yard."

"I don't see anything diff—" There was a new mailbox, sitting on a new post. A heavy-duty, thick wooden post, stained to a dark tone.

Lex was practically jumping up and down. "We have an entirely new mailbox and post instead of what was there last night! Someone stenciled *Salem* on it in cool lettering. There's a chrysanthemum planted at the base! Which Lily says is good luck," Lex added. Of course he'd already discussed the potential issues of surprise mailboxes with poor Lily. Being a smart witch known to excel at research must make for some weird texts. "Who does something like that?"

"Cara did it," Mal said firmly. "I've heard her bitching about the mailbox. She thinks our house is a wreck."

"Our house *is* a wreck," Lex said. "But I'm more worried about logistics. Why didn't we wake up when she snuck onto the property and stole our old mailbox, and then drove a new post into the ground in the middle of the night? We do have wards and cats and stuff, right?"

Dom frowned as he thought it over. "The mailbox is technically not our private property—the postal workers have a legal right to get in there. That must somehow negate the general warding."

"Yeah, but the cats should have noticed a woman stealing the mailbox in the middle of the night!"

"They probably did, and didn't care."

As one, they all looked over toward Behemoth, who was fake sleeping.

"Well, asshole?" Dom asked.

One emerald eye slitted open, like a dragon.

Correct.

Then the eyelid dropped again, indicating the end of the conversation.

"Great protection we've got," Lex muttered. "Mal, you have to ask her why she did it. And maybe slide in a question about whether she cursed it or something."

"Who curses a mailbox? Anyway, I'm pretty sure she doesn't do magic."

"Pretty sure is not enough. Charm it out of her. Not like magically charming, just be nice and friendly."

He'd been trying that tactic for days, and all it got him was Cara's icy death glare.

"I need coffee," he grunted. "It's too early to think."

"Can you sneak into the job site this weekend?" Lex asked over breakfast. "I wouldn't mind seeing the actual design blueprints."

"Not since Cara installed her new security system." As soon as the guys returned from the store on Friday, she'd put the locks on the doors and gates, and rigged the floodlights with motion sensors. Mal was sure she secretly went out on her own and bought a camera too. Whichever dumbass stole that copper piping was making Mal's life hard. "I'll get some more details on Monday. Promise."

Mal was hoping for a calm weekend, but of course right after Lex left for Chicago, they got an emergency call. A terrified man in Arizona had the family scrambling to get a team ready to head out. After assessing the situation, which sounded like a curse put on the client due to an unfortunate run-in with a book that was once the property of a demon, it was decided that Dom and Vinny would go together. Dom was a skilled spellcaster who could handle it on his own, but Vinny was learning the ropes of the family business, so she was excited to go along. Piewicket also volunteered to go. She liked road trips.

Mal spent much of the morning running all over the house helping to get all the needed supplies together. They gathered in the driveway early in the afternoon.

Vinny walked up to Dominic and dropped her bag to the pavement. Dom slipped an arm around her waist and dropped his head to her neck. Whatever he did to her made her squeal and then throw her arms around him.

Mal hid a smile and turned away. It was still weird to see Dom happy, because for years, he'd been, well, *not* happy. But from the moment he'd met Vinny, it was like he'd forgotten the last decade of angst and brooding.

So this was better.

Vinny glanced at her watch. "We should hit the road if we want to get enough driving hours in today." For someone who looked like an anarchist, she was very organized.

Dom nodded. "We got everything?"

"My clothes, your clothes, ritual kit, bag o' demon slaying stuff, extra supplies for curse-breaking, and Piewicket's travel carrier and extra cat food."

"And where is Pie?" Dom asked, looking at the empty carrier.

I am here, Piewicket announced as she bounded over the lawn.

"Ready to go, Pie?" Vinny asked. "We got a long day ahead of us."

Cars are excellent for napping, Pie replied, even though Vinny couldn't hear the response—the cats only ever communicated telepathically with members of the Salem family. The cat wound itself affectionally around Vin's boots.

"All right, let's load up," Dom said. He looked back at Mal. "We should be gone for about a week. Depends on how bad that curse is. And who knows how long Lex's research might take."

"No prob," Mal said. "I've got eyes on the hellhole." He glared up at the house on the hill.

Piewicket also looked toward the house. *The things that house is hiding won't wait long. Don't let your guard down.*

"I'm on it," Mal assured them all.

For what that's worth. That opinion came from behind Mal. He turned to see Behemoth on the porch.

"Nobody asked you," he retorted.

Mal spent Sunday alone. He trained in the basement, working on forms and then shifting to weights, which were surprisingly easy. All his work on the construction site was keeping him in shape.

On Monday, he made sure to be the first of the crew to get to Egan House, except for Cara. Did the woman sleep? He found her in the parlor room, already absorbed in assembling the pieces of marquetry for the summoning circle.

"Hey Cara, how do you like your coffee?" Oops, he didn't realize how cheesy that sounded until the words were out.

Cara sure did. She raised one eyebrow as she replied coolly, "I like my coffee like I like my men. Hot, and without a bunch of piled-on BS masquerading as sophistication."

He handed her the tall mug. "Then you should like this."

She frowned, popping the top off. Intense black coffee aroma floated out. "Why did you bring me coffee?"

"Because it's a nice thing to do."

She still regarded him with suspicion. "You didn't roofie it for a joke, did you?"

Who did this girl used to hang out with? "That'd be a pretty bad joke."

"Agreed. Ok, if I'm not dead from poison by the end of the day, I'll say thanks."

"You're welcome," said Mal. "Oh, by the way…"

Cara crossed her arms over her ample chest, a move that Mal fully approved of. "What do you want?"

"The mailbox across the street," he began.

She raised her eyebrow again. "What about it?"

Doubt ate at Mal. Did she have nothing to do with it after all? Oh, right, that's what he came here to find out.

"Did you fix that mailbox?"

"The old one looked horrible," she said.

Mal took that as an admission of guilt. "You stealth fixed the neighbor's mailbox. Why?"

"Because the old one looked horrible. Pay attention."

"Yeah, I know what it looked like. But why did you go out of your way to fix it? That new wooden post thing is a solid piece of work."

"You bet it is," she said, looking a bit smug. "It's going to take effort to make it look as bad as the old one."

"Ok, but *why*?"

"I wanted to improve the view."

"You're not the seller. You get paid either way. What do you care?"

"I like it when things look nice!" Cara burst out. "What's seismic about that? I could make something better, so I did."

"That's all you had to say." Mal let it go before he got too enmeshed and accidentally admitted it was his own mailbox. Cara was a weird girl, salty and sweet all at once. And definitely someone who tried to hide her softer side.

He would really like to get to know her softer side, preferably without getting smacked in the head with a hammer first.

VI

After Mal left, Cara took a cautious sip from the mug he'd offered her. The coffee was amazing. It was going to be hard to go back to disgusting gas station coffee after this. But she couldn't exactly put in an order with Mal every morning. Especially not after accusing him of poisoning it.

She wished she could have easy access to good coffee, because she was tired after working extra hours all weekend. And there was the little fact that she'd given up her motel suite to sleep in the office trailer. Cara had panicked about the expense of replacing the copper, and if she could recoup the money by sleeping in slightly rougher digs, well, that was what she'd do.

Cara had spent all Friday night working on her special project, which was the replacement mailbox post across the street. Digging out the old one and putting in the new one had been immensely satisfying, even if she did it in the wee hours of the morning to avoid awkward questions from the neighbor she had yet to set eyes on.

She'd thought about the parlor floor all weekend, and even dreamed about it the past two nights. It wasn't totally surprising. Cara often got sucked into her work, the creation of new art consuming her. She stopped thinking about basic things like showering and eating. She crammed in whatever food came close to her mouth, and ignored all bodily signals until the thing she was carving was finished. Only then did Cara realize that she was bone-tired, sick from junk food, and incredibly stinky from her only perfume being sawdust. Not a good look.

But while she was creating, none of that mundane stuff mattered. Bringing the shape and the story out of the wood, hearing it call to her and tell her how to chisel and sand and scrape it into existence...*that* was what mattered.

She started work on the floor with a feeling of relief. Being away from the floor was starting to feel wrong. She continued the painstaking work of assembling the design, and trimming and filing down the edges of the many pieces so they'd fit exactly. She marveled at the intricacy of the design. Little Greek and Egyptian symbols inlaid into diamonds and circles. Five pointed stars laid out to mimic constellations. Strange little faces formed out of minuscule chips of wood, like elves or demons or ancient spirits.

She didn't remember taking any breaks, but the crumpled fast food wrappers near the door told her she must have downed a burger. Or two.

Someone's footsteps echoed down the newly recovered subfloor in the hall, and Dan appeared. "We finished reframing the front wall where that water damage took out the old wood. Figured we're at a good stopping point. Want these things packed up?" Dan asked, indicating her tools. Cara had issued orders to lock up *all* equipment every night.

Cara checked her watch. 4:00 p.m. Time for the guys to take off—they started early and put in a full day's work. "No thanks, Dan. I'm going to use the orbital sander before I call it a night. I'll put these things away when I'm done. Tell everyone they can head out. See you tomorrow."

"All right, boss." Since that first day, Dan always called Cara *boss*, which she appreciated even though she knew it was mostly done for humor.

She rooted around in the remains of her lunch bag, hoping to find some lost fries. There were a few in the bottom, and she wolfed the cold, salty sticks down without enjoying them.

Then it was back to work.

She lost all sense of time, only marginally aware of when it got dark enough for the floodlights in the room to become the only illumination.

Nearly cross-eyed from staring at the floor all day, she'd taken a little break to work on the fireplace design instead.

Cara hummed to herself as she sanded down the piece in front of her. It was the left-hand side of the mantelpiece, and it took the form of a human figure, specifically a long, thin, stylized woman in ancient Egyptian costume. Her hands were raised above her head as if she were holding something. And when the work was done, she'd be holding up the horizontal mantel on one side. The right side was going to be a man, also in Egyptian garb.

The original mantelpiece was lost, and the only photos were black and white, meaning Cara had to guess as to the type of wood. She chose a densely grained oak that held tones of brown, grey, and thin streaks of silver. When finished and polished, the mantelpiece would shine as if lit from within.

But oak was a hardwood, with deep grain that was often tricky to work with. Cara was patient, moving from rough cuts to finer drill bits, carving the piece down to where she needed it to be in order to get to the details of the sculpture.

It was probably eleven o'clock, and she had the floodlights on high. It illuminated her workroom like high noon. Her phone blasted out music from its inadequate speaker, but Cara was only using it for background noise. She mouthed the words to classic rock as she worked, time slipping away from her as she moved deeper into a flow state, the happy place where she was so focused on the wood in front of her that she saw nothing in her peripheral vision, and in fact often missed when people spoke to her until they yelled several times.

However, when the lights flickered and then went out, Cara snapped to attention. At the same time, the music dwindled away as the phone's connection was interrupted.

Cara was working with a handheld chisel, nothing electric, so she held it in her hands, not moving, hoping the power would come back on before she had to start stumbling around in the dark.

A minute passed. No power.

She slowly stood up. "Hello? Who's there? Did you not realize I'm working up here?"

No answer. Did someone cut the power? Or drive over a line, or hit something in the yard? Was this just an accident, or was it deliberate?

Was someone here to steal more supplies?

Still holding the chisel, Cara made her way carefully to her phone. It lit up at her touch—at least the battery was fine. She could call for help if she needed to.

She turned on the flashlight function, and soon stood in front of a cold blue circle of light.

Ok. Time to get to the circuit breaker. Maybe the floodlights were just drawing too much power and something tripped.

She reached the doorway and looked both ways down the hall. Nothing to the left. Nothing to the right.

Except two eyes glowing in the dark.

Cara nearly jumped out of her skin, wheeling her arm around in front of her to hold the flashlight up.

The blue light illuminated the passage. Nothing.

Cara gasped, her heart thumping out of control. She'd seen someone there. Hadn't she? Cara gripped the chisel tightly and moved forward. The shiny metal of nail heads gleamed for a second. She felt like a moron. The crew was putting up new plywood on the walls, driving nails in to secure it to the two by fours. The light must have reflected off two of them, just happening to be at the right height to look like a person's eyes.

"Get a hold of yourself," she muttered.

Then she heard the footsteps.

Just like the first day, the footsteps were light and furtive. Cara knew her way around the house by now, and the darkness didn't slow her down much. If it was the person stealing her equipment, she was going to catch that bastard.

She followed the faint sounds, keeping her own movements as quiet as she could. Not that Cara was especially stealthy.

A floorboard creaked under her feet the moment she stepped into the room on the eastern side.

That's when she saw the little girl.

And the little girl saw her too.

She wore a simple white dress nipped in at the waist, and what looked like lace at the sleeves. Her hair came to her chin and shimmered like silver. Cara could see the outlines of the door molding behind the figure. But the eyes—those were pitch black, and locked on Cara.

Cara dropped the chisel in her shock, the tool clattering to the floor, a horribly loud sound in the otherwise silent house.

The ghost's form swirled, and the impression of it being a little girl faded. Soon, Cara could focus only on two furious eyes.

Then, with no warning or explanation, smoke began ballooning out from everywhere, puffing in sooty grey clouds toward her, rising up past her knees, then her waist. The shadowy figure was swallowed up by the smoke, and Cara had no idea where it might move.

She choked as the smoke surrounded her. Cara raised her arm. Trying to breathe through the fabric of her sleeve, she looked around for the figure with the eyes.

She didn't see it, but suddenly she felt heat. Heat all around her.

Cara's brain stopped working properly. Her body took over, some ancient survival instinct driving her muscles. She stumbled backward, back toward where the door had to be.

She fell to her knees, wincing as the rough floor splintered into her knees and palms. Rather than get up, she crawled through the room, hoping the smoke was less thick here. She got to the doorway, and shakily got to her feet. She half turned, thinking that she should do…something.

Call 911? Get the fire extinguisher?

Cara stood frozen, unable to think clearly enough to make a decision.

Then the dark, shadowy *something* burst out of the smoke and rushed toward her, hurtling into her with a physical force strong enough to push her back toward the stairs. *GO AWAY.*

That was it. Cara ran.

Down the stairs, out of the house, down the hill. She didn't have a plan, she didn't have a destination.

She just had to get AWAY.

Cara was still running when she crossed the street and stumbled up the rickety wooden steps of the neighboring house. She stopped short just before hitting the solid wall in front of her face. She turned and sagged downward, seeking shelter in the corner of the porch, hiding in the darkness, hoping the *some*thing that nearly pushed her down the stairs couldn't find her here.

Cara braved a glance upward, expecting to see the sky illuminated with orange and red, to smell the smoke from the fire that must be ripping across the whole second floor by now.

She blinked. Nothing.

The house on the hill stood silent, the sky scattered with stars.

She sniffed, knowing that she had to be covered in the smell of smoke.

No. Nothing.

Cara's hands pulsed with pain, and remembering the splinters she'd got from her fall into the floorboards, she raised her palms upward.

They were unmarked. The pain was there, just as her knees ached. But the skin was unbroken, and her jeans didn't have any char marks or holes.

The lack of evidence of what just happened didn't make her feel better. It made her want to curl up into a ball and hide until the world stopped being scary.

Dawn. Dawn would come eventually. She wasn't going to budge until the sun came back. And then she was getting out of this town.

Cara shivered, and let her head drop onto her folded arms. Then she heard a meow.

She flinched when she heard it, not connecting the noise to a cat.

But then it meowed again. She looked up to see a gigantic black cat brushing up against her legs. This wasn't the cute calico she'd seen before. This thing looked like it weighed thirty pounds at least.

Cara didn't know how to react. She held still, hoping the cat was just a cat, and not some horrible monster that wanted to trick her by pretending to be something harmless and then killing her right when she thought she was safe and…

"Cara? What are you doing on my porch?"

She looked up to see Mal standing there.

VII

Mal stared down at Cara, who was wedged into the corner of the porch, her face pale and her eyes big with fear.

"What happened?" he asked.

She swallowed once before saying in a choked voice, "There's someone in the house."

Adrenaline rushed through him at the thought of Cara in danger. He reached out and took her by the arm to help her up, even as he looked up at the house on the hill. "They still there?"

"I…I don't know."

Jesus, she was crying.

"Did someone hurt you?"

She shook her head. "Not really. I mean, I'm just scared."

"Ok, come in here."

Cara hesitated, probably because the house was pitch black. Mal reached for the light switch and the kitchen warmed to bright gold, banishing the darkness. "It's ok. Come in. I'm inviting you in, Cara." Mal said the words deliberately. Even though Cara would have no idea of what was happening, his invitation would allow her to pass by some of the strongest wards around the house, the ones that the Salems put up to keep themselves safe.

Cara looked around as she stepped into the light. Sawdust had settled on her hair like snowflakes, and she wore jeans and a simple flannel shirt. Her boots were light brown leather, and also dusted with tiny wood shavings. The scent of raw pine and varnish followed her in, stinging his nostrils.

"You live here?" she asked, puzzlement on her face. "Why didn't you say?"

"Never mind that. Tell me what happened."

Mal was glad he was there alone for the moment. Dom and Vinny and Lex and Piewicket had all left. It was Behemoth who had sensed the presence of a person on the porch and howled a silent warning to Mal.

Now Cara's hands twisted nervously as she started to talk. "I was working late. I do that a lot. The lights were on, bright. Anyone would have known someone was there."

He saw that she was shivering. And not just because it was a nice cool autumn night outside. This was the aftermath of shock. Worried, he grabbed a blanket from the living room couch and wrapped it around her shoulders. Cara gripped the edges of the fabric like it was the only thing standing between her and certain death.

"Better?" Mal asked.

She nodded, her gaze unfocused.

"Want something to drink? Yes, you do. Something hot."

He got the kettle going, pulled out a mug from the cabinet, and rooted around for tea. He found a canister of handmade packets of herbs that Lily had crafted, marked Restful AF. He grabbed one and dropped it in the mug. Then he turned back to Cara, who was standing there, looking lost.

He indicated the kitchen table with its mismatched chairs. "You should sit."

"Hmm, yeah." Cara sat in one, as vacant as a sleepwalker.

Mal's concern sharpened. "Are you sure no one hurt you? Do you want to call the cops?"

"No!"

Mal paused at her vehement reply, the first noise she made that sounded conscious. "Why not?" he asked.

"I don't want to get cops involved."

"You called them when the supplies went missing before. This could be—"

"This is different."

"Why?"

She shook her head. "This is going to sound stupid."

"Just say what you saw. Don't worry about how it sounds."

She took a breath, or tried to. Mal saw her chest working, and then noticed the tightness around her mouth.

"Hey," he said, moving to take her by the shoulders. "You need to breathe."

"I am breathing!"

"Not well. You need to take long breaths. It'll lower your heart rate and get your body back to normal. Listen. Take a deep breath in. I'm going to count to three, then you exhale for three. Ok?"

Cara nodded, and Mal counted slowly, tapping her shoulders in time to help her focus. After the first couple counts, she was breathing more normally and her color came back to her face. Mal itched to push her messy hair back, but he was also very aware that any move that freaked Cara out would blow up the delicate state of trust he just established.

Wait till she figures out that you're lying about your name.

Cara finally sat up straight, letting the blanket slide down from her shoulders. "How do you know about stopping panic attacks?"

"I don't. But I know when people aren't breathing normal. It's a thing that helps right before a fight, when your heart goes all haywire. Different reason, same treatment."

She nodded in comprehension, her eyes now locked on him instead of unfocused like they were before. "Wait, a fight?"

"Yeah, I do a lot of martial arts," he explained hastily.

"Oh. That explains…" A blush crept into her cheeks. "Um, that just explains it."

Behemoth took that moment to leap onto the table, and Cara was obviously glad of the interruption. "Who's this?" she asked, holding a cautious hand out for the cat to sniff.

"His name is Behemoth. Family cat. He's sort of a jerk."

But Behemoth was purring up a storm as Cara began to pet him. Her shocked expression began to fade as she focused on the cat. Behemoth was probably working some sort of cat magic to calm her, which was the first useful thing he had done in quite a while.

"Charm offensive, Behemoth?" Mal asked the cat.

Just my usual charm, the creature replied in his mind. *Are you jealous I can seduce her when you cannot?*

"Shut up," Mal muttered.

Cara blinked. "Excuse me?"

"Nothing. Are you feeling better?" he asked.

"Yes."

"You think you can tell me what you saw now?"

Cara closed her eyes. "I swear it was a ghost."

She said nothing more, maybe waiting for Mal to laugh in her face.

He didn't. Instead he pushed the mug of tea toward her, simultaneously whisking Behemoth off the table. "Drink this."

"I'm not crazy," she muttered.

"I don't think you are. But you are in shock, at least a little." It was too hot to drink, but the solidity of the ceramic mug would be grounding enough to keep her from shivering. And the tea, whatever it was, smelled amazing. Lily was very good with herbs. That had to help.

Cara wrapped her hands around the mug.

Mal kept his voice calm. "Tell me what you saw. I promise I won't laugh."

She inhaled, and in a small voice recounted what happened to her. Mal nearly had a heart attack when she talked about smoke and fire. He'd have lost his mind if he was in that particular situation.

"You say you had a weapon?"

"Not really a weapon. I was using a chisel and I had it…until I dropped it."

Mal nodded. A simple, solid iron tool was exactly the right weapon for a novice to choose. Iron was damn good against anything from the fae otherworlds, and in fact, iron was great against corporeal things too. Anything that could deliver a good whack.

"What did you do then?"

"I followed the noise into the east room. I had the chisel, I figured it was just a raccoon or something anyway."

Cara was bolstering herself up, and he admired her for not caving after her first, terrifying encounter with the supernatural.

She was saying, "I heard someone tell me to get out, to leave and never come back. And I turned when I heard that, because there's not supposed to be anyone else in the house and I saw this shape. A person. But no one could have got there without passing by me. There's no doors, no windows, nothing. But I saw them, and I felt a push toward the stairs, and I was just running out of the house."

"What did it look like? The ghost?"

She shook her head. "I was panicking. I'm sure I'm not remembering it right. For a second I thought it was a little girl, but that's got to be me thinking of horror movies to fill in the blanks. I can only be certain about the eyes. And the voice. Something in that house really doesn't like me."

All of a sudden, tears were rolling down her face. Mal forgot all his good intentions to keep his hands off her and leaned forward to take her in his arms.

Cara resisted for half a second, and then softened against him. Despite everything, despite his goal to ignore any physical reactions to her, Mal inhaled the scent of her sawdusty hair and felt how incredibly soft she was, and he'd be happy to hold her all night.

Do not say anything stupid about how she smells good, he warned himself. *She's scared out of her mind.*

After a moment, Cara mumbled something. Mal leaned back. "What was that?"

"I'm sorry. This is unprofessional. My crying, I mean."

"Cara, it's ok. You had a really weird experience. Ghosts are scary."

"It can't have been a ghost," Cara said, more firmly than before. "I don't believe in stuff like that. There's a rational explanation, and in the morning, it will all make sense."

Mal said, "I believe in ghosts."

She looked over at him suspiciously. "Do not play with me."

"I'm not."

"You, macho workout martial arts dude, believe in ghosts."

"Yes. My physical workout regimen doesn't have any-thing to do with my metaphysical…regimen. Or some-thing." Mal was annoyed at his own statement. "My point is that I one hundred percent know ghosts are real. And I am not surprised to hear that you saw one in that scary house up there."

Cara got defensive, fast. "At least I'm working on it, making it habitable. Not like this place."

"We are working on it," Mal said hotly. "We do what we can, ok? It's not like we *planned* to have pigeons liv-ing in the rafters."

Her expression brightened. "Oh, that's easy. If you know where they're getting in, you can staple chicken wire over the opening. Not while they're in there, duh. But scare them out, and—"

"Cara. Forget about the pigeons. Let's get back to the ghost."

"It wasn't really a ghost."

"What if it was?"

"Are you trying to freak me out?"

"You were already freaked out when you ran over here."

"Yeah." She shivered, and Mal's instinct was to pull her close again and hold her till she stopped shivering. But Cara would probably use a chisel on him if he tried it.

While he was thinking things over, Mal texted Lex, who was still away on his research mission.

Re: Egans. Look up to see if there was a girl living there. Daughter, niece, etc. Cara saw ghost.

Lex texted back almost instantly. *Ghost! OMG. Will do lookup.*

Mal rolled his eyes. Sometimes talking to Lex was like talking to a teenage girl. He blamed Lily. The chica was a bad influence when it came to texting.

Behemoth sunk a claw into Mal's calf to get his attention. *We need to talk.*

"Owww! Ok." He glanced at Cara, who was watching him with wide eyes. "'Scuse me, I just got to go feed him." He grabbed Behemoth and moved into the big pantry off the kitchen.

"What is it?" he hissed at the cat, who was laughing at him.

First woman who places professionalism over fun with you. What will your brothers think?

"Do not tell them! Not Dom, not Lex. And definitely not Lily!" He did not point out that Lily was not a brother, or even a Salem. Lily was basically an honorary sister, and she'd tease the hell out of Mal if she ever found out he'd been turned down flat by Cara.

Behemoth had Mal in a corner, literally and figuratively. *What is my silence worth?*

"What do you want? Tuna? Salmon? What?"

I shall consider my price, Malachy Salem. In the meantime, you must examine that house as soon as possible. Tonight. By dawn the lingering energies will dissipate and we'll learn nothing.

"I can't leave Cara here!" Mal said, almost forgetting to keep his voice down.

I could make her sleep, the cat replied.

"You can't just slap some cat magic on anyone who gets in your way."

Behemoth looked puzzled. *I assure you I can.*

"I mean it's not kosher. By the way, what do you think of her?" he asked. "Apart from the turning-me-down thing?"

The cat twitched his tail a few times, which Mal recognized as a thinking gesture.

She seems on the level.

Mal winced. "Did you just make a carpenter joke?"

Some of your predecessors were freemasons. The jargon was much the same.

"You don't think she's part of an evil plot to reopen a hellhole?"

She is undoubtedly part of a plot. Whether she knows it or not is another matter. Open that can of tuna and feed me. For appearances.

Mal did, grumbling about Behemoth's opportunism. Back in the kitchen, Mal didn't say anything for a while, considering the whole situation. He was unreasonably angry that something scared Cara so much. He started tapping his fingers on the table. "Ok. I'm going to go over there."

She looked up, alarmed. "No way. What if there's…"

"A ghost?"

"I was going to say a real person," she corrected. "A guy with a gun, maybe. Someone did steal copper pipe and fixtures. That stuff's expensive enough that somebody might be pretty serious."

"All the more reason to find evidence of what's happening." Mal stood up. "Wait here with the cat. I'll be back."

Cara stood too, a hard look on her face. "No way. Egan House is my responsibility. If you're going over there, I'm going too."

VIII

CARA FELT A LOT BRAVER with Mal next to her. Walking up the hill, she took in the bulk of Egan House, grim and glowering against the night sky. As ramshackle as Mal's house was, it had a warmth that Egan House lacked.

"You saw the ghost upstairs, in the eastern bit," Mal said, looking at the house. "Not in the parlor?"

"No. I was in the parlor, but the sounds led me upstairs. By the way, how can you even prove a ghost's existence?"

"There are ways, but not many that your average scientist would accept. The supernatural tends to screw with technology. When the creatures from the otherworlds step into ours, it creates all sorts of disruptions. Lex says it's the result of realities clashing. And the effects are to make cameras go wonky and recording equipment fail."

"How convenient," Cara noted dryly. "Who's Lex?"

"My little brother. He's a genius."

"And also into ghost hunting?"

"We're all into ghost hunting. I'll explain later." Mal gave her a sideways glance. "What's reliable is your gut. The feelings you get when you step into a space where the otherworlds are close. All the standard descriptions—a chill down your spine, the feeling of being watched, getting jumpy for no reason—that's real. That's humans reacting to the presence of the supernatural."

"Are you trying to scare me, because you're scaring me."

He shook his head. "Nothing's going to hurt you, Cara. Not while I'm here."

"You're pretty full of yourself, you know that?"

"Yeah, I've been told." He grinned, evidently not offended in the least.

Cara opened the door to her office trailer, grabbing the spare heavy-duty flashlight. Mal hovered in the doorway, taking in everything…including the sleeping bag.

She caught his narrowed glance the moment he saw the sleeping bag, but didn't want to deal with that on top of everything else right now.

"Let's go," Cara muttered, pushing him out of the office and locking it behind her.

They reached the door to the house, still open wide since Cara had torn out of there in a panic. Mal tapped the flashlight. "You're on lighting duty."

They proceeded upstairs. Cara was relieved that there was no evidence of smoke or fire, because it meant the house was intact. But the flip side of that was she'd definitely been hallucinating, and that couldn't be a good sign.

In the room where Cara first saw the…whatever it was, Mal looked around carefully. He put his hands on the walls, as if feeling for secret passages.

"What are you doing?" she asked.

"If there were real flames before, the walls would be hot. I'm just being thorough." He pointed to the east wall. "The old wing used to be over that way, right?"

"Yeah. That wall is an exterior wall now, but it wasn't meant to be originally. That's why the bricks don't quite match on the outside."

Mal tapped a door on the wall in question. He tried the knob, which was purely decorative at this point. "Odd that they'd keep the door." The door was a heavy, dark-stained cherry, with a tall mirror inset. The glass of the mirror was darkened with age, and the silver backing was seriously clouded and foxed, the little spots making it very difficult to use as a proper mirror.

Cara moved across the room to join him, regarding the door with interest. "I guess they wanted to keep the look, even though it's a brick wall on the other side. It's really sort of amazing that more of this house's interior didn't get stripped and end up in a salvage yard. They don't make doors like this anymore." She ran her fingers over the carved decorations with the love that any artist feels for work well done.

"You could do it," Mal pointed out. "You could totally make a door this fancy."

She felt suddenly shy. "Well, if someone's got the money they can custom order anything." Then Cara looked down, seeing a glint on the floor. She bent down to pick up the tool. "Weird. This is my chisel, but I was never in this corner. How did it get here?"

"Maybe you kicked it over here without knowing?"

"Across the whole room? I feel like I would have remembered." On the other hand, she was freaking out at the time.

GO AWAY.

Cara felt the words resonate in her head, and she looked over at Mal. "Did you hear that?" she whispered, her former panic threatening to return in half a second.

He nodded, his expression going very calm. He maneuvered her toward the carved door. "Stay there, ok. I'm going to keep it away from you."

Cara stepped back, and Mal moved in front of her. He shook himself a little, flexing his hands open and closed. Getting ready for a fight. She picked up on his tension, even though she'd never been in a fight in her life.

Without warning, a shadowy form coalesced in front of them. *GO AWAY.* It wasn't speaking, but the words again shot into Cara's mind.

Mal didn't respond with spoken words either. Instead of sensibly getting the hell out of the way, he jumped forward, directly into the shadow.

The logical part of Cara would have said that it was impossible to fight a shadow, or a ghost. But the logical part of Cara was too busy gaping because Mal was in fact fighting it.

It was hard to see what was happening, with the flashlight being the only illumination. She could see Mal, mostly, though parts of him would get eclipsed by shadow every few seconds. Or was it that he was moving faster than normal?

Cara blinked, trying to understand what was happening. It was like Mal was there, and then he wasn't, and then he was again.

The shadow pulsed and roiled around him, and now Cara heard an incoherent scream of fear and pain echoing in her head. Mal kept lashing out, moving it and himself steadily away from Cara.

"You're hurting it!" she shouted, half-excited, half-terrified.

Somehow, he was connecting with the amorphous shape, and just as it contracted into a much darker, almost solid form…it vanished. But for an instant, Cara once more saw the shape of a young girl.

Mal stood alone in the middle of the room, in a ready stance, his eyes darting around, ready for anything to leap out again. After a long moment, he took a breath. His skin had a slight sheen, sweat from his sudden burst of controlled fury.

"It's gone for now," he said at last. "But I only surprised it."

"You surprised *me*," Cara burst out. "How did you do that? Hit a ghost? How *fast* are you? Like, you were weirdly fast."

He shrugged it off. "I practice."

No way was that the whole story, but Cara couldn't worry about that now. She was shaking, her body catching on to the fact that something completely beyond her experience had just occurred right in front of her.

"That was real?" Cara's legs felt watery, and she leaned back against the wall.

Mal made a step toward her, and Cara was about to beg for him to help her up, or even better, hold her and tell her things would be all right. She opened her mouth to embarrass herself, and that was when they heard the crash below.

A giant, unmistakable thump echoed through the house, like someone dropped a ton of bricks.

"What's that noise?" Cara squeaked after a second of stunned silence.

"That wasn't a ghost for damn sure. Did you hear that kind of sound before?" Mal asked in a low tone.

"No! It's coming from downstairs. The parlor! My tools are still out." Cara took a step toward the door, but Mal put a hand out to prevent her from going forward.

"Hold up. I'm going first."

If this was what it was like to be around an alpha male, Cara was all for it. Mal moved down the stairs, as alert as he'd been during the fight. Cara trailed after him, happy that he was between her and whatever had made the crashing sound. Somehow, Cara had complete confidence that Mal could take on anything in his path. Before, she said he was full of himself. But what happened upstairs wasn't bravado. It was cold, competent skill.

Mal paused in the hallway outside the parlor. The sounds were unmistakable now. Someone was moving the heavy equipment closer to the hallway. Cara grimaced, thinking of the cost of the drills and the lathe.

Mal held up a hand, signaling to Cara that she should stop. She halted, very willing to let Mal take the lead on this.

Mal then stepped up into the doorway. "Hey asshole!" he yelled, his voice booming in the echoing halls.

There was a startled silence, and then a shape hurtled out of the darkened room, directly toward Mal.

Cara screamed a warning, but before she could blink, Mal moved so fast he *blurred*.

She halted in midscream, her brain not able to take it in.

Mal had moved out of the way of the attacker and then sort of swooped around to position himself in the hallway, between Cara and the other guy.

The other guy, still nothing more than a shadow, raised an arm, revealing a crowbar in his grip. He howled, and started to bring his arm down, intent on smashing Mal's head in with the wicked hook end.

Once again, Mal moved out of the way too fast to be believed, and then rushed the guy, delivering a brutal kick in his chest. The guy gasped for air and dropped the crowbar as he stumbled backward.

He braced himself, preparing to attack Mal. But then he turned and ran.

She didn't miss it that time. Mal covered the twenty feet like it was two and rushed the other man before he could get out the door. Mal slammed him against the new plywood walls, pinning the guy there.

"Copper piping wasn't enough?" he asked. "Too bad you chose tonight."

"You can't prove anything," the other one replied in a rough tone.

"I installed a camera," Cara said as she moved toward the pair, shining her heavy-duty flashlight around the hall.

Mal gave her a single glance that warned her to stay back. She saw that the other guy was struggling hard, and Mal didn't want her to get hurt if he lost his grip.

She angled her beam of light on the guy's face. A very familiar face. "Holy crap, it's Barry!"

Mal grinned when he recognized the man. "Oh, good. I've been wanting to kick his ass for personal reasons anyway."

"Fuck you and your fat girlfriend," Barry snarled. "You're not a cop. Let me go."

Cara didn't quite see Mal punch Barry, but she saw Barry drop to the ground, moaning in pain with his hands over his face. Blood trickled between his fingers. Mal might have broken the guy's nose.

"Want to kick him in the balls?" Mal asked conversationally, hauling Barry up. "Great opportunity."

Cara took a step back. "Don't want to get my boots anywhere near there, thanks all the same."

"Then I'll do it, just to make sure he suffers. Go outside and call 911, ok?"

She nodded, reaching for her phone while Mal dragged Barry outside to the driveway, pushing him down face-first on the crumbly asphalt, with his arms pinned behind his back.

Barry struggled, or tried to, but Mal simply bent Barry's right arm an inch further and told him to shut up when he whimpered.

Minutes later, the bright red-and-blue flashes of a cop car emerged from the darkness, and an ambulance was not far behind. Thankfully, neither vehicle used its sirens.

Two cops got out of the car, hands on weapons. The driver was a blonde who looked like a poorly disguised superhero, all sleek muscles and a great-fitting uniform. The guy who emerged from the passenger seat was older and bit grayer, but still in shape. The donut stereotype did not apply to these small-town cops.

The female cop looked to Cara first. "I'm Officer Hallihan. You placed the call?"

"Yeah. We found this guy, Barry Field, trying to steal some of my most expensive equipment. I've already reported a previous theft from this site. Copper piping."

Hallihan nodded, and Cara figured that in a town this size, information like that would be known by the whole force. She then looked down to where Mal was keeping Barry immobile. "Mal. Fancy meeting you here."

"How's it goin, Hal?" Mal's voice was casual, but Cara didn't need to be a genius to figure out that these two had a past. It was in the way Hallihan tucked a loose strand of hair behind her ear, and the way Mal didn't quite look at Cara as he stood up. *Hal and Mal?* She almost wanted to vomit at the cuteness of it. Perfect couple.

Barry protested his innocence as the cops hauled him up and cuffed him. However, Cara's account was damning, and the male cop dryly noted that if a lot of copper piping and wire was found where Barry lived, he was going to have a hard time explaining it.

He shut up then, lapsing into a sullen silence. Hallihan and her partner radioed in that everything was under control. Cara answered a slew of questions, mostly about who she was and why she was there at night and why Mal was with her.

That was a little awkward, but Mal stepped up and took over. "She heard a noise and was smart enough not to investigate it on her own. She asked me to come with, and you know I'm a sucker for a damsel in distress."

Hallihan snorted at that. "If you both are so smart, why didn't you call 911 right away instead of going all Scooby Gang?"

"I figured I could handle it."

"What if this guy had a gun? No matter how good at jujitsu or krav maga or whatever else you do, you're not bulletproof, Malachy Salem. Next time, call the authorities, ok?"

"Yes, ma'am."

"And don't ever ma'am me."

"Yes, Hal."

The cops drove off, leaving Cara and Mal standing alone in front of the house.

"Well, that was a weird time. I need a drink. Want one?" Mal started walking down the hill.

"You know her," Cara said, following him. She could tell when someone was trying to change the subject.

"Hallihan? Yeah. We were in an unarmed defense class last year. I mean, I taught it. She took it."

"A teacher-student thing, huh."

"Well, not till after the class was done. We might have gone on a few dates." He rubbed the back of his neck, not looking Cara in the eyes.

"Might have, as in you don't remember?"

"As in, I'm not sure they could be called dates."

"Oh, *really*."

"This conversation isn't going well."

"Maybe not for you," she said. "I think it's very informative."

They reached the road, and Cara saw the name on the mailbox. "Oh, that reminds me. She called you Malachy Salem. Why are you listed on all my paperwork as Malachy East?"

"East is my middle name," Mal said, ushering her into the house again. "One of them anyway. And yeah, I fudged a couple details on my application. I didn't think I'd get the job under my name."

"You have a record?"

"A few misdemeanors. I sometimes get into situations where things get physical. Fortunately I have a cousin with a particular set of skills."

"Hacker skills?"

"The less we talk about that, the better."

She pursed her lips. "I don't like it."

"My record?"

"I don't like that you lied about your name." For many reasons, she didn't like it. A flush of guilt rushed up from her stomach.

"I didn't like it either, and if I could have told you earlier, I would have. And I'm good at my job, right?"

"Yeah. For a liar with no background in construction, you're all right." She sighed.

"Want a drink?"

Cara wanted all kinds of drinks, but she shook her head. "I gotta go. It's late and I'm tired."

"Hold up, Cara. Go where? Was that a sleeping bag in the office? Tell me you're not sleeping on site."

"Hey, I had to make up the cost of the lost copper somehow. It's fine."

"It's not fine at all," he countered. "No way is it your responsibility to give up your housing just to make the budget, and Egan House doesn't even have a working bathroom."

"Not right now. But we'll get the plumbing sorted in about a week," she said, looking on the bright side.

Mal leaned forward. "A week in an office trailer with no plumbing? You can stay with me. In this house, I mean."

"Absolutely not."

"What? It's right across the street. And you can sleep in a bed. And use a shower."

Cara shook her head. "I'm really fine. Now that Barry is out of the way, there's nothing to worry about."

"What about the ghost?" The way Mal said it—totally reasonable, as if he were talking about a water main break—made Cara remember all the creepy feelings she got while she was there. *Trust your gut*, Mal had said. But Cara's whole digestive system was against her, so how could she trust it now?

"There's no ghost," she said, willing it to be the truth. "Maybe Barry somehow made me see something. Like a hallucination induced by a chemical."

"And you still want to go back there all alone in the middle of the night?"

"Um…"

"We have a perfectly good spare bedroom. And plumbing. And coffee."

She hesitated, wavering at last.

"Just for a night or two," he promised. "Let's make sure Barry doesn't have partners, ok?"

Her eyes widened. "Yeah, how did he move all that stuff on his own? It would have taken him all night."

Mal sighed, evidently in relief at winning the argument. "Right. Let's grab your things from the trailer and come back here."

Cara nodded, wondering if she was making a gigantic mistake. Not that she thought Mal would take advantage of her. She knew he wasn't interested, not when he regularly hooked up with women as buff as Officer Hallihan.

But if any of the crew found out Cara was sleeping in the same place as one of her workers, her authority would be totally shot.

"I'll stay here," she said, "but no one on site can know."

Mal gave her a long, considering look that she couldn't read, but then nodded. "You got it, boss."

IX

Cara had a ton of questions for Mal, but by the time they'd retrieved all her things from the trailer, and he showed her to the spare bedroom, she was dead tired.

"There's a lock on the door," he said. "Use it if you want."

What exactly would she be keeping out? A sex-crazed Mal? Unlikely. But she did appreciate that he was trying to make her feel safe. Still, she didn't bother to lock it.

He pointed out his own room and told her to knock if she needed anything. Cara had no intention of doing that. She closed the door and undressed, pulling on the leggings and loose T-shirt she used as pajamas.

When she pulled the covers up, she sighed, fully realizing how wiped out she was.

Then she heard a click. The door handle was one of those lever style ones. It lowered, and the door pushed open a few inches.

"Hello?" she asked. Maybe she should have locked the door after all.

But it was Behemoth who slinked in, then leaned against the door to close it again.

"Wow. You are a smart cookie," she said.

The big cat plopped onto the bed with an *oof*, and then padded over to her. Cara reached out to pet him, scratching gently behind his ears.

She let the cat curl right next to her. "Cat. I have had a *day*. Caught a thief, found out ghosts are real, and I'm sleeping in the same house as my employee. Mostly, though, ghosts are real. I'm not crazy, right? I realize that talking to a cat and asking for non-crazy validation might be all the info I need."

Behemoth began to purr.

"Yeah, I guess it doesn't matter if I'm crazy or not. Still gotta keep on doing whatever I do."

That earned her a meow. Cara smiled at him. Behemoth. It was really a very fitting name for the massive, inky-dark feline. He continued to purr at her, and within seconds she was asleep.

She woke up feeling great. Against all odds, she had zero nightmares. The cat was now curled into a ball near the foot of the bed. When Cara sat up, the cat stretched and yawned.

"Me too, Mr. B," she said. "Shall we get some food? I think I skipped dinner."

Cara dressed in her usual work uniform of jeans and a plaid shirt. After a moment's consideration, she added a layer. The days were definitely cooling down, and Egan House didn't have working central heat.

Behemoth pawed at her, so Cara scooped him up and brought him downstairs with her.

Mal was in the kitchen, standing over a skillet on the stove. The scent of coffee pervaded the room.

"Mr. B wants breakfast," Cara announced.

He turned around at her entrance. "Mr. Who? Oh no, you're holding Behemoth," he said, sounding as if she were holding a bomb.

"Yeah." He was not a light load, but she liked the weight of the cat in her arms, the softness of the midnight-black fur.

"Put him down. Now. You'll get clawed in the face."

Cara looked down at the cat, into his gleaming green eyes. "You're not going to claw me in the face after I brought you all the way downstairs, are you? That would be rude, and you're far too civilized to be rude like that."

The cat meowed, and Cara knelt down, gently letting the cat pour out of her arms to the floor, where he sauntered over to a bowl filled with fishy-smelling food.

"What did you do?" Mal asked. "Behemoth doesn't like anyone or anything."

"That is not true," she protested. "He may look big and mean, but he's really a lovebug."

Mal's eyes widened. "A *what*?"

"Watch your breakfast," she warned.

He whirled around and prodded at the contents of the skillet with a spatula. "Hope eggs are ok. And there's sausage. I should have asked if you're veggie."

"I'm agnostic. And I don't expect breakfast to be made for me. I'm just crashing here for a couple nights."

"Hey, I'm making breakfast anyway. It's not any extra work. Coffee's ready, by the way."

Cara definitely wasn't turning that down. She poured a cup and inhaled the smell with a sense of bliss.

Her good mood notched down when she saw Mal piling scrambled eggs and sausage links onto a plate. The familiar tension of anything food-related hit her all at once. People tended to assume she either ate ALL the things, or deserved NONE of the things, and there was no middle ground. It didn't help that Mal obviously had no food issues himself, not with the shape he was in.

He put down two plates, exactly equal in terms of quantity. "Eat," he said, gesturing to the seat closest to her.

She sat down. "Thanks, but don't do this again. I'm perfectly capable of taking care of myself." In the sense that calling a bag of chips dinner was "capable."

"Ok, here's the thing. You stay here, you're a guest, and if you're a guest, you get fed. Tia Aida would murder me in my sleep if she ever heard that I didn't treat a guest right. Worse, she'd tell my abuela."

"And what would she do?"

"She wouldn't wait for me to be asleep to murder me, that's for sure."

Cara ate some of the eggs, which were tasty. She thought of the word *tia*. And *abuela*. Then she said, "Maybe I'm really dumb and missing something, but neither East nor Salem are Spanish, right?"

"My mom was Mexican, and her name was de Silva. Dad's side was Irish…mostly. And Salem is technically an English name, and it's a bit of a long story. But we—my brothers and me—spent a good chunk of time with my mom's side growing up."

Cara nodded and ate the rest of her meal, and then downed her coffee. "I have to go over to the site."

He glanced at the clock. "Shift doesn't start for half an hour."

"Good. I'd appreciate it if you took the full half hour."

"Ah. Ashamed to be seen with me."

"It's not exactly a good look professionally, ok?"

"You're all about professionalism, aren't you?"

"I am," she said. "My business is my life, and if you mess it up even a little bit, I'll find your abuela myself and tell her you were a terrible host."

"The nuclear option." Mal sighed. "Ok, get to work. I'll saunter in with a minute to spare."

That day was a little awkward at work, not just because Cara was terrified Mal would let slip that Cara was now sleeping in his house, but also because she had to explain Barry's absence.

The crew took it well, and if anything, they seemed happy that Barry was revealed as the thief. Turns out, Mal wasn't the only person who disliked the guy.

Jalen was in such a good mood that day that he actually smiled at her and said good morning when she passed him while he was installing the housing for the electrical.

"Whoa, Jalen. Was that a good morning? I thought you hated me."

"No, ma'am. You're probably the best foreman… forewoman…whatever…I've ever had on a job."

"Then why can't I get the time of day out of you?"

Jalen looked at her, really looked at her, for the very first time. "Remember the first day when you said no flirting, no hitting on you, all that stuff?"

"Yeah."

"You didn't have to tell me that. I know that. I had that drilled into me. And when stuff started going missing, I was just waiting to be called for it. Cops always look at a black man first."

Cara blinked, seeing things from his perspective. "Oh, Jalen."

"It's true."

"It's depressing. I guess it was a good thing Barry was a dumbass and let himself be caught. Well, for what it's worth, I think you're a good worker. If I was local, I'd hire you permanently."

"Thanks." He turned back to his work, but Cara felt like the brusqueness she'd seen before was a little lessened.

Cara spent the rest of the day working on the fireplace carving, wanting it to be done so she could have a nice backdrop for the shots of the floor. She took a ton of process pictures, chronicling her work on the carving and the installation of the whole mantelpiece.

She once again forgot that she'd had no opportunity to make her own lunch. She dashed to the office trailer and found several granola bars. She ate them and washed the sticky rice taste down with caustic orange soda. Then she returned to work.

At four, Mal walked into the parlor. Just like he did every time, he skirted around the edge of the floor and gave the whole room a dirty look. Cara was going to have to ask why he didn't like her marquetry.

"Shift's over. You want help packing up the tools?" Barry was in jail, but Cara had reiterated to the crew that they should still practice caution and put all the expensive stuff under lock and key when it wasn't in use.

She shook her head. "I want to keep working."

"Do you? Or is this a way to avoid being seen with me?"

"Not everything is about you, Malachy *East*," she said, laying on the sarcasm. "I actually want to finish this."

"It looks amazing, by the way," he said, gesturing to the mantel. "The carving on the people's robes and all the little folds and stuff. I'm sure there's a term for that."

"The term is *drapery*. It's easier to render in wood than in stone."

He snorted. "Easy. Sure."

"Go home, Mal. I'll show up when I'm done, ok?"

"Not too long."

"You're not the boss of me. In fact, I'm the boss of you. Go home."

He left, and she heard the rumble of all the guys' cars starting and then fading down the drive. Then it was quiet.

She turned up the volume on her phone speaker and returned to work. A little while later, she had to turn on another floodlight. The sun was going down earlier and earlier, and she walked across the hall to a room with a view to the west. The sky was already bleeding into those intense sunset colors—orange, red, purple—gorgeous right now, but only until darkness swallowed up all the light.

Cara was just turning around when she saw the faint outline of a little girl pass by the doorway. Cara froze for a second, and then moved to follow the shape.

The girl had just reached the turn in the hallway when Cara got to the door. She went left, and Cara followed.

The ghost walked, or seemed to walk, all the way to the basement stairs. Cold crept up Cara's spine, but she pursued the shape down there. She'd been in the basement plenty of times. The crew spent a whole day reinforcing beams in one corner. There was nothing frightening about the basement. Right?

When she reached the bottom of the stairs, she saw a filmy shape illuminating the space. The ghost was in the corner of the basement, near the wall close to the large, sagging back porch. It seemed to be looking up, trying to see something. But whatever ghostly powers it had, levitation wasn't one of them. It was too short to get whatever it wanted.

"Hey." Cara tried to sound friendly but forceful.

At the sound of her voice, the ghost froze and blinked out.

Cara then heard a strange sound, like a baby whimpering, or a mouse squeaking.

She walked closer and heard the weird sounds again. Frowning, she decided to find out what was causing the sound and fix it. No way was Cara going to pull late night shifts when the stupid house was squeaking and moaning at random, making even ghosts get out of Dodge.

She grabbed a stepladder. Beaming her flashlight at the wall, she studied the rough surface and knocked on the crumbling plaster. "Hello?"

Scratch, scratch.

What could be scratching like this? Rats? Someone buried alive, trying to claw their way out of a grave…

"Wow, slow your roll, honey," she told herself.

A thin, high-pitched sound emanated from the hollowed-out spot. Cara jumped, nearly falling from the ladder. The flashlight wobbled and caught a reflection where the wall met the joists of the flooring. There was a gap, and whatever was making the sound was on the other side.

Cara leapt to her feet and stormed up the stairs and out the back door of the house. The night air was cool and dry, a welcome change from the musty, dust-choked atmosphere inside.

She heard the sound again, high-pitched and pitiful.

Cara crawled into the space under the porch steps, crouching down to get a better angle. The damn shrubbery was thick as chain link over here. Something smelled nasty too.

She pulled the flashlight up, but before she could switch on the beam, she saw two glowing spots right in front of her. *Eyes.*

X

Cara threw her hand in front of her face to protect herself, and hit the switch of the flashlight to high.

The bright white beam illuminated a tiny kitten. The glowing eyes squeezed shut and it emitted a mewl of protest.

"Oh, sorry!" Cara said. The kitten was worse than scrawny. It was starving. Its fur was matted and mud-coated. She couldn't even tell what color it was. It wobbled as it took a few steps toward Cara's beckoning hand.

But there was a deep gouge in the ground here, like a miniature canyon, and the kitten would fall in if it kept coming toward Cara. She beamed the light around and saw that the only safe path was to enter the porch from the short side, way on the end of the house, and army crawl next to the foundation wall to reach the cat.

Then she beamed the light back to where the kitten sat and realized that the situation was way worse than she thought.

Bile rose up in her throat. "Hold on," she told the kitten. "Don't die. I'll be right back."

She crawled out from the porch and ran down the hill, nearly losing her footing in her haste. She crossed the road and pounded on the front door of the Salem house before she noticed the doorbell. She knocked again anyway. "Mal! Open the door!"

It seemed like forever before a shadow moved behind the curtained window, and then Mal's bulk filled the doorway. "It's not locked. Did you even try the knob?"

Cara didn't waste time on pleasantries. "I need cat food and a shovel."

He raised his eyebrows but otherwise seemed unmoved. "That sounds dark."

"Not for the same cat!" she sputtered.

Behemoth appeared behind Mal, as if summoned by the mention of its kin.

Cara took a breath. "I found a kitten under the back porch, and it really needs food, like now, and you've got a cat, which means you have cat food, so can you please help me out?"

"Why the shovel?"

She closed her eyes at the grisly image she'd seen. "There's one kitten alive, and some others that…aren't."

"Oh." Mal cast a glance at the black cat, then back to Cara. "Stay with Behemoth," he said abruptly. "I'll be back in a second."

"What are you doing?"

"Getting a shovel."

She squatted down to look the cat in the face. "I'm sorry to talk about cat death in front of you," she apologized. "I'm sorry I have to talk about it at all, actually. Like, what else on this job can go wrong?"

Behemoth's tail lashed a few times, and Cara took a step back. "Are you in a bad mood?" she asked.

"Are you talking with the cat?" Mal asked, reappearing with a heavy shovel gripped in one hand.

"I asked if he was in a bad mood. And he is. I mean, I assumed based on body language that he is."

"Behemoth is almost always in a bad mood." Mal looked at the cat. "We're going over there to take care of this. You stay here. *No*, we're not discussing it."

Cara stood up, realizing that she'd have to confront the scene she'd just left. At least she wouldn't be alone for round two.

Cara led Mal around the dark, looming bulk of the house.

"It was just under here," she said, pointing to the half-destroyed back porch. She flicked her flashlight on. "We have to go the long way. Let me go first. And watch the branches so they don't whip you in the face."

Cara pursued a tortuous route into the dense shrubbery and then to under the porch itself, moving slowly to avoid getting scratched. Behind her, Mal followed, moving with surprising stealth for a guy built like a bulldozer.

"Should have brought a chainsaw," he muttered.

Once under the porch, the going was a lot easier, though the passable area was really narrow. It looked like years of water erosion took its toll. One more task to add to the to-do list.

At last she saw the kitten, hiding in the deepest corner. "Hey, I'm back," she told it.

Mal scrambled up beside her.

The tiny kitten wobbled on its feet. "Come on over here," Cara urged, trying to exude gentleness and love. "You can do it."

"*Aquí, gatito,*" Mal murmured. He was stretched out on his belly to fit under the half-collapsed porch, and he was only inches from her. His voice was mellow and warm, and Cara was distracted from the kitten for a moment, thinking of the last time she'd been this close to any man in the dark.

"Come on, sweetheart," Cara cooed, refocusing. "We won't hurt you. We're here to help."

The kitten paused. Then, with effort, bounded once to reach Cara's outstretched hands.

She gently grasped the ball of fluff, feeling just as much mud as fur. "Ok, I've got him."

"I'm going to deal with the other ones. Can you shimmy out without the flashlight?" Mal asked. "I'll shine it to light your way as much as I can."

Cara nodded. She carefully extracted herself and her precious burden, crawling back the way she came. On the lawn, she cradled the kitten close to her chest, hoping it wasn't too late to save him.

Moments later, Mal emerged from the shrubbery, now holding a heavy-duty garbage bag containing something very upsetting. He picked up the shovel in his other hand. "Come on, let's get back to the house."

"What about…those?" Cara indicated the garbage bag. "We should bury them."

Mal shook his head. "Later. We take care of the living before we take care of the dead."

He said it like a mantra, or a rule he knew so well he didn't have to think twice.

Cara blinked, again trying to realign her assumptions about this guy. "Um, how often do you do this?"

"Save tiny kittens? Hardly ever." Mal smiled then, a flash of white teeth against the darkness of the night. "Come on."

They returned to the Salem property, but before Cara could walk up the front path, he stopped her. Behemoth sat there like a bouncer, his tail lashing to and fro.

"Hold on," Mal said. He bent down right at the edge of the yard, dropping the shovel. Then he took the kitten from her and put it in front of Behemoth.

"What is this, a job interview?" she asked. "The kitten is cold and starving."

"Just wait," Mal said softly, his gaze locked on the cats. "This is important."

Cara was struck by something in his voice, a seriousness that seemed out of place for Mal. Not that she knew him that well. Maybe she wanted to know him better.

She shifted her attention to the black cat, who was examining the tiny, pathetic lump of kitten with what seemed like extreme judginess.

Then, just when Cara was losing patience, Behemoth bent his head, took the kitten up by the scruff of the neck, and spun about, heading for the house.

"All right," Mal said with a relieved sigh. "Let's get this orphan cleaned up."

In the kitchen, Mal filled the kitchen sink with an inch of warm water and gestured for Cara to lower the kitten into it. "Keep hold of the little guy. I'm not sure how he'll react."

It barely twitched as its paws got wet, and only mewed a bit in protest when Cara started spooning the water over its back, soaking its fur. She rubbed her fingers into the kitten's coat, trying to loosen the caked mud and the debris that had got stuck to it. The water quickly turned brown, and the kitten slowly grew less brown.

"I think he's orange," Cara said.

Mal reached for the sprayer, tested the water pressure, and held the sprayer over the cat like a tiny shower. It meowed louder, and started to wiggle more, almost getting free of Cara's grasp.

"He's not loving this," Cara said.

"Yeah, he's too young to appreciate getting into a shower with a hot girl."

Cara blinked. "Excuse me?"

"Sorry. Woman."

That wasn't the word that startled her, but Cara was suddenly way too aware of Mal to discuss it.

Once it was clean, she wrapped the kitten in the towel and gently rubbed him dry. He started purring, and her heart melted completely. "I'm going to call him Pumpkin," she announced.

"Good name. Does that mean you're keeping him?"

"I want to," she said, more hesitantly. Keeping any pet was a big responsibility, and she had a lot on her plate already. "I should take him to a vet before I get too attached. Who knows what condition he's in?"

"I know a vet who's really good. Dr. Amber. But tonight, let's see if he'll eat."

Mal made a disgusting slurry using milk and canned tuna, then put a small amount in a shallow bowl and placed the kitten in front of it. "Behemoth, show him how it's done."

The big black cat was extremely interested in the new arrival, and he took a bite of the food, then waited for Pumpkin to imitate him.

After a second of sniffing, Pumpkin took a bite. Then another. And another. Then the kitten just jammed his snout into the bowl.

Cara was delighted beyond words. "He's eating!"

"Now he just has to keep the food down," Mal said. He looked over at her. "Speaking of food, you need anything? I was going to make dinner right when you came over."

He was probably hungry, and Cara had distracted him with her mission of mercy. "I'm good," she demurred. "Remember when I said I can take care of myself?"

"Sure, but now you have to take care of Pumpkin, so how about you let me deal with dinner? And in the morning I can drive him to the vet."

"You don't have to do that."

"I know I don't. I'm offering. Besides, what are you going to do? Skip work? Do you know *how* to skip work?"

Good point.

"Besides," Mal said with a grin. "I think my boss will understand if I show up late when I tell her I was literally saving a kitten."

"Ok, but that excuse only works once," Cara warned.

Mal turned the oven on and then started pulling items out of the fridge. "How'd you find the cat?" he asked.

Cara sighed, unhappy that she had to confront the reality. "A ghost led me to the kittens. The ghost of a little girl."

Mal paused. "It *led* you there?"

"Well, I saw it out of the corner of my eye and followed it. I don't think it was deliberate. For all I know, the ghost girl was interested in the dead cats, because maybe there's ghost kittens there now? Oh, how horrible." Cara hated the thought of little ghost kittens.

"It's pretty rare for animals to be ghosts," Mal said.

"You say that with a disturbing amount of confidence. You're going to have to explain how you know all this." Cara stood up. "I should bury those poor cats. The sooner the better."

"I'll take care of it."

"It's not your job," Cara said, feeling like she'd really taken advantage of him. Lord, a tiny kitten and the damsel in distress. "I can handle it."

Mal shook his head. "You focus on Pumpkin. I know what to do. If it makes you feel better, I'll be saying a prayer for them. Santa Muerte is fond of cats."

"Who?"

"Santa Muerte," he repeated, more cautiously. "Let's just say Death."

"There's a saint of death? Is that Catholic?"

"Sort of Mexican and sort of Catholic but also some other traditions and it's kind of not important now." He gestured toward the living room. "You could light a candle for the cats, if you want. That'd be good."

Cara looked over at the shelf she hadn't noticed until now. "Is that an ofrenda? Is it for Halloween?"

"Yes, but it's year round."

She walked over to check it out. The ofrenda was chock-full of pictures and candles and little knickknacks, some of them pretty random. Kwan Yin? An elephant? She looked at the photos, some black and white, some very recent.

"Your family?"

"Family and friends, yeah."

"Who's the couple?" She regarded the central photograph in a silver frame.

"My parents."

Cara went still. "Your parents? But they're so young!" The couple was in costume, as if for a Halloween party.

She couldn't date it by clothes. But Mal wasn't that old himself. Maybe late twenties?

"It was an accident," he explained, not looking at her. "Years ago."

"I'm so sorry."

Mal shrugged, obviously not wanting to talk about it. Cara got the impression that whatever happened, it was still raw, no matter how many years it had been. He'd mentioned once, casually, that he'd spent a lot of time with his mom's side of the family growing up, a statement that took on new meaning now. He wasn't just talking about his grandmother as a distant relative. She must have raised him and his brothers.

Cara lit a candle, thinking of the kittens that didn't make it. She didn't feel comfortable praying, since she wasn't particularly a believer in anything. Although now she knew that ghosts were real, maybe she should rethink her assumptions.

"Mal? I have questions."

"I bet." He smiled a bit, and it made her feel better to know that whatever had happened to him, he could still smile.

"What's real?" she asked. "I mean, if ghosts, then…"

"Sit down," he said, indicating the stool by the kitchen counter. "I'll explain while I cook."

She sat, and wordlessly accepted a bottle of beer Mal slid toward her. After a long sip, she said, "Ok. I've never believed in ghosts. But that house up there is legit haunted."

"Yes. Ghosts are real, and at least one is up there. Possibly more than one, I'm not sure. And ghosts aren't the worst part of that house."

"What's the worst part?"

He chewed his lower lip, obviously thinking hard. Just when Cara was about to retract the question, he said, "There's more than one world. There's this world, what we think of as the real world. But there are hundreds of others. Call them different realities or dimensions or whatever. It's like they're separate, but also all sandwiched next to each other, and sometimes they can overlap, and sometimes things can pass through the barriers between them."

"Is this like the Copenhagen Interpretation but with ghosts?"

Mal frowned. "You'd have to ask Lex. He's the smart one. And Dom is the powerful one."

"What are you?"

"The tough one."

She believed that, after seeing him fight once. But she didn't like the way he said it, like it was unimportant. "You're a superhero team? You and your brothers?"

"Basically. Demon-hunting is the Salem family business. Has been for generations. My brothers and I just made it a bit more like a…business. People get in touch with us and we help them solve whatever supernatural problem they're having. That's why Dom is gone now— he's off to break a curse. Should be back by next week."

Cara nodded, and then put two things together. "Wait a second. Did someone call you and ask for you to join the job site *because* it's haunted? Did Morningside hire you?"

He shook his head. "No one hired us. Egan House has been on our radar. A member of the Salem family has been watching it for years, and my brothers and I just happened to take over recently. When the construction was about to start, it was too good an opportunity to pass up. So I applied."

"You're just there to get intel! You don't even need the job."

"Uh, actually the pay is a very nice side benefit," he said. "Demon-hunting is not the most stable business. And I'd like to point out that I *am* working."

"Sure, but you're mostly poking around the house looking for…what?"

"Let's just say I'm looking for supernatural problems."

"You are not getting away with that level of vagueness," Cara told him. "You said this house is a known issue. What do you know about it that I don't?"

Mal used the fact that the food was ready to avoid answering. He offered her a plate of rice, broccoli, and some fantastic-smelling orange chicken. "This looks really good," she said. It also looked ten times more nutritious than what she'd been eating on the job site the whole week.

"It's all out of packages. I'm no chef."

Cara ate, but didn't let it distract her. "Egan House. Tell me."

Mal poked at his chicken. "You studied the history yourself. Rich guy builds a mansion, and it's very fancy and pretty weird, especially when it comes to design and decoration."

"It's called architectural," she said.

"It's called occult. And not in the sense of it was in fashion to use Egyptian designs or whatever. That house was built on that hill for a very specific reason. That location is uniquely suited to be a portal to other realities. That's why Egan moved out from New York City and bought it. The house is just a shell. He wanted access to that spot on the hill."

"You have got to be kidding me."

"I am not. Things have happened there, bad things." Mal started ticking things off on his fingers. "The fire that destroyed the house killed Mrs. Egan, you know that? And Egan himself was basically a raving madman for the rest of his life, which ended in an asylum in the '50s. The sons both died in the war, which probably didn't help Egan's state of mind. According to the research my family has done, the most likely scenario is that Egan built the house to hide the fact that he was also building a way to activate the hellhole—"

"The what now?"

"We call portals hellholes. It doesn't matter where they open up to—it's not always a hell, but it's usually a place ordinary people shouldn't be poking into."

"Ok, there's a *hellhole*..." Cara said, not bothering to hide her resurgent skepticism.

"Yeah. Egan was obsessed with magic. He and his wife were both known to associate with some very sketchy folks in the US and all over Europe. He somehow learned about this location, which is locally famous as a spooky ass place. Settlers wouldn't go there, and there are even a couple of hints in the early place-names that some of the local tribes designated it as forbidden land, guarding against anyone climbing the hill or staying there at night."

"Until they got shoved out west, huh? So no one was guarding later on."

"Bingo. The native knowledge about the hellhole became folklore and then eventually just local spook stories. Egan bought the property because no one was in a position to stop him. And he spent the next two years prepping the site to serve as a working portal to other dimensions."

"Why?"

"Who knows? He wasn't exactly sane enough to answer questions afterward."

"But Egan never actually opened his portal because the fire destroyed the house?"

Mal nodded, but looked uncertain. "Our working theory is that they were in the act of opening it and something went wrong. Spells like that are super complicated, and if you mess something up, dying is the best thing that can happen to you. The fire was likely a side effect of a mistake in spell casting, and it got out of control because the Egans were unable to do anything about it while they were wrapped up in magic. The wife died from the smoke, Egan got away from the physical fire but was already zapped by the magic, and the house burned merrily until dawn."

"So it was over before it began."

"It's not over," Mal said seriously. "The portal itself is still there. And someone—your client or someone who's influencing them—is taking the first steps to reactivate it. We think that fancy floor you're working on is the key. As soon as I saw it in person, I felt how powerful it was, even unfinished."

Cara's back stiffened. "You're saying that what I'm doing is evil?"

"Not directly. You don't have an evil bone in your body. But good intentions can be bent. And your pretty floor is a very large summoning circle. All those symbols aren't just there for show. They have occult significance. You're laying out a spell in wooden pieces, whether you know it or not."

"You're saying it will be my fault?"

"No!" Mal reached across the counter and grabbed her hand. "No one's blaming you. But whatever is happening in that house, you're involved, Cara. And I don't want you getting hurt."

"Why do you care if I get hurt or not?" Cara asked, even as she became exquisitely conscious of the touch of his hand over hers. She could feel the strength in him just by the way his fingers curled over hers.

Mal didn't reply, but he looked at her in a way that sent Cara's heart rate spiking. His eyes locked with hers, and she was getting lost in the deep brown gaze that exuded sensuality, but also something even deeper and more threatening to Cara's carefully guarded peace of mind. Like, maybe, impossibly, he did care about her a little. And what was she supposed to do with that info?

Mal's gaze dropped a bit, letting Cara breathe with relief, until she realized he was looking at her mouth.

He's going to kiss me. A lightning bolt through her brain would not have been more shocking than the understanding that scorching-hot Mal Salem would absolutely kiss Cara in about three seconds if she made the tiniest sign that she wanted him too. Which was why she had to fight the overwhelming instinct to lick her lips, or spread her fingers to stroke the palm of his hand, or close her eyes and let her body take over.

What would it feel like to kiss him? To touch him? Cara's temperature soared. *This is the worst idea ever.*

She swallowed hard and pulled her hand from his, leaning back. "I gotta check on the cat. And then go to bed. Like alone. And right away. And I'll get a hotel tomorrow because this is…not something I should have…I don't need this. And you don't need this. This isn't even a thing. Ok." *Shut up, Cara*, she yelled at herself. She was babbling like an idiot, and Mal hadn't said anything, and she was probably hallucinating that he wanted to kiss her just like she hallucinated seeing smoke and flames the other night.

Cara got up and looked for the kitten. A meow led her gaze to the beat-up couch in the living room.

Pumpkin was curled up in a tiny ball, nestled right next to Behemoth's dark bulk. The black cat's tail was curled protectively around the orange kitten.

Mal was standing behind the island, looking perfectly in control of himself. No hint of lust in his eyes at all. Just a smile for the cats. "See? Everything's going to be fine, Cara. Let Pumpkin settle in. You should go up to bed. You've had a long day."

Did she ever. Cara fled upstairs and when she closed her door, she locked it. Whether it was to keep Mal out or her in, she didn't know.

Cara couldn't be sure what was real anymore, and if Mal was interested in her even a little bit, it meant the world she knew was totally flipped on its axis.

XI

SHE IS NOT YOUR TYPE.

She is not your type.

She is not your type.

Mal chanted the words at himself until Cara was gone from the first floor, and he heard the sound of a door close upstairs.

Wow, he'd been about to do something really stupid.

And he was starting to think he was wrong about what his type was.

Mal took a breath. He was happy to have solved the immediate problem of Cara sleeping right over a hellhole. But having her in the house definitely brought up a new problem, namely that Cara was very close by, and Mal could barely think straight around her. It put him on edge.

When he was on edge, his favorite way to unwind was sex. Fun, fast, furious sex with no strings attached. And that meant *not* with anyone actually living in his house, no matter how briefly.

He could go upstairs, take a quick shower, get dressed, and head out to a bar. He'd find someone up for fun within the hour. Some nice, hot blonde who he didn't have to pretend to be friends with first. A woman who wanted a wild night and then would push him out the door before she got up for brunch with her gang.

He could do that. But he didn't want to.

Mal stood there for a long minute, trying to decide what he did want.

Then he glanced at the two sleeping cats and remembered he had other duties.

He went to the spell supply closet and selected a few items. Then he walked outside to where he'd put the garbage bag and the shovel before.

It didn't take long to decide where to bury the remains of the cats who hadn't survived. There was a particular spot in the vast backyard that was sheltered by a few pine trees, and away from the main yard…assuming they ever got around to making it a proper yard.

Mal checked the cardinal directions and then dug a grave, careful to move clockwise as he did. The hole was much deeper than the pitiful size of the remains, but Mal wanted these cats to be firmly tucked into sacred ground.

Sanctifying the grave was an easy enough process. A sprinkle of sage and mint. A scattering of holy water from a little blue glass bottle. Then a dash of catnip, because cats.

He opened the garbage bag and gently transferred the remains of the kittens to the grave. Five tiny bodies, all taken before they even got a chance to experience life as cats.

"Santa Muerte," he began, instinctively using Spanish, "give these unnamed cats a safe and speedy passage to the afterlife. Keep them from any harm. They died close to a hellhole, and their souls need watching. Gertrude, patron saint of cats, I pray for you to intercede to help these kittens be reborn as cats again. They didn't get a fair shot this time. Francis, you too if you have a minute. I'll watch over the living if you can mind the dead. Amen."

Mal shoveled dirt over the grave and mounded it up. He placed five small stones in a circle around the top, using them as points to trace a simple pentagram in the soil.

He stood up, feeling unaccountably drained. This sort of ritual barely counted as magic, but Mal found it a challenge all the same.

He remained there in silence for a minute, then walked back to the house, returning the shovel to its spot in the garage before walking into the kitchen. He planned to wash his hands about three times, and then pour a serious shot of whiskey.

He was washing his hands when he heard Behemoth's voice in his head.

The little one is sick.

Mal hurried out of the bathroom, his hands still wet.

Pumpkin was on the couch, but he was no longer sleeping peacefully. He wheezed in and out, and his little sides were puffing as he tried to get air that wasn't coming in.

He needs help. And soon, or he too will die.

"I'm on it."

He didn't like to exploit a personal relationship, especially with an ex, but Pumpkin's condition looked like a code red.

Mal grabbed his phone and found the right number. At the beep, he said, "Amber, I got an emergency. I'm driving over to the clinic right now with a sick kitten and you need to be there. He's not breathing right. Oh, this is Mal. Later."

He scooped the cat up and deposited it in the nearest container, which happened to be a saucepan hanging from the rack in the kitchen.

The car started—a minor miracle for which he thanked St. Gertrude, who was obviously paying attention—and Mal drove three miles to the vet clinic in the tiny downtown, talking to Pumpkin the whole time.

A blonde woman stood in the doorway. She waved when Mal pulled up and parked in the handicapped spot. Mal grabbed the saucepan and got out.

"Did you cook for me? That was the emergency?" Amber asked.

Mal showed her the contents of the pan. Amber took it from him and strode into the clinic. He followed, hoping that whatever was happening to Pumpkin was a solvable problem.

"Take a seat. I'll be a few minutes." Amber took the kitten into the back.

Mal waited, tapping his foot against the rail of the chair. He considered texting Cara and then remembered he didn't have her number. Damn. Then again, what could he say that wouldn't make her panic?

He waited. He made a reminder to get Cara's number ASAP. He waited more.

After what seemed like an hour but was probably only twenty minutes, Amber emerged, sans cat.

"The little guy was totally dehydrated and had an obstruction that was impeding his respiration. Probably ate too much after nearly starving. Food chunks can go down the wrong way. I had to sedate him to get the obstruction out, and I want to keep him till tomorrow for observation."

"Will he recover?"

"With proper care, yes. I'll do a more thorough examination tomorrow to make sure that there are no chronic conditions, but my guess is that he's simply a severely malnourished stray. You found him?"

"Yeah. Well, I helped and he's staying at my place for a few days. His name is Pumpkin."

"Cute. I'll note it in the file. Pumpkin Salem."

"Uh, it would be Pumpkin Michaels, actually."

Amber raised an eyebrow but didn't get into it. "How are your other kitties? Piewicket and the other one. Monster?"

"Behemoth. The cats are fine."

"Good to hear. Haven't heard from you in a while," Amber noted.

"I've been busy. Working. Construction. How are you doing?"

"Great."

Mal paused, then asked, "Seeing someone?"

"Yes, actually. It's, uh, it's going really well." Amber smiled and blushed slightly, the universal sign of a satisfied-with-life woman.

Mal was happy for her, and said so. She'd never blushed like that around him. Of course, neither of them were exactly looking for long-term bliss at the time. Mal preferred to stay away from long-term commitments. Or short-term commitments. Or any commitments.

No commitments meant no problems, and you didn't have to worry about endings.

"Thanks," Amber said. "I hope you're doing well too." She shifted back into professional mode. "Come back anytime after noon, and you can pick Pumpkin up and I'll give you, or whoever, a full report."

"You're a lifesaver. Literally."

She grinned. "I know. I'll see you out and lock up behind you."

She let him out and waved from behind the glass.

Mal walked to his car, but just as he got a grip on the door handle, he caught a glimpse of something out of the corner of his eye.

He looked up and around without seeming to. He didn't see anything. No, wait. There was a figure standing a few doors away, watching him.

The guy, dressed in dark jeans and a hoodie, tipped his head once, indicating the passageway between two buildings that led to the alley behind. Then he walked down it, getting lost in the shadows.

Mal sighed. Spooky Dude was really going to do this B-movie bullshit? He considered just getting in the car and leaving, but then thought of Amber, alone in the clinic because he'd asked her to be there. Nope. He couldn't leave while there was the slightest potential for her to get hurt. He slowly loosened his muscles and rolled his shoulders, then followed Spooky Dude.

There were no doors and nowhere to hide along the passage, and Mal was smart enough to come out into the alley fast and crouched down. Sure enough, he felt the air just above him woosh as Spooky Dude took a swing where he thought Mal's head would be.

Mal nearly ran into the opposite wall of the alley before he stopped and swung around to face the other guy. The alley was much wider than the passage, with a lane for vehicles and dumpsters and trash cans behind each building. Plenty of space for a fight.

Spooky Dude whirled around, pointing directly at Mal's head. "Malachy East."

Not my name, but super interesting you used it. "What do you want?"

"I want you to stay away from Cara Michaels."

"She tell you to say that?" Mal asked, shifting his weight to the balls of his feet.

"Doesn't mat—"

That was as much as the guy got to say, because Mal jumped forward, grabbing the edge of the otherworlds as he went. He folded the ripple between realities around himself, giving him more time than the other guy had. He slid into the world next door just long enough to let him move ten feet in an instant. As far as the other guy knew, Mal simply flashed from where he'd been to within grabbing distance.

The flesh Mal grabbed was ice cold. He closed his hand around the guy's neck to make breathing difficult. But this guy wasn't breathing in the first place.

Vampire.

And me without a stake, Mal thought.

Why would he have a stake? He was in his hometown, on an emergency vet run.

The vampire was startled by Mal's unexpected speed, but he recovered fast. He reached up, and with inhuman strength began to pull Mal's arm off his neck.

Don't look, don't look.

Looking into a vampire's eyes, or even letting it talk to you, was an invitation to bitestown. It meant slipping under the vampire's power, and then it would leisurely drain you of all your blood and let you die.

Mal closed his eyes. When outgunned, you have to do something unexpected to stay in the fight.

He bit the vampire.

"What the…" the lurk screeched.

"You can dish it out but you can't take it, huh," Mal said. Or rather, he sort of said, because he still had half a mouthful of undead flesh, which ruined the crispness of his snappy jibe.

Oh, well.

He bit the vampire again, because while a vampire doesn't expect a victim to bite back, it sure doesn't expect the victim to do it twice.

And then he used his free hand to pull out the chain he wore around his neck. He pressed the crucifix to the vampire's body.

The thing screeched again, more from rage than pain, but it released Mal, dropping him to the rough, greasy pavement.

Mal turned and ran down the alley, diving behind a large dumpster about sixty feet on.

"You can't hide from us," the vamp yelled, his feet slamming on the pavement as he chased after Mal. "You get in our way, we get you out of the way. You're lucky I'm only going to kill you."

Mal listened to the rant as he hunted around among wadded-up trash and debris, looking for anything like a weapon. He surprised a few rats, who dashed out into the alley. Then his hand touched something else, and he felt a jolt of hope.

A desperate squeak echoed through the alley and ended abruptly. The vamp just had its appetizer.

There is a dreadful feeling when you're waiting for the inevitable. Mal knew the vampire knew exactly where he was. Vampires were predators. They smelled their prey, they heard sounds no human could pick up on. The vampire could probably hear Mal's heart and know its BPM.

Vampires also liked to play with their food, and Mal wasn't entirely shocked when the body of a dead rat dropped on him.

"Here's your friend," the unseen vamp growled. "But I'm still hungry."

Mal leaned against the brick wall behind him, keeping himself steady, even while his whole being was screaming at him to run, run, run away. No matter how much training he endured, the human instinct was to flee, to survive, to get out of the path of scary things.

The point of training was to help him past that feeling.

The vampire appeared in front of him, stepping beyond the dumpster and rushing forward to grab Mal like a tasty snack.

The strength in the creature was mind-boggling, way beyond what logic told him was possible.

Mal swung his right hand up just as the vampire was leaning in for its first bite. Mal couldn't stop a half-formed shout of pain as splinters jabbed into his palm.

But he'd aimed well, and it was totally worth it to hear the vampire's gasp as the scrap of wood Mal had recovered from the trash broke its skin.

"Just die," Mal hissed, pushing forward with all his own strength. The piece of wood finally connected with the vampire's heart, and the splinters that made Mal wince were doing a lot worse to the monster.

Within seconds, the vampire's body went still. Mal pulled out his trusty pocket knife and slit the vampire's throat, just to be sure. Then he raised his foot and stepped on the end of the makeshift stake, driving it all the way through the dead flesh.

The vampire started to shrivel and smoke, its body losing form as the demonic energy that fueled it was sucked back into whatever hellish otherworld it came from.

A moment later, Mal stood over a pile of ash. He said, "Santa Muerte, I send you one more soul tonight, a particularly crusty one that you can do whatever you want with. Have fun."

He turned and walked back to his car. There was no sound or light from any of the windows of the buildings. He was amazed that the fight hadn't roused a single person's interest.

Mal was never so happy to get home. The feeling of crossing over the barrier that protected the Salem home was a lot like stepping into sunshine after getting dumped on by rain.

He stumbled into the kitchen, his right hand now throbbing with pain, little bits of wood jammed into his flesh.

You smell hideous, Behemoth told him.

"Vampire," he replied, and heard Behemoth's answering hiss. "Keep extra sharp watch tonight, ok?"

You may rely on me. I will protect every soul in this house.

On that subject, he had full confidence in the cat.

Mal was actually shaking with fatigue. A long day, an unexpected burial, a very unexpected vampire, and a fight where he had to slide into the otherworlds just to stay alive. Yeah, time to hit the sack.

He had just enough energy to scrawl a note to Cara, and leave it on the kitchen island. He reached up and unfastened the chain around his neck, dropping it right next to the note. Then he dragged himself up to his bedroom and just managed to fall onto his bed before he lost consciousness.

XII

W‌HEN C‌ARA WOKE UP, THE first thing she wanted to do was find Pumpkin, so she dressed and hurried downstairs. It was totally quiet, no cats or humans in sight. But a note lay on the counter, along with a tangled metal chain.

C—

Pumpkin got sick. I drove him to Dr. Amber, who kept him overnight. But don't freak out. He'll be fine, and I'll get him later today. I'm sleeping in. Don't fire me. Also, here's a necklace. Put it on and keep it on. PLEASE. I'll explain everything later.

—M

Frowning, Cara reached over and pick up the metal chain, noticing it had a pendant. It looked like a saint's medal, though it was rather old and smushed so she couldn't see enough detail to know which saint it might be. Also strung on the chain was a small crucifix, probably brass. Despite the very homely appearance of the jewelry, there was something special about it. Cara put it on, hoping that she wasn't just falling for some occulty mumbo jumbo because she was falling for Mal.

She left the house and walked across the street, grateful that she was early. No other workers had shown up yet.

Cara tilted her head up, examining the exterior of the structure. After everything Mal told her about the secret history of Egan House, it was hard to look at it the same way. Even though the day was bright and sunny, crisp and clear in a way that only autumn days can be, the building looked cold.

Worse than cold. Creepy.

"It's just a job," Cara told herself. "Haunted or not, this is not my problem. And Mal might be wrong anyway."

Cara didn't even get a chance to touch the marquetry work that day. She was too busy running around, directing the men working in various parts of the house. She must have climbed forty flights, from answering questions in the basement, where Jalen and Kevin were patching the walls, to upstairs, where Dan and Reyes had discovered termite damage in the north bedrooms. The only bright side was that the termite damage was from fifty years ago, and no little creatures were currently chomping on the delicious wood.

"We'll have to do a run to the lumber yard," Dan said. "If we don't fix this, it could cause the roof to start sagging."

Cara nodded, calculating the amount of lumber needed. "I'll call Morningside and get it approved as a purchase, but just take the credit card and go. He won't say no to this." Maybe by the time Dan returned, Mal would be there to help with the repairs.

But no. Mal wasn't just sleeping in, he failed to show up the whole day. Cara was sort of pissed, but mostly worried, especially since she couldn't run down to the Salem house without busting the lid off a whole bunch of secrets. Yet another reason to not live with your employee. Keeping things on the DL was practically impossible.

Cara sent the guys home a bit early, waiting only until the taillights on Dan's truck disappeared down the road before she hotfooted it across the street.

Inside, Mal sat on the couch, nursing a beer and a kitten, which was not something Cara expected to see. He had Pumpkin wrapped in a hand towel like a burrito, and he was feeding it from a bottle, while occasionally taking a sip of beer from his own bottle.

She skipped the preliminaries. "What is going on? Where were you all day? How's Pumpkin? Why am I wearing a weird necklace?"

"Sit down." Mal indicated the seat next to him on the couch. She took it only to be close to Pumpkin. *Riiiight.*

He gave Cara the run-down on what happened to the cat, the midnight run to the vet, picking him up this afternoon, and the fact that Pumpkin was on a liquid diet for the next three to five days.

"The vet says he should be fine, but we need to watch him and just take things slow. He had a rough start in life, and we need to give him time."

Cara reached over and petted Pumpkin's ear. The kitten mewed and started purring loudly. "Oh, I love you," she whispered.

"Hey, take things slow, I said. Oh, were you talking to the cat?" Mal grinned at her.

She rolled her eyes, fighting off a blush. "Shut up."

He transferred the burrito of cat to Cara, offering her the bottle of what she presumed was kitten formula.

Then she saw his right hand was bandaged. "Wait, what happened there?"

"Uh, just an accident with a chunk of wood. I'll be fine."

"Did you have a weirder night than you're admitting? And why did you tell me to wear this?" Cara withdrew the chain from under her shirt. "Where did it come from?"

"It's mine. And you're wearing it for protection."

"Yours? Like you were wearing it yesterday and I'm wearing it today?" That felt a lot more personal than Cara was prepared for.

"Exactly. I want to strengthen the protection for you, which means I'll need to do a spell, and I'm going to need your full name for that."

"Hold on. A spell?"

"Yeah. Magic is real, just like ghosts and hellholes. You need more protection than you've got right now, and magic is going to help with that."

"No, I believe you! It's not that. But you're going to do a spell on me?"

"On the necklace, which you'll wear. And not unless you say it's ok, because I can't cast it without you giving me your full name. Just Cara Michaels isn't going to cut it."

"Oh." *This is about to be awkward.* She kept her eyes on Pumpkin as she said, "Actually…Cara Michaels isn't my name."

Mal looked at her with raised eyebrows and took a long sip of beer, then said, "What's your real name?"

She took a breath. Was she going to spill this? Yes, yes, she was. "Caitlin Marine Carmichael."

"Did you not like your name?" he asked, puzzled.

"It's not a matter of liking. My dad was in the construction business in New York and New Jersey. He taught me a lot, and he's why I got into woodworking and why I know as much about building as I do. He was looking forward to creating a real family business. He got very successful, and then sort of got involved with some players who…ok, it was the mob. Things went badly. Dad messed up, yeah. But I know he took the fall for some other people who did way worse things. Dad knew that he was sacrificing his freedom to keep his family safe. Safer anyway."

Mal leaned forward. "Where's your dad now?"

"A federal penitentiary in Colorado," Cara said. For some reason, telling Mal all this didn't seem as tough as she feared. "He's serving ten to fifteen for fraud, embezzlement, and a bunch of other crimes. His company was

Carmichael Construction, and all his clients left and the state seized his assets, and he had to declare bankruptcy. I had to strike out on my own if I wanted to make any money, but having the same name as a convicted felon is not exactly good for business. So I…made a few strategic changes to my identity. Carmichael became Cara Michaels. Michaels is a common name. It doesn't raise red flags. And I can do what I'm good at without needing to worry about Dad's old associates."

"Do you talk to him?"

"We send letters. He doesn't like the phone. And he says I can't visit because he doesn't want anyone there to know he's got such a pretty girl for a daughter." She finished on a derisive snort.

But Mal shook his head. "I totally understand his motivation. Sounds like he made mistakes, big ones, but he did his best to keep you safe. He's still doing it."

Cara wiped away a tear that pooled in the corner of her eye. "Yeah, I know. It's just…it was hard. Not anything like what you went through." She gestured to the ofrenda.

Mal shifted to put his arm around Cara's shoulders, drawing her closer to him. "I've had most of my life to adjust. You've only had, what, a few years?"

"Still not the same." Cara leaned against him, trying not to enjoy the feel of his body. Then she stiffened when she thought of how he was going to react to her less-than-ideal figure. She'd heard plenty of comments about that from…well, everyone, from her family to old boyfriends to random strangers.

"Is it ok to call you Cara?" Mal asked, still keeping his arm around her, evidently not squicked out. Or maybe he just liked being close to Pumpkin, who was snuggling in Cara's arms.

She nodded. "I prefer it, actually. New life and all."

"Wow, I really don't know anything about you. What's your favorite color?"

"Um, red, probably."

"Favorite movie?"

"Impossible question. Try again."

"Ok, favorite fruit."

"Cherries."

"Favorite subject in school."

"Math."

"Whoa, really?"

"I always liked math. And I was good at it."

"I bet. I mean, you're really smart. I just thought you'd say art, because you're an artist."

She shook her head. "I'm a carpenter."

"I've seen your website. All those things you've carved. You're an artist who does carpentry on the side."

Cara grew unaccountably shy at Mal's praise. "Maybe." She'd always been proud of her talents, and she knew she had a level of skill few others did. But it felt different hearing Mal talk about it.

Pumpkin had fallen asleep, his purrs tapering off into silence. Cara put the cat bottle aside. "I should put him somewhere safe."

"Behemoth, come here," Mal called.

"Uh, cats don't come when they're called," Cara told him, but then Behemoth appeared and walked directly toward Cara and Pumpkin. He jumped on the couch, nuzzled the kitten and took him by the scruff, and then stalked away.

"Wow," Cara said. "That was…unexpected."

"Behemoth is a pretty special cat. An asshole, but special."

Cara closed her eyes, her head falling back as everything just sort of overwhelmed her. "Sweet fancy Moses. Magic is real."

Beside her, Mal laughed, a low rumble that did things to her insides. "Yeah it is. But it's not all bad. Some of it is definitely good."

"Like what?"

"Like being able to cast protection spells."

Mal's fingers brushed against her neck. Her eyes flew open to find him leaning even closer to her. But he was only reaching for the necklace.

"Easy there, gorgeous," he said, his mellow voice only making her more fluttery on the inside. "Let me take the necklace tonight and I'll cast the protection spell. Then you can have it back in the morning and we'll both feel a lot better."

Cara scrambled to pull the necklace off, and also to give herself a few inches of space to clear her head. Being right next to Mal was confusing. She put the necklace into his open hand. "What will it protect me against?"

"Let's say evil."

"Let's be more specific."

"Um, ok," he said. "It should help anchor you to this reality and also repel creatures from the otherworlds who have nasty plans for you. It's not a very powerful spell, not compared to some of the stuff good casters can do. But it will help, and I really want to help."

"Why? I mean, you're worried about the house, not me. Right?"

"It started with the house, but you're a bonus. It's not like I'm going to let a girl get in danger when I'm right there to stop it. I'm not a complete jerk."

"I don't think you're a jerk."

"Aww, thanks." He smiled, but his eyes were doing the smoldery thing again, and it didn't help that his smile drew her attention to his mouth, and wow did she want to kiss him.

Which would lead to a super embarrassing situation. She said, "I, um…I've got some stuff to take care of."

"Me too," Mal said, sitting up straighter. "I'll get out of your way. Is pizza ok for dinner? I was just going to order a large pepperoni."

"That'd be great."

"Great."

"Great."

Awkward. Cara heaved herself off the couch and retreated to the spare bedroom.

Things settled down once the pizza arrived. Cara convinced herself she'd been making stuff up before. Mal was his normal chill self, and they watched his favorite movie, *Dark Carnival.* She also learned that his favorite fruit was watermelon, his favorite subject in school was gym ("not a real subject," Cara had objected), and his favorite color was black.

Later that night, she called her mom after she'd tucked herself into bed. She talked to her mother only every couple of weeks, mostly because the conversations tended to end poorly.

Her mom picked up right away, and the first few minutes were the usual small talk. Then Cara said, "I think I might have a new pet. I found a stray cat on the job site. A kitten, actually. He's super cute. I called him Pumpkin, because he's orange."

"Probably full of fleas, or worms, or both. You should take it to a shelter and let them deal with it." Cara's mom had never liked animals in the house. It disturbed her sense of neatness.

"Mal already took Pumpkin to the vet, and got medicine for the fleas and worms."

"Who's Mal?"

"Oh." Cara was grateful that they weren't on video. "He's the neighbor. He's got cats of his own, so I went there to ask for some food when I found Pumpkin." She left out the grimmer part of the story.

"He must be a real animal lover to take a brand-new stray to a vet."

"Well, he's local and he knew the vet. I'll pay for everything." Yet Mal hadn't presented her with a bill, or even mentioned the cost. "You think I can't take care of a cat?"

"I think you take on too much, darling. You're always doing more work, work, work. You should take care of yourself first, then focus on the rest of the world. Why not give this cat to the neighbor and not burden yourself with more responsibility?"

"Pumpkin weighs like a pound and he's not a burden."

"How much do you weigh now?" her mom asked abruptly.

Cara grimaced. "I don't know. Haven't weighed myself in a while."

"This is exactly what I'm talking about, sweetie. You got swept up in this job and you're neglecting yourself, eating junk food and not taking care of your physical condition. You're beautiful when you prioritize yourself. I hate to think of you missing out on life because you're not taking a few simple steps to improve your body."

Cara took a long inhale, trying not to snap. "I am not missing out on life. I am doing exactly what I want to be doing."

"You drive around the country like a vagabond. You're always alone, or worse, surrounded by the sort of men who work in construction…"

"They're fine." Except for the Barrys of the world.

"You know what I mean. Those men who catcall or dog whistle—"

"Politicians dog whistle, Mom. Construction workers wolf whistle. But not my crew, because they know I'll sack them."

"Don't change the subject," her mom said.

"I'm not. You brought up whistling."

"I was talking about your health. What did you have for dinner today? Junk food, I bet."

"Pizza," Cara mumbled. Delicious, soul-feeding pizza.

"You need to keep sensible food around. I'll order you some of those chocolate smoothies and have them sent to you."

"Ugh, no!" Cara hated the little plastic bottles of weird flavored pseudo-milk that her mom always drank. Supposedly, they were calibrated with the perfect amount of vitamins and not too many calories, and if Cara would just drink three of those a day instead of eating actual food, she'd be thin and happy and married.

The stuff tasted like misery in liquid form, and Cara wasn't going to drink a single one. And definitely not in front of her work crew. Hard pass.

Her mom was still talking. "I just want you to be happy, baby. You're smart and talented, and if you tried you could look as pretty as you wanted. You've got the most beautiful eyes. And your hair is a gift. I bet you haven't gone to a salon in months."

"I'm busy, and I don't have money to waste on salon visits. Dad made sure of that."

"Don't ever mention that man!" Cara knew needling her mom about him was cruel, but family was all about knowing which buttons to push.

"Does he call you?" Cara asked curiously. Inexplicably, they were still married. Cara's mom talked about divorce all the time, but always said it would cost too much to actually do.

"If he did call, I wouldn't answer," her mom said with a haughty sniff. "You shouldn't either."

"He doesn't call me," Cara said. It was technically true. He mailed.

"Good. He ruined our lives. I had to move across the country to get a new start, and you poor thing are stuck in some cow town."

"Hey, there's also a lot of corn," Cara noted.

After a bit more chitchat, she said goodbye, and then flipped back onto the bed. Why had she thought this conversation would go differently than the thousand before it? Her mother was convinced that if Cara just lost fifty pounds, she'd be happy as a Disney princess. And more importantly, Ever After like a princess too. Meaning hitched, with kids on the way. No matter what Cara said, her mom refused to understand that she *was* happy. Work made her happy. Craft made her happy. Creating form out of nothing made her happy. The smell of wood shavings and the gleam of woodgrain made her happy.

Would it be nice to have someone in her life? Sure. *If* that someone actually wanted to be with her as she was. And Cara knew that the chances of someone seeing past her weight to her inner beauty were basically nil.

Especially if that someone happened to have a lot of outer beauty himself.

Someone like Mal.

XIII

THE VERY NEXT DAY, A large crate of diet drinks appeared at the job site. Cara silently cursed her mother's good intentions, and the modern business infrastructure that allowed crappy shakes to be mailed anywhere overnight. She hustled the crate into the trailer before anyone could get curious about it.

She'd always kept in steady contact with Morningside, the attorney who was handling all the client's end of the business. Cara had called him the previous day about the extra lumber purchase, and had expected a speedy response, since the lawyer didn't seem to sleep. However, she was surprised when he told her that he'd be coming in person to check on the progress, expecting to be there right at the end of the workday.

Cara was freaking out, trying to get everyone to be especially tidy before leaving. Dan told her that he could get her some Valium if she needed it, and she was pretty sure he was being serious.

Most of the crew left on time, since Cara didn't want to keep them there just for looks. Mal remained, since he volunteered to handle some final tasks in the basement while Cara dealt with the lawyer.

Hoping to look more like a supervisor than a scrub, Cara even dashed into the office trailer to change her outfit. Away went the jeans and flannel shirt. She pulled on her only dress, a jade-colored, high-waisted thing that came down to her knees. She only had black flats, but they'd have to do. Cara brushed her hair and prayed she didn't have iron filings stuck in her eyebrows or something. Why did she choose to operate the drill that afternoon?

A shiny black car pulled up, the lingering purple twilight reflecting off the surface and making it look especially expensive. A tall man in an Italian suit stepped out, and Cara immediately had flashbacks to the men in Italian suits who'd got her father into trouble.

Not the mob, not the mob, she told herself. Morningside was not an Italian name. She was fine.

"Miss Michaels?" he asked. "How very nice to finally meet you in person."

"Hi," she said too brightly, too eager to please. "I'm glad you could come. I think you're really going to like what you see."

"I have every confidence in you, Miss Michaels. Shall we?"

"Yeah! Come on in and I'll give you a tour. Oh, and take a hard hat. We're past most of the worst parts, but there's always the chance of something falling."

The bright yellow hard hat looked somehow classy on the lawyer's head, concealing his silvery hair.

Cara showed him the house, pointing out the good and bad things. He made appreciative noises at all the right moments. He didn't seem to notice the weird cold spot in one of the upper rooms. Cara shivered her way through it, and prayed no ghosts actually showed up.

"How are things coming along?" he asked just as they were about to enter the parlor, which Cara saved for last.

"We're pretty much on schedule. Maybe a week behind due to the scale of some of the water and termite damage." She hit the floodlights, illuminating the room.

Morningside frowned as he looked at the walls and floor. "This room is not anywhere close to done."

"Well, no. But it's better than it looks, I promise. See all those tiles? They're ready to go. It's like a puzzle. It looks like it'll never get done, but then it's real fast at the end. I *promise* it'll be done."

"Promises, Miss Michaels, are very pretty, but contracts are what matter. And the contract did state that November first would be the day the client could be assured everything was complete."

"I know that, sir. I signed the contract, and I'm promising too. Double promise. I won't screw this up."

He nodded, smiling slightly. "Very well. I accept your word."

"Restoration projects are always a gamble," Cara went on. "Old houses are quirky, like old people. We have to allow for complications. Like termites taking out that one bedroom decades ago. We couldn't have planned for that."

"I certainly see your point," he conceded. "The parlor is the top priority. If the other parts aren't done exactly before November first, that's all right. But the parlor is the showpiece of the house. It has to be perfect."

"It will be."

"You're putting your heart and soul into this restoration, I can tell."

He walked over and ran his fingers over the Egyptian female carving that she'd just installed as part of the mantelpiece. "Absolutely beautiful work. My client will be pleased."

Cara breathed a sigh of relief.

Suddenly, an angry voice burst out, "Who the hell is this?"

Cara whirled to see Mal in the doorway, glaring at Morningside. "Mal! This is Mr. Morningside. The *attorney* who's in charge of the project. Maybe use some manners?"

Mal had noticed her change of clothing and narrowed his eyes further.

She glanced back at the lawyer. "This is Mal. He was just finishing up something in the basement."

"Well, he can certainly go now," Morningside said, his voice as cold as Mal's had been hot. "And perhaps not come back."

"I can't lose another worker," Cara said quickly. "Not with the schedule so tight already!"

"In any case, the shift is over, is it not…Mr.…" He trailed off, not knowing what name to use.

"Mal works just fine," Mal drawled as he stepped up to Cara. "And yeah, shift's over and you've seen what you came to see. Let's all leave."

Cara had never seen Mal so murderous, not even when he'd fought the ghost. She gasped when Mal grabbed her by the arm and dragged her toward the door. "Wait! The lights and the locks…"

"Later. Time to go."

Mal did everything short of picking Cara up and hauling her across the street. Morningside paced after them, protesting the whole time.

Mal only stopped once he and Cara stood on the Salem lawn, about ten feet from the mailbox.

Morningside glared at Mal. "Really, sir. It's quite out of fashion to drag women to your cave. Let Miss Michaels go at once."

"No one's tying her down. She can walk off this property whenever she wants."

"Cara, please come here." Morningside gave her a smile. "I'll give you a ride home."

"Don't go with him," Mal warned.

Cara held her hands out, feeling utterly confused. "Sorry, am I free to go, or what?"

"You can leave, but I'm telling you that you're safer here," Mal said, his voice low. "Don't step off the property."

"You're nuts."

"I agree," Morningside said. "Miss Michaels, this man is unhinged. Come back here and I'll drive you home."

Mal reached for her, but didn't actually touch her. "Don't, Cara. That dude is evil."

"By that you mean he's a lawyer?"

"No. I mean he's evil. Don't ask me how I know, but I do. The fact that he's got a law degree is beside the point."

Cara shook her head, stepping back from both men. "I can't deal with this."

"If he's a normal, non-evil person," Mal said, "he could step onto the lot and take you back over the boundary. He's not doing that. Instead he's trying to convince you to return on your own."

"Because she's a grown woman," Mr. Morningside said calmly. He gave Mal a chilly smile. "If I do not step onto another person's property, it's because I respect the laws that govern this nation, and I am too intelligent to allow myself to be led into some trap where you, as a belligerent property owner, will try to bring some false charges against me the moment I try to assist Miss Michaels."

"I don't need assistance. I'm not in danger," Cara said, wishing she sounded more certain. The necklace she wore felt hot against her skin, though perhaps just because she was super embarrassed and her shame was heating the metal.

"I sincerely hope not," Morningside told her. "I'm going now. But rest assured that as soon as I get in my car, I'll call the police to come to this address to respond to a possible kidnapping." He looked at Mal with a clear challenge in his eyes.

"Don't talk and drive," said Mal. "It's dangerous."

"You may be joking, sir, but I'm not. The police will respond to my report."

"Fine," Mal said. "I'd rather have half the county law enforcement here than let Cara go anywhere with you."

The lawyer stalked off. Mal and Cara remained on the lawn until they saw his shiny black car drive away.

Then Cara rushed into the house, basically dying from mortification at what just happened. Behemoth found her on the couch and jumped into her lap. "What is going on," she murmured to the cat. "I am in a horror movie."

Mal strolled in. "Well, that was weird."

"Weird?" she snapped. "That's your word for it? You acted like a complete psycho, and now you're probably going get us both canned."

"Sorry. I overreacted a bit. But I did not like the vibe from that guy, and I think there's a strong chance he's a vampire."

"You've got to be kidding."

"I wish I was, but I'm not. The night I took Pumpkin to the vet, I ran into one."

"A vampire?"

"It knew who I was, and it knew who you were. Mentioned you by name."

"What name?" she asked sharply.

"Cara Michaels. And it called me Malachy East. Both of our construction industry identities, you'll notice."

"What did you do with this vampire?"

"I killed it. I didn't tell you because I didn't want to freak you out prematurely. But yes, vampires are real, and I think some of them are very interested in Egan House."

Cara hugged Behemoth, drawing comfort from the cat's bulk. "Please, please, please tell me this is not happening." The cat did not respond other than to nuzzle her.

"Sorry, Cara," Mal said, sounding sincere. "Can I make you a drink?"

"Wine would be a godsend right now." A full bottle sounded about right.

"We've got wine. Hold on." Mal left the kitchen and Cara took a deep breath. Pumpkin wandered in on wobbly paws, mewing at her.

"Oh, it's feeding time," she said, pushing Mr. B aside.

Cara had stashed one bottle of her mom's shipment into her bag, wondering if it could serve as dinner for a cat on a liquid diet. She opened the bottle of vanilla-flavored smoothie and poured some into a dish. Pumpkin approached it eagerly, lapping it up. Then a startled expression crossed his face and he spat it out. Directing a wounded look at Cara, he began to scrape his tongue against one paw, ridding himself of the taste.

"Totally agree," she said. "Ok, I'll toss the whole box in the trash and leave a bad review. 'Even cat was grossed out—one star.'"

Mal returned with a bottle of wine. "What is that?" he asked, pointing to the smoothie.

"Nothing. My mom sent me some diet drinks."

"Gross. Why?" Mal was rooting around in a drawer for a bottle opener, so he probably missed Cara's jaw dropping.

"Uh, because of my weight?"

He shook his head. "Forget that. You look great, and you can haul heavy drills and two by fours up the stairs faster than any of the guys. You're in perfectly good health. Here. Drink this. It's a…" He peered at the label. "Pinot something? Vinny bought it and she's good at picking out rich people stuff."

Cara took the glass, still stunned by Mal's comments. She took one sip, and decided that whoever Vinny was, she knew wines.

Just then, Mal looked out the window. "Oh, look who's here."

Cara followed his gaze. A squad car pulled up into the driveway. No lights or sirens, but the cops who got out looked damn serious.

"He did call," Mal said softly. "I didn't think he was actually going to go that far."

"Isn't that the cop from before?" she asked nervously.

"Officer Hallihan, yeah."

He opened the front door and stepped out. Cara followed, leaving her lovely red wine in the kitchen with a sense of regret.

The blonde woman walked up to the porch, unsmiling. "Mr. Salem, we got a call to emergency dispatch. Something about a woman being held against her will?" She sounded skeptical, but was clearly going to do this by the book.

Mal held out a hand, indicating Cara. "One woman right here. But she's free to go whenever she wants."

Hallihan looked directly at Cara. "If you wouldn't mind stepping onto the lawn to answer a few questions, ma'am?"

Cara passed by Mal on the way to the steps. He winked at her, which she felt was a little too self-confident, considering he had cops on his lawn. Officer Hallihan took her by the arm and started to walk to the center of the front yard.

Over her shoulder, Hallihan said, with studied nonchalance, "Stay with Mr. Salem, would you, Jim?"

Once they were out of earshot, Hallihan took Cara by the shoulders and turned her away from the porch, presumably so Mal couldn't read her lips.

"Tell me what's going on."

"I think there was a mix-up," Cara said. "You got the call from Mr. Morningside, right?"

Hallihan said nothing.

"Well, Morningside was just on the job site a half hour ago and he and Mal got into kind of a…discussion."

"Go on."

"Mal doesn't like Morningside. Like, hated him right off the bat. And Mal didn't want me to go with Morningside. But he didn't *kidnap* me. It was my choice to stay here."

"Yeah, kidnapping isn't really Mal's style," Hallihan noted dryly. "Just so we're clear, I'm going to ask a few more questions. Do you feel that you're safe in the company of Malachy Salem?"

"Yes."

"Do you feel safe at this location?"

"Yes."

"Do you want a police escort to any other location?"

"No."

Hallihan's eyes narrowed. "Do you think Malachy might have been involved in the theft of the materials from your site?"

"What? No! He was the one who caught Barry in the act."

Hallihan shrugged. "Maybe. Or maybe it was a partnership that fell out. Mal could have sold out Barry when he got annoyed with him. Judging from my few interactions with Mr. Field, he probably annoys everybody."

"Did Barry say Mal was involved?"

"I can't comment on that directly."

"Mal had nothing to do with stealing supplies."

"You're the lawyer for the defense, huh."

"Is he going to be charged with something?"

Hallihan said, very precisely, "Not at the moment. You sure you don't want to be driven somewhere? Where are you staying in town?"

"Uh. Actually here."

"The house on the hill?"

"No. Here. Mal offered me a spare room."

At that, Hallihan actually took half a step back and reconsidered Cara. "Really."

"Yeah."

"Why." A demand, not a question.

"It's close to the site. I was sleeping at Egan House for a bit, but it wasn't…ideal. No running water, no heat, that sort of thing." *Haunted by a ghost, possibly over a hellhole.* "Old house problems. You know."

"I don't, thank the lord. I live in a shiny new condo." Hallihan was silent a long moment, then said, "This lawyer was so pissed at Mal that he chose to call the cops on him? The fight was that bad?"

"Lawyers can be pretty ruthless. I think he was trying to show Mal he could mess with him."

"Yeah, well, it's not as if most people can take Mal in an actual fight, so maybe that makes sense." She sighed, and then led Cara back toward the house. "All right, Mr. Salem. We're leaving. Thanks for your cooperation."

"Anytime, Hal." Mal hadn't moved from the porch, his manner over-the-top casual.

"Walk with us to the squad car, would you, Miss Michaels? I left my cards in there."

Hallihan opened the door, rooted around, and then handed Cara a business card. "Contact me directly if you have any issues. And call 911 if you feel you are in immediate danger."

"Ok. I don't, though. Feel in danger, that is. Not from Mal."

The cop gave her a look that might have been pitying. Then she said, in a lower tone, "Look, there's one thing that I find weird about all this. I'll tell you because it's technically public anyway, or it will be. Yesterday, Mr. Field got an attorney to represent him, by the name of Morningside."

Cara blinked. "What? But Barry stole from him. Or his clients, I guess."

"Yeah. Conflict of interest all over the place. But it was Morningside who filed the paperwork for bail. Just thought you should know."

XIV

Cara walked back inside the house, feeling jittery and ill at ease. Hallihan was very nice for a cop, but Cara's experiences with the law were in general not good. The wineglass called to her like an old friend, and she took way too big a swig.

"You ok?" Mal asked.

"Ugh, yeah, fine. I've interacted with the police more in the past week than since the whole mess with my dad. I know I didn't do anything wrong, but the sight of a badge gives me chills. Sorry."

"No, I should apologize. I handled the lawyer thing badly. Like, he's still evil, but I should have been cooler about it. I was just really worried about you."

Cara took another sip, trying to make sense of what was happening.

"Oh, hey. I got you a surprise earlier." Mal opened the fridge and brought out a large container of juicy red cherries.

"It's not cherry season," she objected, even though they looked perfect.

"Well, they were at the store, so they must be in season somewhere."

Cara took one, and closed her eyes as she savored it. "Ok, these are good. Don't know how, but they're good."

She ate another cherry, almost sputtering with laughter when Mal tossed one in the air and caught it in his mouth. "They have pits! You can't swallow it whole."

"I'm not," he said after a second of chewing, spitting the pit into the garbage. "But I have to keep in practice. Never know when a food-tossing contest might break out. It's a good party trick."

"You're legitimately weird, you know that?"

"I hide it well, though." He winked at her. "Can you do the thing?"

"The thing?"

"With the stem." He took another cherry and popped the whole thing in his mouth, stem and all.

That was when Cara remembered the trick. Eat a cherry and then tie the stem into a knot while it was still in your mouth. Another party trick to impress people, to show off just how good you were with your tongue.

She never learned. What was the point? No one cared how good Cara might be with her tongue, because none of the guys looked at her, or tried to impress *her* with a tied cherry stem. It was the pretty girls, the thin girls, the girls who didn't take shop class.

"I don't think it's a real thing," she announced, the taste of cherry suddenly going sour in her mouth.

Mal just smiled at her, then pulled a perfectly knotted stem from his mouth, handing it to her.

She took it even as she said, "Ugh, I don't want your spit-covered stem."

He laughed. "Then why'd you take it?"

"I wasn't thinking. Anyway, I don't believe you really did that. You probably had one you tied up first and then switched them when I wasn't looking."

"You were looking the whole time, Cara. Want to watch me do it again? For science?" he asked, his voice challenging.

"Fine. I'll choose the cherry." She wanted to be sure he wasn't messing with her.

She picked a fruit with a stem that was a much lighter brown than most of the others. Hopefully she could confirm it was the same one when he was done. "Here."

Mal didn't accept the offering. Instead he leaned closer. "Put it in my mouth."

"What?"

"So my hands aren't involved. I don't want you thinking I'm tricking you."

Cara made a face, but nodded. She raised her hand to his lips and popped the cherry into his mouth, wishing the move didn't feel so…intimate.

"Don't take your eyes off me," he warned, the words slightly mangled as he talked around the fruit.

Cara watched, arms across her chest to make it clear that this was just for science, and she wasn't into it, and the sight of Mal sucking on a cherry didn't send a little—ok, a big—jolt down into her belly, or make her damp between her legs.

He took his time this round, smiling a little as he held her eyes.

"What's the matter?" she taunted him. "Can't get it done?"

He shook his head slowly, denying her assertion. Then his smile grew into a toothy grin. He held a stem between his upper and lower teeth.

"Take it," he said, the words clear enough.

Cara glared at him but reached forward to snap the stem away. He relaxed his jaw in time and the stem fell into her palm.

"Well, Professor Michaels?"

It was undoubtably the same stem, curled into a knot. "I guess you really did it," she admitted grudgingly.

"Of course I did. I'm good with my tongue."

She blushed, because he said it in a way that was meant to make her blush.

"This is the part where you're supposed to say I'm totally full of myself," he prompted.

"You *are* totally full of yourself," she said, happy to have any words to say, even if he supplied them.

"And then this is the part where I counter with an offer to prove that even if I am totally full of myself, I'm still good with my tongue, and I really want to show you just how good I am."

Cara couldn't breathe very well. "How…how are you going to show me?"

He leaned over again, his hands reaching for her, catching her shoulders, drawing her to him. She met him in the middle, and right there over the kitchen island, they kissed.

Cara nearly caught fire at the touch of Mal's lips on hers. For such a hard-edged guy, his mouth was surprisingly soft. Gentle. Sweet, even.

"You taste like cherries," she murmured, not meaning to say it out loud.

Mal made a sound of agreement and used the moment she opened her mouth to slide his tongue in.

Oh. My. God.

Cara had made a flip remark about not wanting his spit, but she did want it. Bad. She wanted his spit, his tongue, his teeth, his lips. All over her.

The sensation of his tongue pressed along hers brought out a little whimper, a wordless way of begging for more.

"This countertop is definitely an obstacle," Mal muttered then, taking a moment to breathe.

She inhaled too, briefly on her own again as Mal pulled away. He stepped around the end of the island, and simultaneously pulled her closer to meet him.

He pinned her there, her back pressing against the edge of the stone. She tilted her head up, wanting another kiss, or whatever it was he was giving her.

You should one hundred percent not be making out with your demon-hunting employee. Cara ignored the warning in her head. She was sick of playing it safe.

She kissed him back. And she was going to make it count. She tilted her head up—Mal was way taller than she was—and reached her hands up to his shoulders. Cara really liked good shoulders, and she'd spent enough time on the job site stealing covert looks at Mal in a T-shirt to know that he had very, very good shoulders. Big, strong, begging for her to sink her teeth into. At the moment, she just dug her fingers in, hoping to prolong the kiss as much as possible.

Mal's tongue against hers made Cara weak in the knees, ready to rip her dress off, and willing to do anything he wanted. She could definitely use her less-than-impressive height to advantage when it came to blow jobs, and judging from what she felt when he leaned into her, he'd be up for it.

"Hey, do—" she whispered, about to offer exactly that. But then Cara whimpered when Mal got her lower lip between his teeth and gently sucked on it. *Yes, please.*

Cara felt like she was rising up, and hoped that she hadn't died and was only getting this brief glimpse of heaven before someone decided she'd get turned away at the door. Because Mal being close to her, being into her, was pretty much heaven.

But no. She hadn't been rising in a spiritual sense. It turned out that on that last epic liplock, he'd somehow just lifted her up so she was now sitting on the kitchen island, and he was head to head with her, his hands twisted in her hair, keeping her in kissing range.

"Didn't want you to hurt your neck," he explained between kisses. "I like your neck." He proceeded to pull her hair away from the right side of her neck and kiss her from her shoulder to her ear.

Cara let out a moan, too lost in the sensation to keep any cool. "Yes, please," she said, saying it instead of thinking it this time.

"What do you want?" he whispered in her ear.

"See you with your shirt off," she said instantly.

Mal straightened up and smiled, and half a second later his shirt was gone. She didn't even see where it landed because she was too busy ogling him.

Perfect. Even better than she remembered from that first day seeing him in the doorway. Tight abs, broad chest, and yes, shoulders she was going to lose her mind over. Cara reached out to get her hands all over them, spreading her fingers wide as she finally felt the skin and the muscles underneath.

Mal closed his eyes, his mouth falling open just a bit. He muttered, "I knew you'd know how to touch a man."

"Why?" she breathed, still mesmerized by the feel of slightly sweaty, gorgeous flesh.

"When you touch things you're into, you get this look in your eye. Like when you run your fingers over all the damn carving in that house, you do it in this way that just says you're all in. It's sexy as hell."

"This better not turn into a joke about how much I must like wood."

He laughed, and she felt the vibrations of it under the pads of her fingers. But then he dropped his hands to either side of her legs, leaning into her. "No joking, Cara. Not tonight."

Cara slid her hands up to his neck and went for another kiss.

Meanwhile he worked his hands under the skirt of the dress, up her legs. When she realized how far up he was getting, she instinctively pulled back, trying to get away, thinking only that he'd be disgusted by the size of her thighs, that he already regretted kissing her.

Instead he just moaned as his fingers hooked around the sides of her panties. "These have got to come off, babe," he said in a low voice.

"Here? In the *kitchen*?"

"Sure. You're at the perfect height."

"The perfect height for what?"

"You know what." His tongue lapped her throat. "Let me, Cara. I want to taste you so bad," he said, sounding like he meant it.

"No way." But it came out not as a refusal but as a disbelieving *no wayyyy*, because Cara flat-out couldn't believe it.

"Yes way. Let me."

"Um…"

He stepped back all the way to the living room area, and then kicked a suede-covered cube that must usually serve as a footstool over to the edge of the counter. He knelt on it, and yeah, it was pretty much the perfect height, because his head was exactly on the level of her…

"Spread your legs, babe." He had his hands on her thighs again, pushing the skirt up and away. "Lean back if you want."

"Mal…"

"Just for now," he said, flashing her a smile that shot pure heat right to where he was heading. "Afterward, we can relocate for more sex."

"Oh." *Oh.*

He was really going to do this. He started with just a puff of breath across her skin, disturbing the curls of dark reddish hair, because waxing down there was approximately one million on Cara's list of priorities. But if that bothered him, he didn't let it show.

Tension ratcheted up her sensitivity, so that she might pass out right there. Then his tongue slipped into the cleft and her mouth fell open at the sensation of being touched like that, by him.

She lifted one hand and reached forward to sink her fingers into the dark waves of his hair. It was natural to curl her hand, fist the hair, pull him to her. "Oh, wow," she gasped.

He made the softest humming sound, which sent a wave of want down her bones. He licked, he sucked, he made her want to melt onto the countertop. He caught her clit between his teeth, drawing a shaky, half-scared breath from her. And then the tip of his tongue right. There.

Cara moaned. "Holy…*yes*. That. Oh, right there."

She was going to come, right on the countertop of the kitchen. And she didn't care. Not caring was a feeling almost as glorious as the feelings Mal's tongue was creating, and Cara let her head fall back as she gave in to the last little lick he offered before her whole body quivered and she had to moan way louder than she ever intended.

Mal shifted his position, rising up to stand, his fingers replacing his tongue over her clit. He barely brushed against her, but the strokes had Cara stretching up and forward, leaning into him as she lost control and bit into his left shoulder. His gasp was intoxicating, and Cara turned the bite into a long sucking kiss.

He slipped his free hand under her hair, and flipped it to one side of her head, his fingers sliding through the strands.

"Let's go upstairs," he said.

She nodded, not trusting herself to use words. She'd say something dumb. Something that was supposed to be clever, but she'd jumble it and he'd think twice about what he was asking.

She wasn't sure how she managed to walk upstairs, but the second they entered Mal's dimly lit room, he moved behind her and started gathering up the fabric of her dress.

"Arms up," Mal ordered. She lifted her arms above her head to let him pull the dress off. Her bra wasn't exactly sexy, but it was lace, and newish. It also didn't match the panties she'd been wearing, but Mal had solved that problem downstairs.

He dropped the dress to the floor as he stepped around to face her. He took a long look, his eyes locked on her chest in a way that probably should have been offensive but was actually pretty…awesome.

"Cara," he breathed. He reached for a bra strap, but she stepped away.

"You first," she ordered. "You're still practically dressed."

"I can fix that," he said, yanking at his belt buckle. A second later, his jeans and boxers dropped to reveal perfect legs, because of course he had perfect legs. Oh, and a cock that was perfectly hard.

"Take the bra off now," he said, sounding a little desperate.

"I will when you get on the bed," she countered.

Mal was on the bed so fast that she knew there was something suspicious about his abilities. No matter how ready for sex men are, they usually don't blur when they move.

But a deal was a deal, and Cara reached up to unfasten the bra's front closure. She freed her breasts and shrugged out of the bra, her eyes on Mal. His hands were clenching into fists, wrinkling the bedsheets.

Cara walked slowly up to the bed, and the moment she get there, Mal reached for her and pulled her down. A second later they were lying on their sides, pawing at each other like teens.

"Hey," Mal said eagerly. "If you flip around, we can—"

"No." She stopped cold. "No 69ing."

Mal looked surprised, but said, "Ok."

"I mean it. That's what no means."

"And I mean that's ok. That's what ok means. If you're not into something, you're not into it."

"I'm not into 69ing." She personally loathed the act, and hadn't done it since the last time an ex-boyfriend inadvertently revealed he only insisted on it because he knew Cara *didn't* want to do it.

Mal shifted a little, easing himself away from her, just a few inches. "Are you still into this? I mean, sex? With me?"

"Yeah. Of course." But she could also tell that her refusal to do what he suggested had already killed the whole mood. She closed her eyes. Why did everything have to be difficult?

Mal's hands cupped her face. "Cara," he said quietly. "I want this to be a good night for you, ok? Tell me how to do that. Can I kiss you?"

She nodded, and a moment later felt his mouth on her own. Not wild, not devouring. Just his lips teasing hers until she forgot the awkwardness of the last exchange and she remembered how good his mouth was.

"Should have brought the cherries up," she murmured.

Mal's lips curved into a smile. "I like the way you think."

She kissed him again.

Mal made a sound of satisfaction and rolled them so she was on her back. He smiled down at her. "You looked nice in that green dress, but this is better. Can I go down on you again?"

"Um. Yeah. That'd be ok with me."

"Deadpan. I like it." He grinned and shifted to move lower down on the bed.

"Mal…you really want to do this?"

"Yeah, Cara." He paused. "But it's going to be a little different this time. I want you to fuck my tongue."

"What?"

"Fuck. My. Tongue. Use your hips, babe. Use my mouth to make yourself come."

She was about to protest that she didn't know what he was talking about, but then she felt his tongue flat against her body, and she knew *exactly* what he meant. She rolled her hips forward, pressing her clit to his tongue, feeling him meet her.

"Oh, right," she managed to gasp out. "Oh, that's right."

Cara gave herself up to it, loving the way she could move her own body and get a jolt of pleasure from Mal's tongue. Control was hot. How had he guessed she needed that, after letting him do what he did to her downstairs, when she'd felt all her own control slip away?

Cara found a slow, easy rhythm that sent electric waves shimmering across her body each time, and within moments, she opened her mouth as the orgasm radiated through her. "Oh, yeah," she breathed.

"Like that?" Mal asked, his voice gruff.

"That was…really nice," she said. It was better than that, but she didn't have much vocabulary at the moment.

He moved so his head was over hers, his divine body poised over her own. *Now for the main event*, she thought, sort of amazed he'd waited this long to get off.

But it was his fingers she felt next, light and teasing. Cara gasped. "What are you doing?"

"Watching you," he said, his eyes intent. "Watching a woman come is one of the best drugs there is. For me anyway. Something about seeing a woman who normally has one look, all cool and calm, just lose it when I touch her…there's nothing like it."

"It's a power thing."

"No. It's a…I don't know. Seeing a secret face thing. Knowing something about you no one else knows. Ok, I guess that does sort of make it a power thing."

"I mean, it works for me," Cara admitted. "It has the last two times anyway."

He smiled. "What's your record?"

"For what?"

"How many times has a guy made you come in a night?"

She closed her eyes. "Two. Tonight beat the old record of one."

"That's unacceptable," Mal said, his voice suddenly harsh. "You deserve a way higher total than that."

"I'm ok. And shouldn't I be doing something for you by now?"

"No hurry."

"Oh, really?"

"Maybe a little hurry," he admitted, angling his body against hers so she could tell just how hard he was.

She slid her hand down, fully intending to play with that erection. But he shook his head. "Later, babe. I don't want to lose focus."

Focus on her? Cara was still reeling from the last couple times he focused on her. And now he was still teasing, his finger circling her clit, bringing her back up to a level she assumed was unreachable so soon after she'd left it. "Mal," she moaned, arching her back. "You're making me crazy."

"You look good crazy," he said. "I cannot wait to get in you."

"But you *are* waiting." Her voice was almost a whine.

"Well, this part is fun too," he said, his voice melting her insides. "The part where I make you need me."

Oh, yes, it was. Cara's hips rocked against Mal's hand in rhythm with his touch. She was getting close to coming again. But Mal was apparently having a good time playing with her. He'd pull his hand away every few seconds, probably just to hear her beg.

"Is this all because I said no to dinner that first day?" she asked. "You have to make me need you? For payback?"

He paused, and not for the same reason as before. "Cara, do you not get that I am into you?"

No, she really didn't. Even now, in this bed, naked. But it was nice to pretend. "Sure."

"You don't. You're going to make me prove it."

He put out a hand, searching for something on the little bedside table, and then he held up a foil packet. "This still ok?"

Cara nodded, her breath fast.

She watched as Mal rose to his knees and rolled the condom on. The muscles of his torso rippled when she put her hand on him and stroked his cock through the slippery latex.

"Wow, Cara," he said, pushing her hand away. "Paws off me, or this is going to be over a little too fast."

"You that close too?" she asked.

He actually laughed. "Do you have any idea how sexy you are right now? I deserve a medal for not coming the second I got your clothes off."

She smiled and cupped her breasts with her hands. "Because you like these?"

Mal let out a huge breath, his eyes widening. "Cara."

"You want me on top?" she asked, suddenly feeling bold.

"Next time. This time I'm on top."

Figures, she thought.

A second later, he was lying over her, his left hand by her shoulder, his arm bracing his body to avoid crushing her. His right hand slid under her ass and lifted her up a little, angling her body to meet his cock.

She was so wet that he slid into her without the slightest resistance, and she heard him groan at the same moment she did.

"Oh, yes," she breathed, even as her body contracted around him. She was coming again. Was that all it took? Was she that ready for him?

Mal's breathing quickened. "This good for you?"

"It's fantastic," she moaned, raising her hips to meet his.

"You're coming?"

She gasped out her yes, and then smiled, too satisfied to be shy. "You feel great."

He withdrew a bit and thrust again. "How about now? It's not too much?"

"Still great. Don't stop."

He didn't stop, and Cara wanted to scream with how good it made her feel. "Faster. Harder."

"You're sure?"

"I'm not fragile. *Fuck* me, Mal."

He shifted his body, gripping her ass harder. "You asked for it."

Yes, she did, and she'd ask again, because Mal was amazing. He went fast, and hard, and rough. Cara reached one hand down to touch herself, sparking an aftershock just as he gasped her name. Mal went still as he came, then closed his eyes and sighed, pulling out.

He climbed out of bed long enough to get rid of the condom and clean himself up. Then he slid back in beside her, pulling her to him. "Get over here," he muttered.

Cara rolled to half lie on him, and smiled when she felt his fingers in her hair. Then his lips brushed her forehead, and her post-sex satisfaction turned into surprise. Mal didn't seem like the affectionate type.

"You liked that?" she asked.

"You fucking kidding me?" was his response.

She giggled. Now *that* sounded like Mal.

They lay together, both relaxing. Cara didn't say anything more, because she learned long ago that guys weren't chatty after sex. In fact, if Mal stayed awake for more than three minutes, she'd award him his medal.

She never got to confirm it though, because she fell asleep two minutes later.

XV

MAL DRIFTED IN THE LIGHTEST layer of unconsciousness, perfectly content to stay there. He was in bed with Cara, and he wasn't fully awake or asleep. He should have passed out after the sex they'd just had. Mal couldn't remember the last time a girl had gotten him that hard. Cara was amazing. The way she tasted, the way she moved, the way she said what she wanted and didn't want, the way she teased him with her tits at the end. But most of all— and he was never going to tell her this—her hair. He loved the way her red hair looked on the pillow, the way it grazed her shoulders. Sexy and pretty and feminine. It suited her perfectly.

She was still lying on her side, curled up on him. He slid one hand over her back and down to her hip, then, because he couldn't resist it, he cupped her right ass cheek. Damn. Curvy Cara was hot. He felt like he'd missed a memo.

Of course, Cara wasn't around before a couple of months ago. And she'd be gone in another month. However long it took to finish the woodwork on the house.

He hoped she enjoyed the sex as much as he did, because he wasn't nearly done with her. There were more positions to try, there was more sweat to lick off, there was more Cara to bring to climax so that he could see her eyes go soft and dark, the pupils dilating in an unmistakable sign that she'd found the peak he wanted her to reach.

He always wanted his partners to have a good time, but he rarely needed to prove himself in the way he was desperate to do tonight. Maybe just because Cara was harder to get? He wasn't used to needing to catch a woman's attention.

Or maybe it was the hint that Cara had settled a few too many times. That she didn't expect much from any guy because she'd had bad luck in the past.

Was he just trying to restore her opinion of men in general?

No. Because the thought of her with another guy made him want to strike out, hard.

What is that about? he thought. Mal was not the possessive type.

Hazy images formed in his brain, sort of like a dream. Mal fought against it just a bit, because he didn't want to fall asleep quite yet, not when he was enjoying being exactly where he was right now.

And yet, there was something intriguing about the feeling, and he finally followed the impulse to go a little further into it.

It was autumn in the dream, not as far into the season as in real life. But the trees wore red and orange, and the sky above was marbled blue and white as thin ribbons of clouds striped the air. Mal heard voices ahead of him. He dream-walked forward—the sort of easy movement only dreams have, gliding like a ghost to wherever you were supposed to go.

He rounded the corner of a house, and a huge green lawn opened in front of him. Kids were running around, chasing each other and shrieking with joy. A dog barked happily, attempting to herd the kids like sheep and failing to do anything but roll in the grass.

"Hey, everyone! Over here!" a familiar voice called out.

Mal's attention shifted to the house.

There was Cara. A little older. Her hair a little darker, more auburn than red. The kids all ran to her, and the dog followed. Three kids. Two girls and a boy, the girls redheaded like her. The boy darker, a little taller.

She knelt down, laughing. The kids swarmed, more like balls of energy than humans, giggling all the time.

Those kids are hers. Cara hugged one of the girls, and Mal felt almost jealous of the love that arced between her and the child. He missed his mom like hell, and the vision, beautiful as it was, still held some pain for him.

She's going to be all right, he thought, suddenly aware that he was seeing not just a dream but a glimpse into Cara's life along the line. The atmosphere around him shimmered and shuddered, and Mal felt a tiny trill of fear as he understood he'd walked into the otherworlds.

He told himself to calm down. There was no danger here, not in this dreamworld, not when his physical body was safe in his own home.

He refocused on Cara and the kids, hoping to regain the calm from before.

But now the kids were gone, and the dog was gone, and the intensity of colors in the lawn and sky faded. Cara stood there, looking exactly like she did in real life, down to a plaid shirt he recognized and the tantalizing glint of metal at her neck. She was wearing the charm he gave her. Good.

She was gazing out over the lawn and into the woods beyond, unaware of him. Mal willed himself closer. He lifted a hand to touch her…and her red hair turned redder. Into flames.

Smoke blossomed all around him, swelling up from the ground and pulsing like clouds in the air, obscuring Cara as she was yanked away from him, backward into the house.

Mal tried to reach for her, grab her away from whatever had her, but he was too slow, too scared to plunge into the flames flaring up between them.

Cara! His howl echoed through the dreamworld, but there was no answer, only a sense of overwhelming fear and pain. He closed his eyes, wincing from the heat of the fire, his feet cemented in place as panic turned his body to stone. He was never, never going to get to her, not with the fire in the way. Mal hated fire. It turned him into a child.

He opened his eyes, telling himself he'd get over it this time.

But the flames were gone.

The house was gone. There was nothing left but a pile of ash.

And in the middle of the ash, a body.

Cara's body.

He saw her burned and broken on the ground, and all around, ashes of what he knew were all the things she'd worked so hard to create. Beautiful carvings and panels of inlaid wood, now destroyed along with their creator.

This is your fault.

The thought came from outside him, and Mal felt the hit in his gut as he understood the words.

You will be the death of her.

Mal woke up, wrenching his real eyes open, wishing desperately to move, but his body felt like lead. He hadn't had a nightmare that bad since the first year after his parents died.

It wasn't a nightmare.

He ignored the nasty voice inside him.

Mal looked over to see Cara deeply asleep beside him, her features relaxed, and her mouth open a little. Her eyelashes fluttered, signaling a deep dream. She looked perfect and lovely, and he couldn't stand to remember the hideous image of her skin cracked and burned. What could possibly want Cara dead? She was an artist. She made beautiful things and she hurt nobody.

But he couldn't rid himself of the idea that something wanted—even needed—Cara to die.

He had to get away. Far, far away from Cara, from the memory of flames, from the heat her body gave off.

He eased himself out of the bed, praying to every saint he could think of to keep Cara safely asleep. A glance at the clock told him a couple hours had passed. His walk into the otherworlds must have lasted much longer than it seemed.

Mal dressed in the first things he could find on the floor. Then he snuck downstairs, like a thief in his own home. He grabbed the keys to Dom's motorcycle just as a black shape drifted in front of the doorway.

Behemoth. Blocking his way.

"Dude, let me out. I gotta go."

Where?

"Anywhere. I just need to drive."

She is still here.

"Yeah, she's asleep. Keep an eye on her, ok?"

I watch the creature while you run away? How brave you are.

"Please shut up. And she's not a creature. She's a woman."

We are all creatures, created by chance and destined to be destroyed.

"You're a ray of sunshine, you know that." Mal moved around the cat and opened the door. "I gotta get out of here."

The bike glittered in the faint glow of the night sky. Mal needed to move, to get out of his head, to feel the wind rush around him so loud that the sound of fire was drowned out.

He'd forgotten a helmet. Oh, well. He swung one leg over the bike. Started it, revved the engine just to get her moving.

And then he tore out of there.

* * * *

Cara slept better than she had in ages, wrapped up in hazy, pleasant dreams that meant utterly nothing and made her feel like her soul was swathed in cotton candy. She woke up alone in Mal's bed and sat up. The clock on the table said it was 5:00 a.m.

The space next to her was cold. Mal must have got up a while ago. Maybe he was attending to the cats. Cara saw a bathrobe hanging from the back of the door, and she hoped he wouldn't mind her borrowing it. She shrugged into it and crossed the hall to the bathroom.

One steamy shower later, Cara emerged feeling clean and smugly satisfied from her previous evening of red-hot sex.

She heard footsteps in the hall and stepped out with a smile for Mal.

Except that it wasn't him standing there. "Holy crap! You're not Mal." Cara grabbed the edges of the robe tightly to her chest, feeling horribly naked despite the floor-length fabric.

"Nope," the guy said, just as alarmed. "I'm Lex. His brother." He was smaller and skinnier than Mal, but the resemblance was there, all right.

"Oh. I'm…Cara. And I'm going to get dressed before I say anything more, if that's ok?"

"Sounds like a really good plan," the guy agreed. Not once did he look directly at her, just as embarrassed by the situation as she was. "I'll be downstairs in the kitchen."

Cara dressed super fast and almost ran down to the kitchen, where Mal had to be. And then everything would make sense.

But he wasn't there either.

Lex was talking to Behemoth and Pumpkin, asking them about what happened while he was gone.

"Do you regularly talk to cats like they're people?" she asked.

"Uh, no. Not regularly. Except our cats."

"Because you know them?"

"Sure."

"How about dogs?" she asked then.

"What about them?"

"Do you talk to them like people?"

"My conversations with dogs tend to revolve around the question of who's a good boy. Or girl. And I gotta say, it's amazing how often the best boy—or girl—is right there in front of me."

Cara laughed, despite her lingering embarrassment. She liked Lex immediately. He looked quite a lot like Mal, but with all the dangerous edge removed. He had the same coloring, though his eyes were much lighter. He wasn't musclebound, and he didn't have Mal's smoldery gaze. He must be the good brother.

"Where's Mal?" Lex asked, looking vastly relieved that she was dressed.

She looked at the kitchen island, the scene of the crime that led her to say yes to everything Mal suggested last night. The bottle of wine was still there, open and probably gone bad. The cherries sat in their package and mocked her for being a damn idiot and letting one spectacular kiss get in the way of all rationality and common sense. "Um, actually, I don't know." Lord, she sounded stupid. "He was gone when I woke up. I know that sounds weird, but…"

Lex was already shaking his head in a way that made her heart sink into her feet. "Nope. That actually sounds pretty spot-on for him."

"Oh." *Oh.*

"You're staying here?" Lex asked in a very carefully neutral tone.

"Yes? For a few nights. Because across the street is sort of…"

"Haunted."

"Yeah. Mal said it was ok for me to stay." But then again, Mal said a lot of things. And he wasn't here anymore.

"I'll text him," Lex said. "Maybe he's got a good reason and he's not being a total dumbass. I mean, we do get emergency calls."

"He's responding to a demon-hunting emergency?" Wow, she sure sounded hopeful about that absurd scenario.

"It's possible." Lex flashed her a sweet smile. "Don't worry. Everything will make sense eventually."

"Look, I, uh, have to go to work in a little bit. Which is right across the street."

"Yeah, I know. Mal's been keeping us informed."

"Right. Is it ok for me to come by after I'm done and pick my stuff up then?"

"Is that what you want to do? Where will you stay?"

"Got any recommendations?"

"I've only ever stayed here," Lex admitted. "Look, I know this is awkward, but maybe there is a good explanation. Don't jump to conclusions, ok?"

"I'll do my best," she muttered.

Cara started a pot of coffee and tried very hard not to overhear Lex on his phone. "Dom, hey. You guys about done over there? Because I think you both need to get back here now. No, I don't have any idea where Mal is." A pause, then Lex giving a little sigh. "Ok. *Hurry*."

By the time Cara was pouring coffee into a mug, Lex was hunched over his phone, texting furiously. She would never be happier to get to work.

XVI

MAL RODE THE MOTORCYCLE FOR hours, trying to outrun his own mind, which was impossible to do. He'd not just gone into the otherworlds, he'd stumbled into a legit vision of Cara's future, or futures. Mal was not even slightly trained for such events. And he'd always been terrified of stepping too deeply into the otherworlds, especially when it was mental, not physical. Dancing on the edge of the otherworlds, keeping one foot in and one foot out…that was fine. He could do that as easy as breathing. But giving up his link to his body and wandering into the strange, illogical reality beyond his own gave Mal the creeps.

And he'd done it by accident.

Because getting close to Cara had lowered his defenses.

Dawn was streaking the sky by the time he got his head out of his ass and realized that he'd messed up on a whole lot of levels. Mal had never aimed to be the Perfect Boyfriend, but he knew that running away from your partner while in your own house was not a good move. Cara was going to be confused and probably pissed, and if he was smart he'd get home to explain…what? That he saw her die?

He returned home with a nearly empty tank, a headache, and the sense that things were about to get a lot worse.

Lex was sitting on the porch when he rolled up. He had a mug of coffee in his hands and judgment in his eyes as Mal approached.

"She went to work," Lex said before Mal got out a hello. "You want to give me a report on what's going on?"

"I need coffee."

"I need answers." Lex held out the mug to Mal. "You drink this one and I'll get another."

"No way, you put sugar and cream in and it's gross."

"Malachy East de Silva Salem. Every human and cat around is pissed at you right now, so drink the coffee you're given and start talking." Lex went inside to get another mug, but yelled out, "Talk! I can hear you!"

"I don't know where to start." He stared into the mug.

"Start with why I ran into a strange girl in our hallway at five in the morning!"

"I invited her."

"Yeah, I got that. And based on the fact that she was wearing your bathrobe and nothing else, I assume that you didn't just want to give her a safe space out of the goodness of your heart."

Mal took a sip of the creamy coffee and immediately regretted it. "Things…kind of progressed."

"You don't say." Lex reappeared on the porch, a fresh mug in hand.

"I didn't mean for it to happen. Exactly."

"Going to bed with her? Or leaving your own bed afterward?"

"I freaked out."

"About her? She seems nice."

"She is," Mal said. "It's complicated."

"Hope you're more articulate when you talk to her. Speaking of, shouldn't you be getting ready?"

"I'm not sure I still have my job. Cara might have fired me already."

"It's only eight in the morning. Get your butt to work so we don't lose our access to that hellhole. Ok? Think about someone other than yourself for once."

Lex was normally an easygoing guy, so seeing him angry was a novelty, and a novelty that felt particularly bad. Mal decided that he didn't want to pick a fight with his little brother on top of all his other problems today. He drank down the coffee and stood up.

Mal dressed in his usual uniform of heavy-duty jeans, tank top, and hoodie. At Egan House, he went directly to the parlor room and saw Cara on her hands and knees, absorbed in her work.

"Cara?" He waited. No response. "Cara?"

"I'm not talking to you right now," she said coldly, not even raising her head. "Go find Dan and do every little thing he tells you to do."

"Can we talk later?"

"Get to work, Mal Sa—East."

"Ok." He didn't like the way she was staring at the design of the floor, but he didn't have a lot of leverage now, considering that he'd just ghosted her.

Thankfully, Dan was his normal self, and Mal spent the day doing mindless jobs like carrying materials around, which was all he was good for anyway, considering the limited amount of sleep he'd gotten.

He was doing all right until he paused for a break after hauling up more plumbing fixtures. He leaned against a wall in an unoccupied room and closed his eyes.

He'd screwed up. In a major way.

If he'd known that sleeping with Cara was going to result in a vision, he wouldn't have done it.

Oh, yes I would. And I'd do it again if she let me.

His skin prickled as a cool draft swirled around him.

All I wanted was a chance to prove myself. And I failed. And I'll be stuck here forever, always waiting for the fire to get me.

Wait. What?

These weren't his thoughts.

"Stop it," Mal hissed. "Get out of my mind right now, you little creep. Or I will hurt you a thousand times worse than before."

The sensation intensified briefly before fading away, leaving Mal tired but in possession of his own thoughts again. He made a mental note to bring up some rowan and scatter it around. Pushy ghosts generally hated it.

First a vision, and then a drive-by haunting? Today sucked.

He glanced in the doorway after lunch. Cara was still there. She hadn't taken a break, judging by the crumpled silver wrappers of granola bars and the empty corpse of one of those disgusting diet shakes.

Mal didn't say anything, and Cara didn't acknowledge his presence. After a second, he left and took a detour to the office trailer, where he hefted up the crate of diet shakes and walked out to the dumpster. He tossed the whole crate in. One good deed to edge his karma into a slightly better direction.

At the end of the day, Mal had to move like molasses to allow the other guys to get ahead of him and drive off. He'd managed to keep the fact that he lived across the street a secret. There wasn't a need for it, but he didn't want to get into it.

Naturally, Cara was still hard at work on her fun hell-hole restoration project. She had big goggles on to protect her eyes and she wielded a thing that looked like a space weapon but was in fact a very expensive nail gun.

He assumed she was ignoring him, but then he noticed how intently she was staring at the floor, how still she was.

"Cara?" Mal walked into the room and immediately felt a frisson of creepiness, the feeling he got when he knew he was being watched. But in this room, there was no cold draft or little ghost girl. No one but them. The feeling must be coming from the proximity of the hell-hole, and the rapidly growing design of the summoning circle Cara was building piece by piece.

"Cara?" he repeated once he got closer to her. "Cara, you doing ok?"

"Darkness is coming as a cloud to engulf the stars."

"What?" He touched her shoulder, intending to help her stand up.

What happened was that Cara recoiled, her head snapping up as she rolled back onto her heels, looking for all the world like a cornered animal. She even brought the nail gun up as if to squeeze the trigger at him.

"Whoa, there," he said. "Just asking if you're all right."

Cara's breathing was rapid. "How about getting my attention first before pouncing on me, ok?"

"I called your name three times."

Her brow wrinkled. "You did?"

"Yeah. Why did you say darkness is coming as a cloud to engulf the stars?"

"Why did I say *what*? What does that even mean?" Cara frowned at him. "Is this some weird joke? Like your vanishing act last night?"

"Look, can we talk? It's cool, everyone's gone. No one will see you chatting with me."

She stood up, the nail gun hanging at her side. Her eyes narrowed. "Sure, let's talk. Why'd you leave last night? Why'd you leave me alone in *your* house?"

"I'm sorry."

"I didn't ask for an apology, I asked for an explanation."

"Hey," he said, suddenly unwilling to reveal any more of himself to this woman who he barely knew. "What I do is my business. If I want to go for a ride at night, then I do it. Just because we hooked up doesn't mean I owe you anything."

Cara's eyes widened and her mouth formed a little "o" of shock.

He should not have said that. He didn't even mean it. It was just the sort of cavalier, casual shit he'd say to a woman who was getting too clingy.

But before he could backpedal, Cara's expression reverted to the icy calm she'd worn when he met her the first day of work.

"Yeah," she said. "You're right. Sorry I asked. Tell you what. I'm just going to get my stuff from the spare room and then you won't have to worry about me anymore."

"Cara. That's not what I meant."

She was already past him, walking down the now painted hallway. Mal could easily intercept her, but he instead trailed after, uselessly trying to get her to stop so he could talk to her.

That was what screwups did, and Mal was a total screwup. He deserved this.

Cara made it all the way down the hill and to the Salem house. Lex sat on the porch and wisely made himself scarce the second Cara crossed the property line.

Mal didn't make himself scarce, because he was not the smart brother. He followed her as she went upstairs and threw her things into a large duffel bag. From the bathroom, she retrieved her few toiletries and added them to a little pouch. She was very efficient, prepared for a life on the move.

"Cara," Mal said, trying again. "I was just trying to clear my head. I thought I'd be back before you woke up."

"Clear your head of what?" she asked, suddenly pinning him with her gaze.

"Uh…" *A vision of your death.* No, he couldn't say that. "A nightmare?"

"Oh, it was a nightmare." Cara shook her head and gave a strange, bitter laugh. "Figures."

Mal moved to the doorway. "Not what we did. That's not what I meant. What we did was great."

"You mean the hookup?"

"Yes. I mean no." He stopped, confused. "Wait. Was it a hookup to you?"

"Hey, look at you," Cara said, with a shrug. "Why would I turn that down? Even fat girls need to get laid occasionally."

Stunned by her words, Mal just stood there like an idiot as she more or less shoved him out of the way and went downstairs.

He caught up to her in the living room, and only because she'd taken a moment to pick up Pumpkin and cuddle him. "I don't know if I can take you along, buddy," she was whispering. More longing for the cat than for Mal. Ok. Maybe he really didn't know Cara.

Lex, who was standing nearby, said, "Pumpkin can stay here while he gets stronger. You're welcome to stay too."

Cara's jaw tightened, and she replied, "Thanks for the offer, but I think I've had more than enough Salem hospitality for now. I'm going to find a decent hotel."

She pulled the chain around her neck in an absentminded way, then suddenly stopped. She reached to take off the necklace.

"Keep it," Mal said. "It's useful. Even if I'm an asshole, vampires are still real."

Next to him, Lex nodded. "Yeah. Both of those things are true."

Cara rolled her eyes but returned the necklace to its place under her shirt. "Ok. I'm going."

"You've got my number now. Text when you decide where you're staying," Mal said.

"I'll text when I damn well please."

"It could be really important to reach you," Lex pointed out.

Cara looked at him, and her expression softened. Mal was deeply annoyed that Lex was able to get through to her when he couldn't, but then again, Lex hadn't badly screwed up…everything.

"I'll let you know where I end up," she said at last. "And Mal, you're still on the job, so show up on time."

"Whatever you say, boss."

XVII

After calmly getting into her car and calmly driving away—without bursting into tears once—Cara pulled to the side of the road and proceeded to absolutely lose it.

A hookup. A *hookup*. That's all it was to him.

Even though she should have seen it coming, the truth still slammed her sideways. She grabbed the box of tissues in the back seat and wiped her nose, letting the hot tears flow for a while.

She'd really let him get to her. Cara chalked it up to the long gap in her relationships and the extra weirdness of a ghost and also to, yeah, Mal's smoldery eyes that seemed to be way deeper than he evidently was.

She knew he couldn't be for real. When he'd seemed interested, she'd let things get out of hand. Mal never said anything more than that he was into her, and well, by the end of the night he *was* into her, so that line must be really effective.

"Idiot!" Cara hurled the wadded-up tissue toward the windshield, but the aerodynamics were way off, and it just fell into her lap. "Damn it." She grabbed another tissue, not at all done with crying her eyes out.

She liked him. That was the worst part. Cara wasn't just taking advantage of a hot guy taking advantage of her. She'd really gotten to like him. To want to get to know him, his strange ghost-hunting hobbies, his sad family history, his delightful cat Mr. B.

But right after he'd gotten what he wanted, he was out of there. Literally.

Cara took a deep breath. "This is not the end of the world."

She had options. She could fire him. She could quit the job herself. She could suffer through the last few weeks of working with him…ugh.

"First things first." She couldn't stay in her car all night. She blew her nose, wiped her eyes dry, and pulled out her phone.

Cara found the name of the Calendar Inn among the depressingly short listings of lodgings in the county. It was in town, which was great, although the price made her want to faint. She drove there to check it out, and found a large, all-white Victorian home that had been converted to an inn.

The front porch was both wide and deep, with the sort of tasteful lighting that magazines implied was easy to do, but was in fact an expensive proposition. Rocking chairs sat on the porch, just waiting for a guest to while away an hour or two. The place was decorated with pumpkins and corn shocks for the season, harvesty without being Halloweeny.

Wouldn't it be nice to be a guest, to be someone who could afford a room at the Calendar Inn without blinking, who could sit on a rocking chair for hours without worrying about where her next job would be?

Before Cara quite knew what she was doing, she'd parked, walked in, and handed over a business credit card to the perky girl behind the front desk.

The place was technically a bed-and-breakfast, but it wasn't twee and fussy like Cara had expected. The building was a Victorian, but the interior had been updated to a more modern, clean aesthetic. Lots of blond wood and white walls, accented with good art that Cara would bet her last dollar was local.

Her room was one of the larger ones the inn offered. The king-size bed looked incredibly inviting, with a fluffy duvet and lots of woven pillows stacked against the mid-century headboard. Cara peeked into the bathroom, and found that it was entirely modernized, with a walk-in shower and a glass wall to keep the water mostly in. The only nod to the house's age in here was an oversized mirror with fancy molding. The blend of styles should have been jarring, but it worked.

It was a room she'd never pay for on her own, but after the shitshow of her life the past few days, Cara felt that she was owed a break. Morningside could afford it, after all. And she didn't intend to stay in the inn forever. She'd find a cheaper motel in a few days.

Cara sat on the bed and leaned back against the pillows. Feather pillows. The faint scent of lavender puffed up, and she closed her eyes. Oh, right, this was why people paid big bucks for a nice room. It was totally worth it.

Her phone beeped. She looked at the text message.

Hope you're settling in! Don't forget that we have a full tea and coffee bar in our lounge. If you pine for a latte but don't want to be social, just reply with your request and we'll bring it up!

This place was way nicer than the highway motel. On an impulse, Cara replied, and then leaned back against the pillows to rest.

She was startled when she heard a knock on the door. She must have nodded off.

"Who is it?"

"It's Thalia with your drink!"

Cara opened the door to find the perky front desk girl holding a small silver tray.

She beamed as she handed it to Cara. "Chamomile tea, with extra hot water in the carafe. The shortbread cookies are baked daily in house. Enjoy."

"This will just get added to my bill?" Cara asked, not seeing a receipt.

"It's all included." Thalia chuckled. "Welcome to Calendar Inn."

Cara thanked her. If she was smart, she'd drink her tea, call her mom to sob, and go to sleep early.

Instead, she ate the cookies, fixed her makeup, and left the inn to find a decent bar. Tea wasn't going to do it for her tonight.

It was not a big town, and Cara had little fear of walking alone at night, even though she didn't know the layout. Still, she was a little unnerved when she thought she caught the sound of someone walking behind her. But when she looked, no one was there.

She'd hit the first bar she saw, just to get off the street.

Sadly, she was not in the boozy part of town. Cara kept walking, turning at random whenever she encountered a street that seemed more likely to host retail establishments. Damn, why didn't she ask Thalia at the desk? Oh, right, she had a phone.

Her phone had gone dead. Cara grimaced and shoved it back into her pocket.

Once again, she thought she heard footsteps. And she was no longer entirely sure where she was.

She walked faster, and just when she thought she might start running in a panic, she heard the faint sounds of music. There was a narrow street up ahead, with a glow emanating from it, almost gold, like magic.

Cara stopped and turned when she reached it and saw lightbulbs strung across the space at second floor height, illuminating the otherwise sketchy-looking street. There were several doors and a few outside tables and chairs suggesting a restaurant or two, but only one door was propped open, and the music came from there.

She hurried closer. It was a green painted door, and over it was a sign announcing the By and By Bar.

Cara expected it to be a dive, but the interior was more cozy than dingy.

Glancing behind her and seeing only an empty street, Cara tried to shrug off her creeped-out feeling and walked up to the bar.

The girl behind the bar gave her a lopsided grin. "Evening. ID, please."

Cara realized she left her wallet at the hotel. "Oh, *no*."

"Rough night, huh?" The bartender smiled conspiratorially. "Tell you what. I won't tell if you don't. Bargain?"

"Absolutely."

"Just tell me your name so I can make like I did see an ID if the cops come by."

"Cara Michaels."

"I'm Una. What can I get you?"

Cara slid onto a bar stool. "Something strong enough to erase a bad memory of a bad decision."

"Ooh. Money or a man?"

"Man." Cara winced even as she rushed out with, "His name is Mal Salem."

"Oh, sweetie. I'll take care of ya. Hold up." She turned away from Cara and, like an alchemist with seriously shredded arms, mixed up a drink using about ten different bottles. The result looked something like a latte, creamy and light brown, with a foamy head. The bartender put down a coaster and placed the drink on top. "On the house," she said.

"What is this?"

"I call it an AfterMal."

Cara had two options. She could hurl the drink to the floor and break the glass in a tantrum, or she could suck it up.

She took a cautious sip. It was good. She drank deeper. "Wow," she said at last. "I'm guessing it's popular?"

The bartender gave her a wink. "Sadly, yes. I've had a lot of chances to refine it. Lot of customers in need, if you know what I mean."

"How many?" Cara asked, hating herself for asking.

"Enough to require a special drink. Leave it at that. You are not alone, my dear."

"You a victim too?"

Una shook her head. "Strictly an observer of the human plight. Like a priest, I am here to comfort the afflicted."

Cara smiled. "Thanks for the comfort. I really needed it."

"Live to serve is the bartender's motto. Take your time with that, it's not for the faint of heart." Una tucked a dishrag in her back pocket and moved to the other end of the bar where a man had walked up to order.

Cara took another sip, mindful of the warning about the drink's strength. She glanced around the bar. Irish music floated dimly out of the sound system. The Pogues? Maybe. The bar had fewer than a dozen customers, most of them tucked into tall booths, virtually hidden from her, known only by the sound of conversation and occasional laughter. Cara drank more, the alcohol dulling her emotional pain.

The drink dulled her sense of time too. Or was this the second drink? Cara squinted at a clock on the wall and saw that it was after midnight. Crap, it was a work night, and she wouldn't even get to bed for another hour. Did she miss dinner again? Or had Una supplied her with bar snacks?

She was drunk.

"Una?" she asked. "How far is it to walk to the bed-and-breakfast?"

"You're too wobbly to walk it. I can call you a ride."

"No, I'm not drunk," she lied. "But earlier tonight… actually it's the reason I came in here. I felt like I was being followed."

Una's eyes narrowed, and she suddenly looked dangerous. "Really?"

"I can't prove it. I didn't see anyone, exactly. It's probably just nerves and—"

Una put one firm hand on the bar. "Trust your instincts. Cian!" she called out. It sounded like *keen*. She made a gesture to someone behind Cara, and the bouncer walked up to the bar a moment later. He was a tank on two feet, his shirt straining over a huge torso. His shaved head gleamed in the dim light.

"S'up, Miss Una?"

"Cian, my friend Cara needs a ride to her place. She's at the Calendar Inn. Drive her personally, and wait till she gets in the door, will you?"

"Pleasure," he rumbled. "Do I get to teach some asshole a lesson too?"

"Only if he's dumb enough to show up with you around," Una replied.

"Fingers crossed," Cian said. "Ok, Miss Cara. Your carriage awaits."

The ride only took about five minutes, and Cian barely said a word on the way, instead humming along with the radio.

He pulled up to the Calendar Inn and looked around. "All quiet, Miss Cara. Want me to walk you up?"

"No thanks, I can manage. I, er, can't tip. I'm cashless."

He waved it off. "Just following my boss's orders. You have a good night now."

Cara got out and walked up the pretty stone path to the front porch of the inn. Cian watched her go, and she turned to give him a final wave before she went inside.

She saw that he was holding a phone, but of course she didn't know what he texted.

Package has been delivered.

A simple thumbs-up hovered over it.

Cian texted again. *Why did I just do this? She's not a Salem.*

No, the reply came. *But whoever is of interest to the Salems is of interest to us. And we keep our end of bargains.*

Cian nodded once, then glanced at the peaceful scene. Content that he'd held up whatever end of whatever bargain he was hovering on the edge of, he drove back to the By and By.

XVIII

After Cara had left, Mal went immediately for a beer, ignoring his younger brother's gaze.

"Don't lecture me, ok," Mal muttered.

"You like her."

"Of course," said Mal. "She's nice."

"No, I mean you *like* her." Lex raised an eyebrow. "I thought you were just being your usual Malefactor, but you act weird around her. Is this not just about getting her in bed?"

"Don't tell Dom. Or Lily. And definitely not Cara."

"Hey, not my job. I'm just doing lookups."

Mal recalled Lex's recent assignment. "What did you find out?"

"Lily and I went to the library, and we went through all the old records and books. Not just the files the family put together on Egan House before, but a bunch of books on hellholes in general and spells to seal them. Then we drove to the regular library and looked up the Egan name in the public records. Genealogists have way more resources than even a few years ago! We got a ton of fresh info."

"You're such a dork. What info?"

Lex seemed to be in a slightly better mood than he'd been in the morning. Maybe he was just excited about research. "One thing I found was that there *was* a birth record for a daughter. Her name was Marigold. But no death date that I can find. And no general records from a later date that seem to be the same person."

"Because she died in that house," Mal said, believing it without having any evidence to back it up. Demon-hunting was a business that demanded a certain kind of trust in your own instincts.

His brother chewed his lip. "Then why wasn't it mentioned in any of the newspaper reports? Her name's not there at all. And the Egans were rich. That fire was a big story, the first media circus in this area. And a surviving child would have gone for the inheritance, right?"

"Lex, Marigold is dead. There is the ghost of a little girl over there. If her body wasn't found in the wreckage, it doesn't mean it wasn't there to find. Forensic science wasn't spectacular at the time."

"Seems like a pretty big oversight." Lex sighed. "Oh, that's not all we found out during our lookup. Lily uncovered an account in the old Salem family files from a hunter who ran into a man named Egan who was caught trying to rob the crypt of a church in Romania."

"Let me guess. It was in the district once called Transylvania."

His brother grinned at him in approval. "And they always send me to do the lookups! Yes. It was in Transylvania, and our guy Egan was trying to raise a vampire. The hunter stopped that from happening and got the authorities to arrest those involved for desecration. But Egan was able to use his money and influence to get out of the country before things went further. And then he sort of dropped off the map—or at least out of the spotlight of the Salem family hunters. If Lily hadn't found that old record, we wouldn't have known."

"There are definitely vampires involved in what's happening with Egan House today." Mal told his brother about the vampire attack, and his suspicions about Morningside.

"Dom's going to be pissed when he hears about this," Lex muttered. Their brother got very…emotional when vampires were involved. Specifically, he got stabby.

"Maybe we'll have it wrapped up by the time he gets back."

"Doubt it," said Lex. "He and Vinny should roll in tomorrow or the next day. When you went MIA, I told him to get back here pronto."

Mal looked down at his phone. No word from Cara. If he encountered a vampire while he was out and about, maybe she was in danger too. Then he remembered what the one vamp said.

"He told me to stay away from Cara."

"What?" Lex asked.

"The vampire I killed. He ordered me to stay away from Cara Michaels. At the time, I was just freaked out by the fact that he knew who Cara was. But now I'm wondering if the vampires have another reason to be watching her."

"Well, it seems pretty clear that this Morningside guy is using Cara to rebuild the summoning circle. If the vampires are secretly the ones behind the rebuild, they want Cara alive to complete it."

"They're protecting her? From me?"

"They might just want to keep her from being distracted. And you do tend to distract the ladies," Lex pointed out in his mild tone.

"A vampire stalked and tried to kill me with the goal of keeping Cara's attention on the project?"

"Vampires are such assholes," Lex said. "We should check our supply of stakes and holy water."

"I already did. It's good."

Mal looked at his phone again. Nothing. Maybe Cara was still driving. Maybe she was fleeing the state, having given up on him, this town, the whole haunted house, and the entire messed-up situation. He wished he felt better about that possibility.

"Where do you think she's going to spend the night?" Mal asked absently.

"Not with you, player." Lex stood up. "You should text her and ask. And then wind down and get to your own damn bed, alone. You look like crap and you need to work tomorrow. Hopefully, she'll show up too."

Mal was dead tired. But sleep was hard to come by when he kept thinking of Cara, alone and unprotected… wherever she might be. His text message to her went unread and unanswered.

In the morning, he was woken up by Behemoth landing squarely on his back.

Get dressed and follow me, the cat ordered. *The night was not without interest.*

Mal shoved the cat off him and struggled into his sweats. It was appallingly early, not even proper dawn.

He followed the cat outside, seeing Lex already standing near the Salem property line, right where the lawn met the road.

Lex was staring down at a pile of grey ash, visible in the light of his phone. He announced, "The good news is that the wards against vampires are working perfectly."

"I see that," Mal grunted. The vamp must have incinerated on contact with the invisible boundary that marked the Salem property.

"The bad news," Lex continued, "is that a vampire showed up at our place in the middle of the night."

"Yeah." There was zero chance of it being coincidence. Mal looked worriedly up toward Egan House, praying that Cara hadn't been stubborn enough to camp out there again, where there was no anti-vampire protection to speak of.

"Think the vamp was after Cara or you?" Lex asked.

"I have no idea. If they're watching her, they probably know she's not here anymore. If they're watching me, one of them might have decided to get a little closer." In most situations, a vampire would have no problem crossing a property line. They were only forbidden from entering actual homes uninvited. Luckily, the Salems laid down extra protections to extend the zone of safety past the house itself. The vampire was probably really surprised, right before it got really burnt.

"We have to tell Dom the second he gets back home."

Mal sighed. "Yeah. He's got to know. And Cara should be told, well, something. I'm not sure she believes what I said about vampires, but I'm not about to trust their desire for her to finish the floor to keep her safe."

"Yeah, vampires can do carpentry too," Lex noted in a way that was not at all reassuring.

"They're not going to turn Cara into one of them!"

"Why not?"

Mal struggled to find an answer.

Splinters, Behemoth suggested. *The undead would not excel at woodwork.*

"This whole conversation is getting bad," Mal said. "I'm making coffee."

As soon as it was reasonable, Mal rushed to work, actually arriving before Cara did for once. He waited on the porch of the house, not having a key to unlock the place.

He watched the clouds in the sky turn pink, then orange, then white as the sun climbed above the horizon.

When a vehicle pulled up, Mal stood to be ready for when Cara came around the corner. She looked red-eyed and a bit sleepy.

"Where'd you stay last night?" he asked.

"I have a room at the Calendar Inn. It's nice."

"It's not safe."

"At the prices they charge, I don't think petty crime will be an issue."

"That's not what I mean. Are you still wearing the necklace?"

She pursed her lips. "Yes," she said, unwillingly.

"Good. Don't wander around at night, ok? In fact, you should come back to the house."

"Uh, how about no," she snapped.

"Cara, there are vam—" The arrival of the other workers cut him short. "We'll talk later."

"Dream on."

Cara steadfastly ignored him for the rest of the day, choosing to lock herself in the parlor and work diligently on the stupid summoning circle, despite all his warnings. Mal tried to talk to her half a dozen times, and each time got shut down before he could even get a word in.

He planned to get her to listen after the shift ended, but a text from Dom changed that plan too.

Home. Get over here ASAP.

Mal sighed. Dom sounded pissed. Whether it was because of Mal's mistakes, the presence of vampires, or something else, he didn't know.

Mal sent a text to Cara, asking her to contact him, and then went home.

He found his brothers, Vinny, and three cats in the kitchen. The humans sat at the table. The cats had taken over the couch. Piewicket was diligently bathing Pumpkin, so at least something was going well. Pumpkin saw Mal and let out a little squeaky mew.

The little one thinks you are the person to feed him, Behemoth informed him.

"In a bit," Mal said.

Now.

"Fine." He got out the formula and wrapped Pumpkin into a hand towel burrito, the only way he could get the kitten to stay still enough to feed. He tucked the kitten burrito into the crook of his arm and sat down at the table.

"Ok," he said to everyone. "We can talk while I feed him."

But no one talked. A moment later, Mal looked up to see the others staring at him. "What?"

"It's just very…domestic looking. In a weird way," Vinny said after a second. She exchanged a wide-eyed glance with Dom.

His older brother shook his head. "We've missed a whole lot."

"I got them up to speed on everything I know," Lex told Mal. "But we need to plan our next moves. Did you convince Cara to come back here?"

"No. She barely talked to me today. She's staying at the Calendar Inn, which is moderately safe, as long as she doesn't invite anyone into her room."

"She needs more protection than that," Dom said.

"I cast a protection spell on my medal and crucifix," Mal said. "With her true name. She's still wearing it, I think."

"Your own necklace?" Dom asked, surprised.

"It's what I had. And I figured my connection to it would strengthen my otherwise weak-sauce casting ability."

Dom nodded thoughtfully. "Yeah, that could help a lot. But I'd still like her to be here."

"So would Mal," Lex murmured.

Mal kicked him under the table.

"Tell us more about the summoning circle," Dom said, mercifully not noticing Lex's comment.

"It's progressing. Cara is still working on it, despite what I told her. I think she either doesn't quite believe me, or she's thinking that she'll be gone before anything magical happens with it."

"You couldn't convince her to stop?"

Mal shrugged. "How does that one quote go? The one about getting paid to understand?"

"'It is difficult to get a man to understand something when his salary depends on his not understanding it.' Upton Sinclair," Lex said.

"Or 'If there's a steady paycheck in it, I'll believe anything you say.' Winston Zeddemore," Vinny added.

"Cara's getting paid to do it," Dom said, "and that matters more to her than stopping a hellhole from opening."

"It's not her fault," Vinny argued. "She has no context for all this, and a girl's gotta eat. A few months ago, if you'd suddenly showed up and told me that by playing a gig, I'd let evil into the world, I'd have thought you were high."

"But Cara knows magic is real now," said Dom.

"Sort of. She's seen a ghost," Mal said. "She's seen me *fight* a ghost. But she's never recognized a vampire, or seen any spell cast."

Lex drummed his fingers on the table. "We'll have to show her. Convince her that we're not joking around."

"I could cast a spell that's more…theatrical than usual," Dom said, "but if she's determined to be skeptical, she could just say it's a trick."

"That's what would happen," Mal said miserably. He looked down at Pumpkin, wishing none of this was happening. If the present was this messed up, what would the future bring?

Oh, right, he'd seen what the future would bring.

Mal said, "Dom, I have to talk to you."

"Shoot."

"It's sort of…can we move?"

Dom raised an eyebrow. "Ok."

The brothers walked to the porch, leaving Vinny and Lex caring for Pumpkin inside.

"What's up?" Dom asked, his expression serious.

"I had a vision."

"Didn't figure you for a prophet."

"Think how I felt."

"What happened?"

Mal began, "I was lying in bed, and I was sort of asleep and sort of awake, you know…" He explained the branching visions, and the terrifying sense of finality in the future filled with fire. He finished with, "I don't know any more than that. Dom, I'm not good at this sort of thing."

"You mean sticking around for more than a night?"

"I mean visions. You're the magic master. Tell me what this means."

"Maybe it means you shouldn't sleep with every woman who crosses your path."

"It wasn't like that."

"No?"

"Cara's not some random chick I picked up in a bar."

"I agree. She's a chick who is not random at all. She's linked to the house on the *hellhole* we've been watching for the last year. If you weren't thinking with your dick, it might have occurred to you that by inviting her into our home, you actually slapped some protection on our enemy."

"Cara is not our enemy."

"Maybe not, but regardless, it was a dumb-ass move. Hope you had a good time, though."

"I did! Right up till the moment where I had the vision of her body all burned up on the ground! If I make the wrong choice, she'll die, Dom. I know it. I will have killed her."

"Mal, you said yourself that you were almost asleep. How do you know it wasn't just a nightmare?"

"I know the difference between dreaming and walking into the otherworlds."

"Do you? You're not a huge fan of the otherworlds. You tend to avoid actually being in them at all. Maybe that was part of the nightmare."

It was no nightmare. He wandered into the otherworlds. I sensed it.

They both looked at Behemoth, who'd followed them onto the porch.

"He did?" Dom looked more worried.

Mal tried to ignore the fact that Dom was taking the cat's word more seriously than Mal's.

"What do I do about this?" he asked his brother.

Dom looked helpless. "Avoid flammable things? I don't know, honestly. We're going to have to do some lookups."

"We could try to talk to Marigold too," Mal suggested.

"Sneak over at night and do a seance? That could work."

"Except for all the locks and floodlights and cameras."

"Well, you do know the foreman," Dom pointed out. "Maybe you could come to an arrangement."

"The foreman hates my guts right now."

"This is a radical notion, but what if you apologized?"

"She won't even listen to me. I can't get as far as an apology."

"You generally get as far as you want with women. And you need to let Cara know about this danger."

"She just found out that ghosts and vampires are real, and she barely believes in those things. She's going to freak out if she hears I had a vision of her death."

Dom said, "I don't care what a mess you're making of your personal life. This is way more important. You need to get her back here so we can figure out what's happening with that hellhole and how to stop it."

XIX

CARA SUCCESSFULLY AVOIDED ANY ONE-on-one with Mal since he ghosted her. She ghosted him back by ignoring all his texts, and basically hid in her office trailer or in the parlor on the job site. She thought she was safe when she got to her room at the Calendar Inn after work. But not long after, the landline phone rang.

"Hi, Miss Michaels," Thalia said. "I'm sorry to bother you, but you have a, um, visitor down here."

"Who?" Cara asked.

"Mal Salem." Thalia lowered her voice. "He's being pretty insistent. But if you don't want to talk with him, I can tell him to get lost."

She sighed. "He'll just come back."

"Yeah. Mal's used to things going his way."

Thalia spoke with a lot of authority on the issue. "Let me guess," Cara said. "You dated him too."

"Me? No way. But my sister did for a little bit."

Of course. Cara stared at the ceiling. "Where is he now?"

"I told him to wait in the lounge. But if a paying customer comes in, he'll have to go. He does not match our *hygge* aesthetic, you know?"

"I'll come down and talk to him. Thanks for checking first."

Cara fully intended to go down there and just tell him to leave. But for some reason that meant she needed to change into less schlubby clothes and brush her hair and wash her face first. Damn, she didn't have time to shower and she still smelled like a construction site. Oh, well.

The lounge was the old living room of the house—a large space with big windows and a lot of modern couches. Mal was sitting on a midcentury number in green velvet, looking distinctly out of place in his long leather duster and his raw good looks and his smoldery....

"What do you want?" Cara snapped out, just as annoyed at herself as she was at him.

Mal practically rocketed off the couch when he looked up and saw her. He smiled at her, then faltered. "Cara. Thanks for coming."

"I was already here. Since I'm staying here."

"I mean, down here. To see me. I know you didn't have to."

"How's my cat?" she asked, hating that Mal knew Pumpkin's status better than she did. But she needed to know how her little fluffmonster was doing.

"He's fine, but he misses you."

"Tell him I'll get him as soon as I can." She wanted that little creature in her life, with his soft coat and his insistent head-bops.

"Yeah, Pumpkin's doing fine. But that's not why I'm here."

"Then maybe tell me why you bothered to come bother me?" she prompted after he just stood there like an oaf.

"It's about Egan House. Something we need to talk about. About...that one thing you saw?" He was looking over Cara's shoulder, and she realized Thalia was in earshot, and definitely interested.

"Which thing?"

Ghost, he mouthed.

"What about it?"

"We learned some more about it and we've got a plan. Look, this is all a little X-Files. Can we talk in your room?"

Cara took one more look at Thalia and decided that yes, it was better to keep talk of ghosts and vampires and whatever else quiet.

"All right," she said. "You've got ten minutes to talk and then you're out."

He nodded.

Hoping she wasn't making giant mistake number two, Cara led Mal up the stairs to her room.

"This place is nice," Mal commented when he got inside.

"I don't need your opinion on my living arrangements, Mal Salem."

"Ok. Skipping directly to the main topic, the ghost you saw is very likely the spirit of Marigold Egan, a daughter who lived in the house and probably died the night of the fire. We want to do a seance to talk to her."

"Then do it. You don't need me."

"Actually, we do. Because it needs to be at night, and you have the keys to the place and we need you to turn off the alarms and the floodlights and the cameras."

"Oh." Cara nodded slowly. "I get it. First I was convenient for a hookup and now I'm convenient as a property manager. Great. Is there anything else I can do for you? Run to the post office? Get you some beer? Blow job? 'Cause I'm super into helping you after what you did the other night."

Mal sat down on the edge of the bed, without asking. "Are you really mad about that?" he asked hesitantly. "Like, still?"

"Yeah. I did not like waking up alone in your bed in your house with your brother telling me that you running out on a girl was pretty standard behavior post hookup." By the end, Cara's words amped up, and she realized the whole place could probably hear her.

Mal looked nonplussed. "I wouldn't describe it as standard."

"That's your defense?" Cara gaped at him. "You're such a trilobite!"

He blinked. "I'm a what?"

"A trilobite. A lout. A caveman."

"You mean *troglodyte*."

"Don't tell me what I mean, especially when you're the caveman here," Cara said. "Don't cavesplain to me."

"*Troglodyte* means caveman," said Mal. "And you said *trilobite*."

"What's a trilobite, then?"

"It's an extinct prehistoric sea creature."

She glared at him. "Now you're just making stuff up."

"Nope. I know because I once had to memorize all the state fossils. The trilobite is Wisconsin's. And Ohio's. And Pennsylvania's. Which makes it easier to memorize."

Furious, she took her phone out and googled it.

Fact.

That made her more furious. "Well…you're still a caveman and I hate you."

"Ok."

"Like I seriously hate you."

"Sorry to hear that. I like you."

"Ugh, just shut up."

"Can I get you a soda or water or something? You just yelled a lot."

"Water. There's a beverage station in the lounge. And I still hate you."

A few minutes later, Mal returned with both a glass of tap water and a can of sparkling water. "Just in case," he said, setting them both on the table.

Cara took the tap water and sipped it. Her throat was kind of raw. She sat down on the edge of the bed and watched Mal uneasily.

Mal walked over to the window that faced the front lawn and peered out in the night. He pulled the curtains closed. Then he withdrew another can from his coat. Cola.

He popped it open and took a long drink. He said, "I shouldn't have left that night. I'm sorry."

"Too little too late."

He finished the soda, absently crushing the empty can. "Can I tell you why I left?"

"Would it matter?" she asked.

"I think it might."

Mal wasn't looking at her. His eyes looked everywhere but at her. Cara got a glimmering of his discomfort, the fact that he was maybe as upset by that night as she was.

She crossed her legs and sat up straighter. Her paying attention pose. "Tell me."

He gestured to the bed. "Can I sit down?"

"No."

Mal blinked, then nodded, as if chastised. He shrugged out of his coat, seized the nice leather armchair, and dragged it to the end of the bed. He sat down facing her.

He said, "First off, it wasn't a hookup."

Cara's breath caught, and her heart did a weird flippy thing before she could tell it to calm down. "Wasn't it? What do you call a non-date that results in sex and ends with one person leaving real fast?"

"I don't know what to call what we did. And I know that I shouldn't have hit on you. For a lot of reasons. But I did, because I wanted to, and you seemed to want me to."

"I did," she admitted. "The poor decision making was mutual."

Mal's eyes held hers. "Afterward, in bed, you fell asleep, and I sort of fell asleep too. And then…this is going to sound weird, but I swear it's true."

"You should get that on your business cards."

"Cara, let me talk. This isn't easy."

"Ok. What happened?"

"Do you remember when I told you about other-worlds? That there are these different realities and dimensions and some people can cross the boundaries?"

At her nod, he went on, "One form of that is what you might think of as astral projection. Practitioners can sort of go into a trance, and their body stays here in the real world, but their spirit or soul or consciousness or whatever you want to call it can travel to the otherworlds. And there you might see auras, or find a lost soul, or see the future or the past or whatever you need to do. It's an important skill for anyone who deals with magic. And in my family, where fighting evil is our thing, it's essential to know how to do it."

"Ok." Cara was wondering where this was all leading, but she was snared into the story by this point.

"I can do it, but I'm not comfortable doing it. I hate separating myself from my body." Mal actually gave a shake of revulsion as he talked. "I don't know why, but I always have and I always will. Walking into the otherworlds that way is a horrible feeling, and I avoid doing it unless it's absolutely necessary."

He put his elbows on his knees and his head in hands, like a person nursing a terrible hangover. "That night, when I was falling asleep, with you right there, I thought I was dreaming. But I wasn't. Without intending to do it, or even knowing I was doing it, I'd walked into the otherworlds."

"Is that…bad?"

"Not necessarily. But damn, you want to be alert when you're doing it. Luckily, the otherworld I was shown wasn't imminently dangerous. But I did get a vision."

"Like…a vision of the future?"

"Yes." He looked up at her, his expression dead serious. "Your future."

Cara suddenly had trouble breathing. "What?" she gasped.

"Two futures, actually. One good one, and one…bad one."

"Some details, please!"

"I…shouldn't."

"Excuse me?"

"Visions are tricky things. Telling you a future I saw might change what you do, and change the futures."

"Well, isn't that the damn point? If you saw a bad future, tell me so I can avoid it!"

"I saw you trapped in a fire. Burning to death. And I couldn't get you out."

Cold rushed over her, followed by a wash of sweat, her skin prickling in instinctual dread. "A fire?"

"Not just that. The vision made it clear that something I do will make you die. That I'll screw up, and you'll be the one who suffers."

In a fire.

"No." Cara shook her head, over and over. "No. No. You can't. You don't get to decide things like that!" She started shivering, almost convulsing in her distress. No one but her should ever get to decide her life.

Mal pushed himself off the chair and knelt in front of her on the bed, his hands cupping her shoulders. "Easy, Cara. I need you to keep it together, ok? There's a good future too. One where you live. Where you're happy."

"How do you know that? Why did you see that? Is this even real?"

He reached up to stroke her hair. "Cara, sweetheart, take a breath. Count your breaths, ok? I think I saw your futures because we had just been…"

"Fucking," she choked out disbelievingly.

"Let's say…involved. And also, we've both been very close to a hellhole for a few weeks. And everything combined to sort of…spin my mind off into an otherworld."

"But then you left me."

"That was a mistake." Mal sighed. "Cara, I have to tell you something. About my parents. It's not an excuse, but it might help explain why I bolted."

She took a long, deep breath, trying to calm down. "Your parents?" What could that have to do with anything?

"My parents died when we were just little kids. They went away to fight something really bad—something that required a lot of the family to go and fix. Mama and Dad, they loved us, but they were powerful, and they'd never give up their calling just for us. They would save the world because if they didn't, who would?"

"They left you?" Cara whispered.

"With Mama's family. It happened pretty often. But this time they didn't come back." Mal's voice grew gruff, and Cara took his hands in hers.

"We were told they'd died. No details, not for little boys. Nothing but the fact that they were heroes and they saved a lot of people, more than would ever know it…but they died."

"I'm so sorry."

Mal squeezed her fingers tightly. "I started having nightmares after that. Awful things, but mostly fire. Blazing hot flames, and my mama screaming."

"Mal."

"There was no reason for it," he rushed on. "We still don't actually know how our parents died. Not exactly. But in my head, I imagined it as a fire. When you're a kid, you do fire drills, and you're always told not to touch hot things. What's the scariest thing to a kid? Fire. And for years, that was my worst fear, and it's still my phobia. Irrational, but there it is."

"And then you dream I was in a fire too."

"Not a dream. A vision. You got pulled away from me, into a fire, and I was too chickenshit to go after you and get you back. And then I saw your burned body on the ground, and everything you ever carved all burned up too.

And I lost my shit, and I ran the second I could physically move, and I'm sorry."

Cara's emotions were going completely haywire. She whispered, "Mal, why didn't you just tell me that? Instead of running away and acting weird."

"Because it's personal."

"You had the dream while we were in a bed after sex. Is sex not personal? You know what, don't answer that." Of course sex wasn't personal for him. It was just a thing he did.

"I didn't mean it that way," Mal said. "I just meant that I'm not used to talking...with...you."

"You mean you're not used to talking with women you sleep with."

"Ok, that too. I'm really sorry, Cara. I acted like an ass afterward because it was the only way I could not think about what really happened, and I wasn't ready to do that, especially not in front of you, because I'd have to explain all this, and...yeah."

She bit her lip. "I thought you regretted stuff."

Mal leaned back, regarding her. "You mean the sex? No regrets about that, Cara." He lifted one hand to her face, running his fingers along her jawline, making her all shivery again, for a different reason.

She bent her head, not able to look at him. "Ok. That's good. I mean...I'm glad that's not yet another thing to feel awkward about. It's been a weird few days."

"Tell me about it." Mal leaned forward once more, pulling her into a semi-embrace. Then he kissed her, very gently. No pressure, and no promises. Just a kiss, and Cara thought her heart was going to explode.

She inhaled shakily. "Are you still freaked out about the idea of me catching fire?"

"Little bit, yeah. I know it sounds stupid, but...yeah."

"Think the shower would be safe?" she whispered.

XX

MAL WASN'T SURE HE HEARD correctly. "Go on."

Cara still looked somewhat freaked out after he'd told her the whole *vision of your death* thing. But now there was a tiny smile at the corners of her mouth. "This suite comes with a very modern shower."

Now this was the sort of resilient personality he admired. "Go on."

Her smile widened. "I was thinking that we start the water running, and see how things go."

"I know exactly how they'll go," Mal said, his mouth on her neck. "I'm going to strip you bare and have fun with you till the hot water's gone."

He worked open the buttons on her shirt, eager to get to the naked part as soon as humanly possible. He opened the shirt to reveal a lace bra different from the one before. This one was black and mostly sheer. He cupped her breasts and felt her nipples harden under his touch. He said, "I really like the idea of you wearing this sort of stuff under your work clothes."

"Don't think about it on the site, or you won't get any work—" Cara's response was cut off by her gasp when Mal bent to tease her with his teeth through the lace.

Her back arched toward him, and he ran his hands around her waist to her back, loving how smooth and soft she was. He liked the way her hair fell over her shoulders and back, brushing against his hands. He found the clasp of the bra and undid it, pulling the straps down, sliding the whole thing off while Cara was making little sounds of pleasure.

"Lie back," he said.

She did, putting her arms over her chest to hold her breasts, blatantly teasing him with her seemingly innocent movements.

Mal loosened her belt, unzipped her jeans, and started peeling them off. Cara closed her eyes, and turned her head to one side.

Hiding.

"Hey, why so shy?"

"It's nothing," she said, barely audible. "Maybe hit the lights?"

"And miss this?"

"Mal. Don't pre—"

"You think I'm faking being turned on right now?" He was suddenly sort of insulted. He grabbed Cara's hand and drew it right to his crotch. Her eyelids flew open when she felt how hard he was.

"Ok, I believe you," she whispered.

The jeans came off. The panties followed. He kissed her stomach, and ran his hands along her hips and thighs. "I can't wait to get you in the shower, sweetheart."

"I need a shower anyway. I still smell like sawdust."

"You always smell like sawdust, did you know that? Also coffee. And also I like those smells on you. Believe me?"

Cara nodded. "Now your turn," she ordered, pushing him away and sitting up once more.

He stood up, perfectly happy to put on a show for her. One by one, each piece of clothing got ditched. Last were the boxers, and he realized that even though this wasn't his first time with Cara, she'd never properly seen him naked before, not in the light.

Now she took her time looking, unconsciously licking her lips in a way that made his erection almost painful.

"Not bad," she said at last. "If I were into superficial things like you being totally hot."

"I work hard to be this superficial," he admitted.

He realized she'd somehow pulled the bedspread over her torso, and he reached forward to grab the edges of the fabric to flick it off her. "Cara. Don't hide. You need to get over this right now."

"Get over what? A lifetime of conditioning?"

"Yeah. Would sex help with that?"

She bit her lip. "I guess there's one way to find out."

"Good. Shower time," he told her.

She nodded, her expression a little dazed. She got up off the bed and drifted toward the bathroom. He admired the rear view, but didn't follow immediately. Instead, he reached for his jacket. He was always prepared for the possibility of sex, and one pocket was designated for condoms. He grabbed two, putting one on the nightstand and keeping the other in his grip. He hoped he'd need more by the end of the night.

The bathroom was dim. Cara hadn't hit the lights on, and he didn't either, deciding that there was only so much reprogramming he could push in one night.

She was already leaning into the big walk-in shower, her hand in a spray of water to test the heat. Mal put his hand on her backside, to test the heat. Yes. She was hot.

Cara turned around, the water steaming behind her. "Um, I just remembered I don't have a—"

He held up the packet. "All taken care of."

"You came prepared." Her eyes narrowed.

Mal laughed as he bent his head to kiss her. "You never know when a hot girl might invite you into a shower. Sorry, *woman.*"

Cara's response was lost in the kiss. She opened her mouth and let him taste her. Then her tongue started doing things to his mouth just when her fingers curled around his cock, and Mal nearly lost his mind.

She let go and turned around again, stepping into the shower. "Get in here," she ordered, pulling her hair up on top of her head to keep it out of the stream of water.

Mal followed like he was on a leash. The water hit his skin, deliciously warm.

The shower was tiled floor to ceiling on three walls, with the fourth side being a glass panel to keep most of the spray in. There were two showerheads. Mal turned the second one on too. Soon the bathroom was so steamy that it was difficult to see to the far wall.

"Wasteful," Cara chided.

"Nothing that makes sex more fun is wasteful," he returned. He reached out and released the pile of hair she'd just put up. Redness tumbled down around her, and he smiled.

"I was deliberately avoiding that," she said, not looking that upset.

"You said you needed a shower anyway." He angled her so she stood under the spray, thoroughly soaking her hair and skin. "I don't want to be wasteful."

Mal grabbed the bottle of shampoo on the ledge and proceeded to lather Cara up, running his fingers over her scalp, and then making waves of foam all over her shoulders and breasts.

Cara's eyes were closed, probably because of the suds, or maybe because he'd started to play with her breasts, using the slipperiness of the steam to glide over some very sensitive areas.

Her lips parted. "That feels good," she murmured. "Just…touching like that."

"Like this?" Mal toyed with her nipples. Pinkish, round, perfect.

She nodded slowly. "Yes. Do that while I, um, rinse."

She tipped her head back to get the shampoo out, and Mal loved the way her breasts caught the water as she lifted her arms up to her head. He continued to tease her and the second she was soap-free, he moved to take her wrists.

He turned her around to face the tiled wall between the showerheads. "Hands on the wall, babe."

She obeyed and moaned when he stepped right behind, his cock hard as he pressed against her. "You feel clean enough?" he asked.

"Don't think I'm going to stay that way," she replied.

"I did say I was going to have fun with you till the hot water's gone."

"You can't."

"You doubting my stamina?"

"Not exactly. Just saying this place prides itself on energy efficiency and there's a tankless water heater, so the hot water will never run out."

"You're an adorable home improvement nerd and if you think talking about energy efficiency is going to distract me from my plans, you are wrong, Cara Michaels." He pushed her into the wall with his body, slipping his hands between her and the wall so he could still play with her luscious tits.

"What are your plans?" she asked with a little moan.

"Just stand there and look pretty and you'll find out."

He bent down and kissed her neck, licking off the water droplets accumulating there. Then he moved his hands down to her waist and kissed her back and her shoulder blades, and wow, she had a scattering of freckles on her back, and he kissed each one of those. He worked his way down to her lower back, moving his hands to her hips to keep her in one place, because she started getting a little jumpy when his mouth got within a few inches of her bottom.

"Turn around, babe." He was on his knees now, and he leaned back just enough to let her rotate.

Cara leaned back, staring down at him with wide eyes. Mal smiled up at her, his hands running along the inside of her thighs, up and up until she gasped, and he slipped a finger inside her body.

He bent forward and kissed her upper leg, licking the water off even though more rivulets kept sliding down her skin. He listened to her breathing, the gasps she let out when he knew he did something particularly right.

She felt wonderfully wet, a wetness different from the water on the outside of her body. The thought of sliding into her made him groan.

Mal stood up abruptly, fumbling for the foil packet he'd placed carefully on the ledge.

While he was ripping it open, Cara got her hands on his cock again and started stroking him. He groaned again, louder. "Cara, please."

"Please keep doing this, or please stop doing this?"

"I don't know." It felt so good. Her touch sent his nerve ends into overload. "I want to get off like this, and with your mouth on me, and inside you, and I want all of them at once."

"Poor baby," she said with a lash of sarcasm that was totally forgiven when she rolled the palm of her hand over the tip of his cock. "You'll have to pick one."

In that moment, he knew what he wanted. Cara up against the tiled wall, her legs around him, screaming his name.

"Hands off," he ordered. "I know exactly what I'm doing with you."

He finally got the damn rubber out of the package and stepped away so he could roll it on without getting distracted.

"You don't need the condom," she said suddenly. "I mean, not if you're…all clean. I am, and I have an IUD. If you want to skip it…"

He paused. "You just telling me that to make me happy? I don't mind using one."

"You'd like it better without."

Ok, that was technically true. But… "But you would feel better if I used one. Right?"

After a second, she nodded.

"Then just say that," he told her.

"I just want to make it good for you."

"Cara. It will be good for me."

He proved it then by picking her up and pinning her against the wall again, her back pressed into the tiles.

She gasped. "Mal! You can't do that!"

"I just did." He encouraged her to wrap her legs around him, until he was practically surrounded by sweet, beautiful Cara. He kissed her, delighted her face was level with his. Cara's hands were on his shoulders and she was kissing him back hungrily.

He angled himself and slid into her slowly. Yes, she was hot, and slick, and winning the lottery might be good, but this was better.

Mal's head fell back as he felt the first wave of pleasure hit him. "Fuck yes, Cara!"

"Quiet down! People are totally going to know we're having sex."

He grinned. "I don't care. People should assume that's what's happening when I'm around anyway."

"Well, unless you advertise it, no one will believe you're having sex with me."

He thrust once, and yelled much louder, "Fuck *yes*, Cara!"

She gasped, but before she could say anything, he thrust again. And again. Making her gasp for different, better reasons. And soon they were both way beyond words, just pawing at each other and moaning as the pleasure built up to a peak.

"Mal," Cara whimpered, her arms tight around his neck at this point. "Finish me."

"Promise to scream my name," he told her, his kiss ending in a bite.

"Yes," she gasped out.

He buried himself in her, drawing out every little bit of bliss. Cara rolled her head against the wall and gasped his name.

"Louder," he ordered.

"Mal."

"Louder."

"Mal! *Mal!*" That was it. Cara was done, and he let himself go too, coming hard and loud and not caring if he could be heard across town.

He withdrew a second later, easing Cara down so she could stand on her own cute feet.

Peeling off the condom, he took a few heavy breaths, then stepped into the water for a final rinse.

And the shower water was piping hot. Five stars.

Cara was still leaning against the wall when he turned the water off. She indicated a fluffy bathrobe hanging from a hook and he fetched it for her.

She put it on. "Well, they're going to figure out who's having sex with who now."

"Let them envy me," Mal responded, wrapping a towel around his waist. He found a second towel and handed it to her for her hair.

Cara took it and covered up the lovely red, now almost dark enough to be brown. She padded out to the bedroom. He followed, finding her taking a long sip from the glass.

"Didn't get enough water in the shower?"

"I didn't swallow," she retorted.

"I didn't give you a chance," he admitted. "But I could be persuaded for round two."

"How many rounds are you expecting?" she asked, arching her eyebrow.

"How many do you want to give me?"

"I don't know."

Mal stretched out on the bed. "You can think about it while we dry off. Come here."

Cara finished the glass of water, then walked over to the bed. She sat on the side of it, then flipped her head down, toweling her hair dry. It was a habitual motion she'd probably done three thousand times before. It wasn't sexy, and he might as well not be in the room. Oddly, watching her perform such a mundane task pulled something in his chest.

To avoid thinking about that too much, he said, "I should probably point out that I was supposed to come here to convince you to meet up with us to discuss important demon-hunting stuff. Operation Hellhole, Lex calls it."

Cara pulled the towel off, revealing damp, wavy red hair. "The sex was part of the campaign?"

"No. The sex was because I can't keep my hands off you."

She rolled onto the bed, lying beside Mal, both on their backs, staring up at the ceiling.

"Look, I don't *not* believe you," Cara said. "I just don't know what it has to do with me, exactly. Even if I walk away from the job, someone else could complete the floor."

"That's why you need to talk to Dom and Lex. They're way smarter than me, and they'll know what to do. I'm just the muscle."

"That is not true. Yeah, you're tough. Someone would have to be an idiot to want to fight you. But you're really sharp too. You notice things, you put things together in time to do something about it. You know the difference between troglodyte and trilobite." Cara rolled her head to look at him fully, a little smile in her eyes.

Mal took a breath, then rolled on his side to curl up against her. Cara let him rest his head on her chest. After a breathless second, she put her hand on his head and ran her fingers through his hair.

He sighed, feeling like he maybe just passed a test. "I know I'm not the best choice for a good guy. I want to fix this whole mess, Cara. But I can barely think."

"You're tired. We're both tired. Let's take a little nap and worry about it later."

He mumbled, "I don't get women in bed just to sleep."

"Oh, you were going to seduce me again?" She laughed softly.

"Hoping to," he said, his voice slurring. Mal cuddled closer to her.

"We'll talk about it later, trilobite."

XXI

THEY MUST HAVE BOTH DOZED off. Cara woke up slowly, moving by degrees through layers of unconsciousness until she realized she was awake again, still with Mal sleeping next to her. They hadn't even got to the point of getting under the covers. She was still in the bathrobe, but Mal was only wearing a towel, his upper body completely exposed. His very cut upper body.

Cara shifted to her side, figuring now was as good a chance as any to ogle him. There was a lot to ogle, and before she really planned to, she was running her fingers along his arm, feeling the strength in his biceps, and noticing just how nice his clean skin smelled.

She sidled a little closer, opening her robe to put partway across him, a makeshift blanket because she was too lazy to get up and find the extra one in the closet.

Cara laid her hand on his chest, idly teasing his nipple the way he'd done to her.

Then he turned his head and kissed her.

A slow roll of pleasure hit Cara, starting with her mouth, where she could feel the sweet, velvet softness of his lips pressed to her. Then it went lower, sending a wave of heat right between her legs.

Mal's tongue ran along her lower lip and the heat doubled.

"Mal. I thought you were asleep."

She felt him smile. "I wasn't. I was just being real quiet while you were pawing at me."

"I wasn't pawing. I was…"

"Groping?"

"*Appreciating.*"

He laughed and said, "You're supposed to ask before appreciating people that way. Especially if you think they're asleep."

"I couldn't resist. Besides I was pretty sure you'd be into it."

His hands slid under the bathrobe. "You were right."

Another long kiss had her ready for more.

Within a very short time they were both sweaty and short of breath. Riding the pleasant buzzy calm of her orgasm, Cara curled up on her side, ready to sleep for another few hours.

Then Mal asked, out of the blue, "What would happen if you stayed? I mean, after all this is over."

She blinked, puzzling her way out her haze. "Mal, how much work do you think October County can offer for historical restoration? I need to go wherever my next job is."

"I knew you'd say that." He was quiet for a long minute. "Want to fix up our house? I'll pay you."

She kissed him on the cheek. "You can't afford me. Anyway, I don't date clients."

"Good. I mean, unless I ever get to be a client."

"You won't," she said firmly. "You'll just have to get your sex on while I'm here."

When she got up at last, Cara packed up some of her stuff, and they walked outside into a chilly evening. They left her car at the inn, since Mal didn't like the idea of her driving alone at night, even for a little while.

It was very late when they reached the Salem house, but the lights were on throughout the first floor. Mal had Cara's bag over his shoulder and dropped it in the hall.

"Where's everyone?" he called out.

"Where's Pumpkin?" Cara added, feeling that was the most important consideration.

"I'm in here! Behemoth and Pumpkin are sleeping upstairs, they'll be down in a sec." Lex was reading at the kitchen table and didn't even look up from his book. "We didn't know how long your…convincing would take. Dom is upstairs giving Vin a magic lesson."

"Is that a euphemism?" Cara asked Mal quietly.

"Nope. He's been teaching her how to cast spells."

Lex added, "I'm not sure if he's teaching her regular spellcasting, or Dom-style spellcasting."

"Is *that* a euphemism?"

"Nope. Most spellcasting is done with rituals, and it requires a lot of setup and research and double-checking because if you screw up, bad things happen. You can't just fire off a spell off the top of your head."

"But Dom can. He's got a gift. First born," Lex noted. He closed his book and looked up at last.

"Yeah, that's usually who gets something like this," Mal explained. "Dom can basically decide what he wants to do and whip up a spell on the spot—no research, no vetting, no generations of study and refining and casting from a book. And it works."

"It's maddening, sometimes," Lex added.

"Yeah," said Mal, "especially because his spells are so powerful. It'd be less annoying if his stuff was like *poof, I made the chicken cook faster*. But Dom is like *poof, I just locked a demon up in this circle of Pop Rocks I happened to shake out on the floor*."

"That sounds pretty useful," said Cara.

"Don't get us wrong," Lex said. "It's very cool Dom is that strong. And good for business."

"I almost wish he'd make more of a big deal about it," Mal grumbled. "He's so modest about it that showing off would be better."

Lex rolled his eyes. "Like you do with fighting?"

"Well, I'm *good* at fighting," Mal said.

Cara knew that to be true. She asked, "What are you good at, Lex?"

"Nothing, really. I'm the spare Salem. Support staff and bottle washer."

Mal said, "I told you before, Lex is a genius. Don't let him be all humble."

"I'll save that job for you," Lex noted sarcastically.

A small orange mass streaked toward Cara, and she scooped up Pumpkin right before he crashed into her feet. "Sweetie, I missed you!"

Pumpkin started purring the moment she cuddled him to her chest. Mr. B looked on, blinking after his interrupted nap.

Lex smiled at Cara. "We're really glad you came back. Will you stay here for a little while? It's safer."

"I packed my stuff, but I still technically have a room at the Calendar Inn."

"Good. Some misdirection might come in handy. I wanted to ask about the ghost you—"

A couple walked in, interrupting his question. The man was clearly a brother to Mal and Lex. The same basic coloring and features. He had more visible tattoos on his arms. He looked a little older, but not much.

He noticed Cara and immediately walked over to her. "Hey, I'm Dom. I bet things are really confusing right now."

"It's been an interesting few days," Cara allowed.

She looked at the woman who stepped up by Dom's side. She was everything Cara was not. Tall, platinum blonde, and without an ounce of fat on her. She wore her outfit with the sort of confidence that reminded Cara of the cool girls in high school, even though this woman looked like the sort who was voted Most Likely to Burn the School Down.

The sort of girl who would never be friends with a Cara.

But this woman gave Cara a brilliant smile. "I'm Vinny. We've heard a lot about you. And we cyber-stalked you a bit. Your website is amazing."

"Oh, um, thanks."

"Mostly, it was reports from Mal." Vinny's gaze slid from Cara to Mal, and then back again, her eyes widening. Whatever Vinny noticed, it left Cara feeling very shy.

Lex jumped in. "I was just about to ask Cara ghost-related questions. That seems to be the most interesting aspect of this whole situation, and probably our best chance to find out more of what's going on."

"I only saw the ghost a couple times," Cara said.

"But you saw her when no one else did. Little girl, dressed in clothes looking like the 1920s? We're almost certain that it's the spirit of Marigold Egan, the Egans' daughter."

"I thought there were only two sons."

"There's a birth record for a Marigold Edith Egan, and the presence of the ghost suggests she died there, and the lack of a death record suggests no one found the body… which might explain why her ghost is still haunting the place."

"We want to ask her questions via a seance." Dom said it like it was the most normal thing in the world.

"Weird, huh?" Vinny laughed. "But they're serious. The guys can conduct a seance to communicate with the ghost, but we need your help to get into the house."

"And it might be good if you were there since you did see the ghost most often," Lex added. "Any positive vibes improve our chances of speaking with her."

"Whoa. I don't know about positive vibes. I think she tried to kill me once. I was convinced I was caught in a fire and she maybe tried to push me down the stairs. And was she the one Mal fought? How do we know that a seance won't get her really mad?"

"It's a possibility," Dom said. "But we have to risk it if we want to get more information."

"Demon-hunting and ghost-chatting is a risky business," Mal told her. "The good news is that you only have to unlock the house and turn off the alarms."

"When would this happen?" she asked.

"Tonight," said Dom.

"Tonight?"

"Sooner the better. If we go now, we can start the seance at midnight. Perfect timing."

That sounded like atrocious timing to Cara, who didn't even like the idea of raising a spirit in broad daylight. But what else could she do?

"All right. Let's get this over with."

It didn't take long for the Salems to prepare for the seance. Vinny stayed with Cara in the living room while the guys assembled everything. Cara focused on Pumpkin, the most normal thing in her world right now. Cuddling the little orange kitten, she smiled. "At least I found you in this mess."

Behemoth jumped up on the couch, causing Vinny to scoot a foot over, giving the cat a wide berth. He settled between the two humans.

Cara reached down to scratch his ears. "Thanks for looking after Pumpkin, Mr. B." He began to purr.

Then Mal stepped into the room. "Everything's ready. Let's go."

Cara put Pumpkin down carefully and stood up. Behemoth jumped down as well.

Mal looked at the cat. "Oh, you're coming too?" he asked, then paused as if the cat was speaking back.

"It's a thing," Vinny whispered. "Piewicket does it too. I wish I could hear them, but I can't. It's just the family."

"Wait. The cats really *are* talking?"

"Yeah. They're not regular cats. Not at all."

Cara's list of questions about the world was getting longer, but then the whole group was out the door, walking up the hill to Egan House.

She got out her keys to unlock the gate and the back door. She deactivated all the alarms and motion lights, and unhooked her cameras.

"Ok," she said at last. "Coast is clear."

"Should we set up in the parlor?" Lex asked Dom. "It's the place with the most power."

"I'd rather not," Dom said. "Cara, you first saw the ghost upstairs, right?"

"Yeah, I can show you which room."

"Let's go there. Maybe the ghost has its reasons for being in that space."

When they reached the room where Cara first saw the ghost, and where Mal fought whatever supernatural shadowy thing, she took up a position by the mirrored door and watched as Mal and his superhero team went to work.

The floor was pretty clean, but Vinny swept it with a hand broom she'd pulled out of a bag. Lex measured out a big circle and traced it in chalk. Then he and Dom started marking out a bunch of weird symbols and shapes around the perimeter of the circle. They talked as they did so, using terms that sounded like five foreign languages and a chemistry class mixed together.

Meanwhile, Mal and Vinny started placing a bunch of candles around the room. "Want to help?" Mal asked Cara.

She took half a dozen votives. "What are these for?"

"Light. Just put them anywhere where they'll be out of the way. Vinny is placing the candles that will actually matter for the ritual."

"Oh, what have I gotten myself into?" Cara muttered. "No one is allowed to light a single one of these till I get a fire extinguisher in here."

Lex laughed and gave her a thumbs-up, then bent down to work on his cryptic drawings.

Within ten minutes, Cara was standing just outside a twelve-foot wide circle surrounded by a dozen candles in glass jars, with twice as many in the corners and sides of the room to give additional light. Some were little white tea lights, but others were the colorful tall glass ones she usually only saw in Mexican groceries.

She had to admit that it did create a certain ambiance that flashlights couldn't match. "What do all those symbols mean?" she asked.

Mal responded, "These ones are primarily for safety, welcome, and binding. Marigold's name is there." He pointed to the one legible bit of the design. "We want her to know it's ok to show up, but not ok to make trouble."

"Please tell me you've done all this before."

"Oh, lots of times. And Dom knows what he's doing. You'll see. I shouldn't have to kick any ass at all."

"But don't nod off," Lex said. "Just in case everything goes horribly wrong."

Behemoth meowed in what sounded suspiciously like agreement.

"Are these candles placed right?" Vinny asked Dom.

"Yup, perfect. And I see Cara has a shiny fire extinguisher at the ready. Let's do this."

"Who's in and who's out of the circle?" Lex asked. It was very clear that both Lex and Mal deferred to their older brother without question when it came to magic.

Dom looked at Behemoth for a long moment, as if the cat was offering opinions.

"Yeah, that makes sense," Dom said to the cat. Then he looked around. "Lex and Mal, stay outside the circle. You'll watch in case there are problems. Vinny and Cara, join me in here."

"I thought I was just observing," Cara squeaked.

"You are, but you did see the ghost more often than anyone else, and your presence could help get her attention. You don't have to do anything. Vinny and I will handle all the spellcasting."

Cara stepped over the chalked lines carefully so she didn't smudge anything. "Should I sit?"

"Yeah, however makes you comfortable," Vinny said.

"That would be a mile away in a well-lit, non-haunted house, please." She sat and crossed her legs. Vinny and Dom sat too, so they formed a little triangle. Lex and Mal looked pretty relaxed where they were. Behemoth sat in front of the mirrored door, his green eyes glowing in the candlelight.

"You'll be fine," Dom told her. "A seance rarely gets physically dangerous."

"How reassuring."

Despite her worries, Cara was fascinated by the whole process, especially because everyone was taking it seriously, but not theatrically. Dom was wearing a T-shirt, not some hooded robe. Vinny leaned over and gave Cara's knee a squeeze, whispering, "Once Dom starts talking, don't say anything or disrupt the casting if you can help it. Just think about Marigold, and when you saw her, and how you felt during those times. Try to keep an open mind and an open heart, however bonkers you think we are."

Cara smiled, relieved to know that Vinny understood.

Then Dom began to speak. He didn't use English. Cara assumed it was Spanish at first, but quickly figured out it was Latin.

Dom lit a few remaining candles in a diamond shape at the center of the circle. He sprinkled some powder or crumbled herbs over the flames, and Cara inhaled the scents of rosemary and maybe mesquite, something green and wild.

He spoke again, using Marigold's full name, and when he did an immense feeling of sadness descended on Cara. It was similar to the times she'd felt sad in this house before, but it was much, much stronger now.

Vinny's brow wrinkled in distress—she must have felt it too.

Outside the circle, Cara saw Lex and Mal shift a little, uncomfortable.

Dom paused for a moment, but then straightened his posture and went on. His voice changed, becoming more certain, more assertive.

The sadness lessened for a moment. Cara tried to shake off the feeling, and the sense that maybe it was better to let the dead be. Something awful happened in this house…why stir it up again? Why make this poor little girl speak about the terrifying end of her short and lonely life? What could be gained? Why not talk to her parents, the ones who hurt her and betrayed her…

"Marigold Edith Egan, come speak to us," Dom said in the sort of tone that made you want to obey him.

Cara waited, breathless. The candles flickered slightly. Probably just a draft.

Then a wave of blistering heat hit her, followed by a deadly cold. She tried to breathe, but felt utterly frozen.

She opened her mouth, and words that weren't hers came out.

"*I am here.*"

XXII

MAL KNEW SOMETHING WAS WRONG the moment Cara stopped moving. And then he heard the words coming out of her in a voice nothing like her own.

She was still sitting in the circle, flanked by Dom and Vinny, who was already leaning toward Cara.

Vin touched her arm and pulled back suddenly, startled. "She's freezing!"

He didn't need to hear more. No ghost was going to mess with Cara when he was around to—

Lex rushed over to him and grabbed him by the arm before he could enter the circle. "Don't do anything dumb!"

Do not cross the border, you fool! Mal heard the warning in his head from Behemoth. *I will handle this.*

Behemoth leapt across the chalked lines—all cats possess the ability to cross boundaries, magical or not—and moved to Cara. The humans held still, waiting for the cat to act. Lex kept a very firm hold on Mal, talking fast in a low voice. Mal didn't catch most of it, and the words didn't matter. Nothing mattered but Cara's safety.

The cat sniffed around her, and then sat down directly in front of her and locked eyes with Cara.

Why do you not manifest as you did before?

"It's easier this way," Cara-but-not-Cara whispered. "I won't hurt her. She's just like me."

Behemoth's tail twitched, then he climbed directly into Cara's lap. *Be aware then. If you hurt any living being here, I will hurt you.*

"Can I pet you?" Cara asked, seemingly unconcerned by the threat.

Yes, he replied after a moment.

Cara's hand dropped to pet the black cat curled in her lap. "I do miss cats. I had one, once."

Mal hated the childish voice, the non-Caraness of it. "What do you want?" he asked.

Cara turned her gaze to him, and the eyes in her face were all wrong, nearly black and seemingly vacant. "*You* called me here."

"Marigold," Dom said with a warning gesture at Mal to shut up and let him deal with the ghost. "We need to ask you about this house. About the hell—the portal. Do you know what I'm talking about?"

She nodded. "How could I not? I can't get a moment's peace, not with the otherworlds so close, all the beings banging on the door, begging to be let in. They always want to find ways into our world. The souls here are so sweet to them…they are desperate for more. Always more."

"How do you know this?"

"Oh, I can hear them, just on the other side of the veil. Slobbering from hunger, smelling me and telling me to step through and let them eat me up. They promise anything, everything. Light, peace. Freedom."

"You never accepted?"

Her expression grew hesitant, almost ashamed. "I sometimes wanted to. More than sometimes. But I can't. I'm bound here."

"What happened? Why are you bound?"

"It's the gate," Marigold said. "He said he would create a gate of gold. A gate pharaohs would envy, a gate to make Lord Netjerunakht proud."

Dom's eyes widened. "*Who* said that?"

"My father. And I was to be the key."

"What?" Vinny broke in, horror in her voice.

Cara looked at Vinny, the sadness and pain evident on her face. "All I wanted was to make him proud of me. But I wasn't a boy, and he didn't think much of me at all. Until he said I could do something very important for him. A great honor. And he gave me a pretty dress and pretty jewelry—grown-up jewelry. Like a Halloween costume but much fancier."

"You wore those clothes? When? What happened?"

"My parents set up the parlor with candles and a fire in the fireplace. My mother was singing. Not any song I knew. It was a strange tune. And then Papa led me into the center and drew a knife. And then I got scared and I didn't want to be there anymore. But no matter how much I cried and screamed, he wouldn't let me go. And Mama was screaming too, and then it was brighter. Something caught fire that shouldn't. I think the thing that caught fire was Mama.

"Papa was distracted. Helping Mama. I ran away, upstairs and into my room." She pointed to the mirrored door. "That way. But the flames followed, and Mama followed, and Papa followed, yelling that we couldn't stop, that the door must stay open, but there was so much smoke all of a sudden. So much fire…"

"Ok, stop," Dom ordered. "A fire interrupted the ritual. You ran upstairs to the old wing, and that's how the fire spread."

She nodded once more. "It was a mistake. My father was screaming. Mother too, but then she stopped. I heard it all and felt it, but as if through the other side of a looking glass. Somehow distant. And then I saw myself—my own body on the floor, not breathing, not moving. I tried to get to myself…I wanted to be *together* again. But everything was horribly wrong and then I didn't know which direction to go or which way was up and I was just floating in darkness for…I don't know how long. And then I came back from the darkness, and I was still here. But the house was all broken and burned, and everyone was dead and gone. Except me. I'm still here, always here. Always listening to the other side of the gate, always wishing this would end."

"When people came back, you tried to scare everyone away," Mal said. "You tried to scare Cara, and then me. And you creeped out the workers by making them feel cold or sad when you could."

"It's too dangerous for anyone to be here! And to re-build the gate? That's worse! I wanted you all gone, but it takes…concentration to manifest. I couldn't do it more than a few times. And it wasn't enough, especially after you attacked me! No one else has ever been able to reach me, not even when I wanted to reach them. But you did, and it hurt."

"Sorry. I thought you were trying to hurt us."

"No. Just to scare you away. I used my memories, sent them to her and to you so you would see the smoke and fire I see all the time. But it wasn't enough."

Cara's expression looked totally defeated, wrung out by nearly a century of imprisonment. For just a moment, Mal caught a hint of the scope of the ghost's suffering. Poor Marigold, who wanted so badly to be free, and would have succumbed to the demons that were eager for her little ghostly soul, except that her soul wasn't hers to give.

Suddenly, Cara's head turned sharply, and she raised her hand in a warning gesture. "Someone is here. Outside the house."

Mal shifted uneasily, torn between wanting to check it out and wondering if it was a ploy.

But Behemoth also sat up and sniffed. *There is a presence. Not human.*

Dominic nodded. "Ok. We'll end this." He spoke a few more formal Latin phrases, words of severing and sealing. Then he said in the kindest tone he used all night,

"Marigold, you need to leave Cara now. You can't keep using her body."

Cara seemed frozen once more, and then let out a thin sigh. "I'm sorry."

Cara, who'd been sitting ramrod straight ever since Marigold possessed her, now hunched over, cradling Behemoth and hiding her face in the cat's fur. Her red hair cascaded down like a final curtain. The sound of her crying ripped up Mal's soul.

Dom quickly finished the ritual, making a slashing motion with his hand that signaled the dissolution of the magical border.

As soon as he saw that, Mal crossed the chalked outline and reached Cara in two steps. He knelt beside her. "It's ok. It's over, and you're fine."

"She hurts so much," Cara moaned, her eyes still closed. "She's all alone and she can't ever get away."

"It'll be ok," he repeated, the age-old nonsense people say when it is most definitely not ok. "Come on. Get up and we'll get you home. Just across the street, ok?"

Behemoth zipped away, allowing Cara to stand. Mal put one arm tight around her shoulders. "Come on. We're just going downstairs."

Lex and Vinny were moving swiftly, snuffing out candles and rubbing out the chalk symbols.

Dom stood in the doorway. "Behemoth took scout. He's says there's still something lurking."

"Get a stake handy," Mal warned.

Dom never needed that advice. He pulled a wooden stake from the vicinity of his boot. "Can't wait."

Lex tapped Mal and handed him a stake too. "Just in case this turns into a party."

"I hate vampire parties," Vinny said. She was also gripping a stake, though considering she was carting around half the seance equipment, she could also just swing her bag at a vamp and knock it off its feet.

As a group, they moved out of the newly de-magicked room and went downstairs.

First floor clear, Behemoth advised them from somewhere below.

They all hurried past the parlor and to the back door. Cara mumbled that she should reset the alarms, but Mal hustled her past the electronics.

Dom, nearest to the door, gripped his stake tightly in his hand, then opened the door. Behemoth darted outside into the night, and they all heard his furious howl.

"That's it. Mal, you and me. Everyone else, stay inside and don't invite *anything* in!"

Mal handed Cara off to Lex and Vinny, then followed his brother into the darkness. He ran toward the sound of cosmically pissed off cat, and found Dom and Behemoth already engaged with something that felt very vampy.

Since Dom had a special hatred for vampires, Mal always wanted to keep a close eye on his brother in case he let his emotions get the better of him during a fight.

But it was Mal the vampire smiled at, showing viciously sharp fangs. "Oh, it's the boyfriend." It leapt toward Mal, dodging out of the way of the others.

He reacted in time purely due to training, stepping to the side and using the vampire's mass to hurl it further past him. He reached for the crucifix around his neck… and remembered he gave it to Cara.

Well, there was still the stake.

Mal yelled for his brother to back off, then took a short dive into the edge of the otherworlds, just long enough to confuse the vampire. It would look like Mal disappeared. He reemerged in a spot he hoped would be behind the vampire, and went for a kill shot, basically jumping at the vampire's back and hooking his arm around to plunge the stake in.

But this vampire was much tougher than the previous one. It shrugged Mal off, tossing him in the dirt.

Ow.

Mal's vision briefly exploded into stars. Then the vampire was right there, over him. He wanted to spring up, to kick this thing's undead ass, but he was unable to move, pinned by both the strength of the vampire, and its mental assault.

"You won't taste as good as she will," the thing hissed. "But you'll do."

It opened its mouth, fangs bared, and then gave a shriek of pure agony.

Behemoth's head appeared past the vamp's shoulder. The cat had leapt onto the thing's back and sunk all his claws in.

Mal used his precious second of clarity to slip out from under the creature. Dom was there, hauling him up.

"You ok?"

"Not really," Mal snapped, rage replacing his fear. "I'm going to knock this asshat on its back and then you stake it."

Dom nodded.

The vampire was staggering around, trying to throw off Behemoth, who was clinging to it in a way that was wholly improbable. The cat hissed and spit, adding annoyance to pain.

"Behemoth, let go now," Mal said in a low voice.

The cat did, leaping off the vampire's back as if it were a springboard. Mal caught just a glimpse of Behemoth's retracting claws, which were way longer than any cat's should be.

But he didn't care about that. Mal put on a burst of speed and hit the vampire right in the stomach, a move an offensive lineman would be proud of.

He pushed it back, and then used his momentum to topple them both over. The vampire grunted, but wasn't hurt. It shoved Mal away.

The hurt happened when Dom jammed a stake directly into its chest, impaling the heart. The vampire's eyes went wide, and it opened its mouth like a fish gulping for breath.

It struggled against fate and the inexorable result of living wood in its non-living body. Then it sort of crumpled and collapsed, a balloon running out of air. The skin turned grey, the hair withered. Then the vampire simply dissolved into a pile of ash.

Behemoth trod across the ash on his way back to the house. No disrespect like feline disrespect.

Dom dusted his hands on his jeans. "Neighborhood's going to hell."

"We should just burn this place to the ground," Mal said.

Vinny saw them through the window and opened the door. "All clear?"

"Yeah," Dom told her with a tired smile.

"Vamp?" Lex asked, peering into the darkness behind them.

"Dusted. Behemoth nearly filleted it first." Mal took hold of Cara again. She was shivering. "Let's get back home."

Cara was silent as they walked down the hill, Behemoth leading the way. When they crossed the property line that also marked the beginnings of all the Salems' magical wards, she nearly fell over.

"It's ok," Mal whispered, tightening his arm around her. "I got you."

XXIII

MAL PUT CARA TO BED in his own room, promising that he'd join her as soon as he could. She curled up on her side, pulling the blanket around her.

"Why did that have to happen?" she asked in a broken voice.

"Sorry. Dom didn't know the ghost would try to possess anyone. The idea was just to summon her."

"Not that. I mean Marigold's death. Why would anyone use their own child like that?"

"I don't know. People are assholes sometimes. That's all I got."

Cara huddled into the blanket even more. "Mal, don't leave me alone."

"You're not alone. In this house, you are totally safe. We're all here, there are wards up like you wouldn't believe, and we got two guard cats."

"Where's Pumpkin?"

"Pumpkin is not a guard cat."

"He's mine and he's fluffy. I want him here. Tell Mr. B to bring him up, ok?"

"I'll ask him," Mal promised. "Now get some rest."

He reached out to touch the chain around her neck. "You're safe, Cara."

He kissed her and left the room, meeting Behemoth and Pumpkin in the hallway.

"I was just going to find you," he said.

We are found, Behemoth responded. The cats slipped through the cracked-open bedroom door.

Downstairs, everyone was sitting around the long dining table, except Piewicket, who was sitting on the table.

They were mid-conversation. Vinny was talking when Mal pulled out a chair and sat down.

"I think she's telling the truth," she was saying, "or at least as she understands it. I felt it when Marigold kinda slipped in my head, right before she possessed Cara. There was a lot of…um, resonance there. I had a pretty cold upbringing too. Not that my parents tried to kill me, but…"

"Why did it pick Cara?" Mal was still unreasonably mad about that.

Vinny said, "Maybe the fact that she's interacted with Cara multiple times? She's the one who's been in the house, working on the floor that will be the summoning circle to open the hellhole. Marigold has clearly been paying attention to her. And the pull of the familiar can be very strong."

Dom nodded in agreement. "That's logical."

"I don't want it to happen again," Mal said.

"We probably don't need to conduct another seance with Marigold. She told us what she knows."

Lex looked up from his phone. He'd been texting intensely for the past few minutes. "Lily's already started a lookup on that demon Marigold mentioned. Hopefully we'll get something useful soon. Then we can finally figure out how to shut this stupid hellhole down for good."

"Can we…" Vinny hesitated, then went on, "Can we help Marigold too? I know most exorcisms are performed on ghosts that don't want to go, but…"

"We can try," Dom told her. "I don't like the idea of her hanging around any more than you do. But the hellhole is the most important thing."

"Working on it," Lex said, once again texting. "I'm going to look up more on the specific rituals Egan might have used. But I might have to go back to the library to do it." Which would take days.

There is another avenue, Piewicket said. *We do not have much time, so while it is costly, it may be worth it.*

"What do you want to do?"

The Salem family has many assets. One of your predecessors encountered a powerful demon by the true name of Ihithiltalas. That being owes this family a debt. Now may be the time to call it in.

"Pie, how old is this debt?"

Older than you, but not so old Ihithiltalas can even pretend it has forgotten it.

"We're going to summon a demon?" Mal asked, looking at his brothers.

"I mean, sure why not?" Lex said. "It should know about this Lord Netjerkface. And right now, we know nothing. And who knows how long it would take to learn enough on our own?"

Dominic turned to Vinny. "I know you're getting an education, but this isn't going to be part of it, ok?"

"Hey, no problem," she said. "The last time someone summoned a demon near me, it sucked. I'm going to go read a non-magical book."

Dom insisted that he was in perfectly decent mental shape to summon a demon, despite having gone through the earlier seance. As for his own mental shape, Mal wished he hadn't been almost killed by a vampire, but he shook it off.

The brothers gathered outside on the shabby concrete patio for the summoning—it was generally not a great idea to let demons in the house, even within a protected circle.

"If we ever get neighbors, this is going to be hard to explain," Lex said as he measured his second circle of the night.

Mal set up the candles in their windproof jars, while Dom chalked symbols onto the concrete. These were quite different from the ones he used for Marigold's circle. Piewicket directed the choices, and there were a lot of symbols for protection, truth, and binding.

Mal was skeptical about the wisdom of this whole thing, but it got worse when Dom handed him a knife—Dom's own wickedly sharp blade that had magic laced all through the metal. "If things go badly, don't hold back on killing any demon you see."

He took the knife. "Kill mode activated."

The cat remained in the circle with the brothers as Dom began the casting. There was something very comforting about the little calico, right there in the middle of the circle.

When Dom spoke the name of the demon, the candle flames all trembled and turned a deep reddish hue. Shadows began to dance around the circle, shadows that didn't correspond to any light source in the real world.

Then a figure seemed to emerge from a gash in the air, just in front of Pie. Mal tightened his grip on the dagger, and adrenaline hit his veins.

The demon was nine feet high, but thin, like a person stretched too much. Its arms were long, hanging to its knees, and wicked nails sprouted from its four digits. It glared around at them all, its orange eyes blazing beneath its heavy eyelids.

"Who summons me? Let them come forth and be known, lest I pursue them even unto the ending of all things!" the demon intoned.

"Did you just intone?" asked Lex.

"No," said the demon.

"You did. You have the look of an infernal being who just intoned."

"Fool mortal! I shall destroy thee where thee stands!"

You will do no such thing, Ihithiltalas, Piewicket said. *For you recognize me, and you ought to know that these mortals are members of the Salem family, to whom you owe a debt.*

The demon hunched over, losing about a foot of height, but none of its menace. "Did you summon me to remind me of my past debt?"

No, we summoned you to pay it.

"Then I shall listen to thy pleas," the demon said. "And decide if such petty desires are worth my attention." It straightened up, an aura of power surrounding its twisted body. It intoned, "And woe to those who displease me, I who have devoured thousands of souls!"

"You're intoning again," Lex said.

"Fine. I intoned a *little*." The demon looked affronted. "Fuck me for trying to display some gravitas."

"Ihithiltalas," Dominic said, pulling its attention to him. "We have questions."

Ihithiltalas looked more alert. "A bargain, then?"

"My bargain is that you answer all our questions tonight honestly and to your fullest knowledge, and in turn, you will no longer owe the Salem family a debt."

"With nary a soul attached? Not a great bargain."

"We can skip directly to destruction," Mal said, holding up the dagger.

"I did not say I would not accept thy bargain! Just don't mention this to anyone else," Ihithiltalas said. "The sooner I can put the shame of a debt to mortals behind me, the better. There is little glory for the weak."

"Do you accept the terms?" Dom pressed.

"Though it pains me, yes. I shall answer thy questions."

"Tell us about someone who goes by the name of Lord Netjerunakht."

"Ah. That one."

"Then you know who I'm talking about."

"The Prince of Riimara, Realm of Gold and Glory. His is a famous name."

"Famous why? What's his interest?"

"Much interest, of all kinds. For Netjerunakht is a banker, a giver and taker of gold, of magic, of jewels, of ivory, of flesh…anything and everything that can be traded."

"So a gate to make Señor Netjeruwhosit proud would be…" Lex's eyes widened as he realized the answer even as he asked the question. "A toll booth!"

"Thou art clever, young mortal," the demon acknowledged with a bow to Lex. "Yes. Such a pathway would be a true monument to the greed of the Prince of Riimara. Every exchange of coin, every promise of payment would glorify him. And strengthen him."

"What was in it for Daniel Egan? Why would he have been interested in this particular demon?"

Ihithiltalas sighed. "Must I remind you that many who come to us have little notion of who they summon, knowing only that we have more power than they and are willing to bargain for the paltry price of a soul. We are asked over and over for the most banal of gifts. A million dollars. A hundred years. A beautiful face. Nothing that begins to test our powers. Depressing, really."

"Do demons get depressed?" Lex asked.

"We have eons to think on the failures of creation. Of course we get depressed."

"Uh, back to the main topic," Dom muttered. "Does this Prince of Riimara have a lot of dealings with vampires?"

The demon shook his head. "Now that is a question I truly cannot answer. My guess is that he would have dealings with any creatures willing to trade. That would include vampires. Particularly old vampires, ones who had centuries or more to amass wealth and power and acquire ever more…exotic desires."

Then Dom said, "Netjerunakht has a true name, and you know it. Tell me."

"Not that," the demon protested. "Such a breach of etiquette, to reveal the true name of another of my kind! Ask something else!"

"Cut the crap," Mal told it, holding the dagger up. "You guys love screwing each other over even more than you love screwing mortals over."

Ihithiltalas's face cracked into an unpleasant smile, just for an instant. "Ah, but it's not good *etiquette*."

"Tell us the true name we seek," Dom said. "And if the one called Netjerunakht happens to be destroyed someday, well, that leaves a throne in Riimara that needs filling, doesn't it?"

"A most interesting family, the Salem clan," Ihithiltalas said. "Very well. I shall tell you."

"Write it down as well," Lex said quickly, holding out his ever-present notebook and pen.

"I shall, young sir." The demon ignored the pen, and instead used one long nail now dripping with something like blood to inscribe the true name of his rival onto the paper. "His true name is pronounced as thus: Netjerunakhnalasatloth. Use this knowledge as you will, and may the fate of it fall only upon you. Now release me."

Dom raised his hands. "Ihithiltalas, your debt is paid. We release you to return to your home in peace."

The demon sighed in relief, then the gash it entered from appeared once more. "I leave you now, mortals. But one last thing I will tell you—out of our deep and caring bond. You sought me out to learn the true name of one who threatens you. I happen to know that others are seeking true names as well—names that contain Salem within them. Be wary, fool mortals. You are in deeper than you think."

Grinning like a maniac, Ihithiltalas slipped through the gash into his own hellish dimension before anyone could react.

And then the gash was gone, as if it had never been there. The candle flames reverted to their usual yellow, and the night was quiet.

XXIV

CARA WOKE UP NEXT TO Mal, and despite a deeply weird and upsetting night before, she found she was still turned on by a ragingly hot guy. At least there was that.

She managed to keep his volume down—that was the only thing he kept down—and eventually they were both sweaty and sated without waking up the whole house.

Afterward, he grinned and rolled to a sitting position. "I need coffee in a serious way. You want breakfast in bed?"

Cara shook her head. "I'll be down in a little bit. Just got to clean up."

He leaned over. "Is that another invitation to the shower?"

"Not when *siblings* are listening. Ew!"

"I can be quiet. I just proved that."

"Get some coffee going, Mal Salem. I'm speaking as your boss."

Cara hurried through her morning routine, hoping to avoid a bathrobe-only hallway meeting like before. When she was dressed, she went downstairs. Mal was the only person in the kitchen, but he was cooking a meal for what looked like twelve.

"Are we expecting guests?"

"Don't think so," he responded, cracking yet another egg into a bowl.

Just then, the doorbell rang.

"Or maybe we are? Uh, can you get that?" he asked.

Cara opened the front door and was met by a stack of books on two slender legs.

"Little help, please!" the books said.

Cara pulled the top few books off the stack, revealing the face of an Asian woman about her age.

"Morning! You must be Cara! I'm Lily," she said far too cheerfully at this hour of the day. "I brought research materials."

"Oh, yay," Mal said from the kitchen.

Cara pulled most of the remainder of the stack from her and placed them on the table. Lily followed her, dropping the rest.

"There's more in the car. From what Lex told me last night, it seemed like you guys needed more on-site help, so I popped into the archives and grabbed everything that seemed relevant."

Mal regarded the ancient tomes. "Are you sure you're allowed to take these out of the archive?"

"I got special dispensation from Sam. But I have to return them all undamaged, or I'll be killed."

"That's a joke, right?" Cara asked nervously.

"We'll take good care of the books," Mal interjected, leading Cara to think it was not a joke.

"Damn right you will. Hey, is coffee ready?" Lily walked over to the coffee maker, grabbing mugs on the way. She was certainly at home here.

"I'm assuming you want some of this, Cara?" Lily held up a mug.

"You bet."

"Excellent. We're going to need a lot of caffeine to get through all the books."

"I'm, uh, not exactly part of this superhero team," Cara warned her.

"That's what Vinny said, and now she's going through Buffy Boot Camp." Lily handed her a mug of steaming coffee. "Sugar? Cream?"

"Unnecessary."

Lily smiled in approval, becoming even cuter. Cara was hyperaware of the other girl's figure. She was just as slender as Vinny, but shorter, which made her seem delicate. The fact that she was wearing a pink skirt and kitty-cat print tights made her even more adorable. *Lily is what women should look like*, a voice whispered inside Cara's head, a voice that sounded a lot like her mother.

Cara stepped around to the other side of the kitchen island, using it to hide her body from the others.

"Heard you got possessed last night. Lex tells me everything," she added.

"Lily is one month younger than Lex, and she's basically our extra sister," Mal explained as he turned to the stove.

Cara nodded. "Ah. Yeah, I got possessed last night. First time."

"It's really startling, isn't it? I've been possessed a bunch of times, but it's always a bit weird."

"Being possessed by the spirits of your own ancestors is different," Mal argued. "No one knew Marigold was going to hop into Cara. It's not like she asked permission."

"Oh, now you're on the #MeToo bandwagon? Well, whatever works to get you on board." Lily stuck her tongue out at Mal. Then she said to Cara, "You know about Mal, right?"

"Uh, yeah."

"Ohhhhh." Lily's eyes widened as she figured things out. "Lex didn't tell me *that*."

"That's because I don't care about Mal's love life." Lex bounded into the kitchen, wearing flannel pajama pants and a T-shirt. "Morning, Li! You drove fast." He squeezed Lily in an exuberant hug. "What, no one poured coffee for me?"

"Get it yourself," Lily said post-hug. "And pour a lot. I brought books."

"Oh, yay!" Unlike Mal's *yay*, Lex's held no trace of sarcasm.

Dom wandered in, fully dressed but bleary-eyed. "Coffee?" he asked no one in particular.

Lex handed him the mug he'd just poured and proceeded to start brewing another pot.

"Breakfast ready soon," Mal announced. "Pancakes, beans, eggs, and bacon."

"Vinny's not back?" Dom asked. "She went out on errands."

"Do you want us to wait?"

"No way. Let's set the table."

Cara watched the kitchen chaos somehow result in a set table piled with a ton of food in practically no time. She was directed to a seat next to Mal. Lex and Lily sat opposite each other, next to the towering piles of books. Dom sat across from Mal and grabbed a pancake off the stack before he even sat down.

"Dude!" Lex chided him. "Now you have to say grace."

"Crap." Dom put the pancake down. "Ok. May this meal feed us and bless us, and give us the strength to fight evil and stand for those who cannot fight for themselves. Those we love who cannot be at this table in the flesh, may your spirits always be welcome. Amen. Now eat."

Cara took eggs and beans, holding off on the pancakes. She was surprised by the formality of a breakfast grace, but then again, these were people for whom *ritual* had a specific and tangible meaning.

Lily spread jam on her pancake and rolled it up tight before eating it. Mal shook his head at her. "Weirdo."

Cara asked, "Excuse me, Lily. But you could just grab a bunch of arcane books in the middle of the night and drive to Ohio and it's fine?"

"I'm a grad student," Lily said with a shrug. "Pretty flexible schedule. Speaking of, catch me up on what the demon said."

"Wait, *what*?" Cara asked.

Mal said, "Oh, we summoned a demon last night. Strictly for informational purposes. It's fine."

"Wow." What else had she slept through? "This isn't one of those pop into another dimension things, is it? Mal said he hates going into the otherworlds."

Lex looked pained. "You know the story of how NASA invented the ballpoint pen? They needed a way for astronauts to write in space and fountain pens don't work in zero gravity. They spent millions of dollars testing inks and barrels and delivery systems and voila, they invented the ballpoint pen."

"While the Russians used a pencil," Cara finished. Her dad told her that story when she was little.

"Exactly. Mal is like the NASA of otherworlds-walking." Lex pointed almost accusingly at his older brother. "He was so fixated on avoiding this one particular situation that he basically perfected a bananas workaround where he doesn't just send his consciousness into the otherworlds, he sends his whole being. Which is way harder, and about seven hundred times more dangerous, and any other rational person would have just sucked it up and learned to do it the way it's always been done. But Mal invents a brand-new thing, and then uses it to just sort of pop into an otherworld for two seconds and pop out again to *win fights*. Which is the most Mal thing ever."

"Look, it's just what works for me," Mal defended himself. "And anyway, that's not what happened. We summoned the demon to this world. And only because it was important."

The brothers told Lily and Cara what their demon said, and Lily evidently got more out of the info than Cara, who was starting to feel very lost at sea. Then she felt a foot nudge hers, and saw Mal smiling at her over his coffee.

Don't worry, he mouthed.

"But why are vampires getting involved?" Lily asked toward the end of the debriefing. "What's in it for them?"

"They're long-term thinkers," Lex said. "They'd love the idea of a gift that keeps on giving. They must have learned about the hellhole, and the fact that there's a big ol' house on top of it. They see a multidimensional investment opportunity, and bam: Morningside's Friendly Portal to the Mortal Realms."

"The vampire's monetizing a demon gateway?" Lily asked. "That's some late stage capitalism."

"But he can't monetize it until it can be activated again," Mal jumped in. "So he hires Cara to remake the floor, and the rest of the restoration work on the house me and the other guys are doing is actually just cover for that. But he didn't count on Marigold still hanging around with all her memories of the original night the gate was almost opened. She even remembered the name of the demon who was supposed to run it. And no one counted on Salems being on watch either."

At that moment, Vinny walked in through the door to the garage. She held a canvas bag in one hand and a big flat box in the other.

"Ooh, donuts!" Lex said, jumping up to grab it from her and put it on the table.

Lily's eyes lit up. "Are those from Mora's Bakery?"

"Of course," Vinny said, pouring herself coffee.

"Yay! They're the best." Lily plucked a donut covered in pink sprinkles from the box and took a bite, a blissful expression coming over her face.

"Cara, pick one. You can't go wrong." Mal pulled the box toward her.

Cara confronted the box of colorful, delicious-looking donuts. It might as well have been a box of cocaine. "No thanks, I'm good."

"But they're fresh. You should eat one."

"Malachy Salem," Vinny said, "Never tell a girl to eat."

"Or not eat," added Lily.

"In fact, generally just don't tell girls to do things."

"Or not do things," added Lily.

Mal scooted his chair back, looking a little hunted. "Ok, ok."

"Thanks, though," Cara told him. She shot a glance to Vinny, and then to Lily and felt the connection between them, all women, all living in this world. *We're all in the same boat*, the glance said. And Cara took a slightly deeper breath, relaxing.

Meanwhile, Mal took three donuts. She rolled her eyes at the unfairness of the world.

Vinny shoved a donut into her mouth and pointed to the books. "Whashh all thisshh?"

"Chew first," Lex told her. "These are all books on the topics of the portals, hellholes, the specific demon dude Marigold mentioned, and old spells that sort of match what we think Egan did."

Mal leaned forward. "And that's it? That's all we need?"

"Hopefully," Dom said. "We were at a dead end until Marigold told us the name of the demon that was involved. And after last night, we know the demon's true name, so we can shut him down for good."

"Assuming Morningside doesn't open the gate up for business first," Mal said.

"If there's a gateway Morningside is trying to open, that means there's a way it can be closed. Find it."

Lex and Lily exchanged glances. "Yes, your honor," Lily muttered.

Cara wanted to help, but knew that she was way out of her depth. Mal pulled her aside and said that the nerds would ask for assistance if they needed it. "Meanwhile, let's get some fresh air, ok?"

Mal took Cara on a long walk, heading out the back door of the Salem house and crossing neighboring woods and farm fields, onto a narrow country highway, the kind no one ever bothered to paint lines onto. The late October day was cloudless and warm in the sun.

They walked in silence for a while, and Cara was surprised by how non-awkward it was.

They passed a white clapboard farmhouse that had jack o' lanterns sitting in a line on the porch.

"We gotta get our pumpkins this year," Mal said then. "We've been distracted, and there's only a few days left."

"Halloween is a big thing? What does it mean for demon-hunters?"

"It's more that we're into Día de Muertos," he said. "Because of our mom. She did it up big. I was pretty young, but I remember that. It was a huge party every year. And she decorated, and dressed up, and there was food. It was great." He smiled, kicking a few pebbles on the side of the road.

"You must still miss her, and your dad."

"It's not something you get over."

"I keep thinking about Marigold," Cara said. "I can't describe how awful it felt, feeling her emotions. She's had a really rough afterlife."

"Maybe we can fix that," Mal said after a moment. Then he asked abruptly, "Did you really not want a donut?"

"Of course I *wanted* a donut. But I shouldn't have donuts."

"But a donut would make you happy."

"If you want to make me happy, stop talking about food."

"Ok. You're gorgeous, by the way."

Cara bit her lip. "You are."

"I know. But we were talking about you." Mal grinned at her, taking her hand. "Should we head back?"

"Yeah," Cara said. "You know you're full of yourself, right?"

"It's called confidence. I'm told chicks dig that."

"As long as it doesn't spill over into dickishness."

"I'll keep that in mind," he said. "You'll have to tell me when I veer into dickish territory."

"Count on it." But privately, Cara's head was whirling. Mal talked like she'd be around to tell him, like they were going to be together. Like maybe they were a *thing*.

When they got back to the house, the two nerds, as Mal called them, had taken over the living room, scattering papers and books around, most of them held open with other books, kitty-themed sticky notes, or in one case, a sleeping Piewicket.

In addition to the books, they each had multiple screens active for consulting the most recent records, and to confer with other practitioners. Lex paced the kitchen during a phone conversation in Spanish and Latin with a guy he addressed as *Padre*.

Mal explained in a whisper, "He's a priest who also happens to be a third cousin once removed on our mom's side. Padre Leandro works in the Vatican's, er, less public archives, and he knows demonology."

Vinny was acting as secretary, writing down any notes Lex or Lily recited to her.

"This is going to be a while," Vinny warned them. "But if you want to be useful, Dom said we need pumpkins."

Hours later, Cara and Mal returned from a day of errands—pumpkins acquired. Mal had spent a good half hour deciding which thirteen to get, and the pumpkin patch vendor was delighted to take his money.

Cara helped him unload the haul onto the porch. "You're going to carve all these by Halloween? Are jack o' lanterns really a priority now?"

"On Halloween, you bet. They help lead lost souls to a warm place and scare away more troublesome spirits. Ours especially scare away bad things, since we add wards into the carving and the candles."

"Does that mean I can't carve one of the pumpkins to be a cat like actual Pumpkin?"

He grinned, putting the last and largest pumpkin onto the wooden porch. "You can definitely do that."

They walked into the house to find an excited-looking Lily.

"We think we know what's up," she announced.

The family and Cara gathered at the table once more, all three cats in attendance as well, though Pumpkin was just there for the string toys.

"How can we close the gate?" Dom asked.

Lex sighed. "You're not going to like it."

"I haven't liked anything about that house."

"There's one ritual that should work," Lex continued, "but there are a bunch of things that need to be in place. First, the summoning circle needs to be whole and complete, without flaw, and consecrated."

"We can do that." Dom then glanced toward her. "I mean, if we can convince Cara to work on it."

She nodded. "I want to finish it. I know maybe I shouldn't, but I do. And I'm close."

"Ok. Once the floor is ready…" Dom said, looking to his little brother again.

Lex went on, "We need a bunch of herbs and supplies, nothing we can't get our hands on. The ritual ought to be done on a night of power."

Dom nodded. "Halloween. Easy."

"And the last thing, which is not easy."

Lily exchanged a glance with Lex. She said, "A successful closing ritual requires the sacrifice of a willing participant. Someone who chooses to enter the gate and seal it shut at the moment they're on the threshold between here and hell."

Cara felt the pressure in the room drop.

Vinny leaned in. "Guessing they don't come back," she said.

Lily shook her head slowly. "No. And they don't get to go forward either. They're just there, forever. It's the ultimate sacrifice."

"So they die."

"No," Lex said. "According to Padre Leandro, the ritual basically draws their soul out and makes it into a seal that will render the gate inoperable, but the person isn't dead. Or alive. They're…in between."

"That sucks." Mal's forehead was wrinkled up in consternation.

"Yeah. He says it's why the church won't condone it. It's tantamount to suicide. The details of the ritual are kept in the archives only for historical purposes."

Dom looked over all the notes. "How are we getting around this?"

"The whole Catholic Church couldn't solve it for a couple millennia, but I'm sure we'll figure it out." Lex sighed.

"I wonder if that's why the opening ritual got messed up," Vinny mused. "Marigold said she ran away—maybe because she became an *un*willing participant, that's really what fouled the whole spell. And she's stuck near the blocked up gate because she changed her mind halfway through the casting. She's half in this world and half in the other, and she's a ghost, but also sort of a key jammed in a lock that's all rusted."

Dom looked at her. "Damn. Why are you so smart?"

"It's just a theory."

"A good one," Lily said. "Opposing rituals tend to mirror each other! It totally makes sense that the opening ritual would require a similar sacrifice."

"How confident are you about this?" Mal asked.

"Look, there aren't a lot of peer-reviewed journals in the secret occult libraries of the world. We do our homework, try to make sense of it all, and hope we're not too far off."

That sounded dubious. Cara looked over at Mal, hoping a sight of his natural confidence would bolster her own flagging spirit. But he just sat there, frowning at all the books and papers. And for some reason, Cara felt a shiver in her spine.

XXV

Mal did not like the phrase "willing sacrifice." He did not like the way Lex and Lily glanced at each other when talking about it, or the way Dom got that distant look on his face, the look he used to have before Vinny entered his life, when he seemed to exist solely to destroy evil and didn't especially care if he came out unscathed.

His do-gooder little brother and his equally do-gooder best friend would be at each other's throats in order to win the right to sacrifice. Dom would think it was his duty to jump into a hellhole, and Vinny would probably do it herself just to keep Dom safe.

But it was Mal who'd had a vision. A vision that made it very clear that *his* choice would determine whether things ended up aces, or in flames. He'd only seen Cara in the vision, but what if she represented all that he loved? He'd seen her in a house like his, with happy kids, and a dog. That was the good outcome, the outcome everyone deserved.

And on the other hand, he saw a world of ash, a world that destroyed everything: people, homes, the little things that made life worth living. He'd seen Cara's body, but who knew how many others were reduced to ash in that future? How many lives would be lost?

Or, maybe just one could be given up. Mal's.

Really, he was the ideal candidate for a sacrifice. He didn't have the gifts of the people around him. He was good for one thing: fighting. And wasn't this sort of the ultimate fight?

He could go big or go home. Except that if he didn't go big, there wouldn't be a home to go back to.

He looked up to see Cara standing right in front of him. Everyone else had cleared off, intent on other tasks. He'd just been staring into space, lost.

"Mal?" she asked worriedly.

He couldn't let on what he was thinking about, not yet. And not to Cara.

"Upstairs," he told her, his voice gruff with sudden, undeniable need.

Cara raised an eyebrow. "You serious?"

"Find out." He stood up and hooked his hand in hers, leading her up the stairs without another word.

In his bedroom, he didn't bother to hit the switch, despite the swiftly setting sun. By now, he didn't need any visual aid to know where to touch Cara.

Clothes came off fast. He didn't say anything, and Cara kept silent too, probably partly because she had a shyness about getting it on when others could hear, and probably also wondering what sparked Mal's latest lust.

It was the idea that this might be the last time he'd have her. The last time he might be with her like this, or at all.

You will be the death of her.

He swallowed painfully, his throat dry. Ok, one last time. Then he'd do the right thing, and say whatever he needed to say to get her out of the danger zone. Which was apparently anywhere near him.

Mal had no plan, other than hopefully screwing his brains out so he'd stop thinking of the short, shitty road ahead. A second of perfect bliss with Cara, pretending everything was going to be all right.

He inhaled sharply when he felt Cara touching him. Touching him just right, all in, just like Cara when she got interested in something. Her hands all over him, perfect, possessive little hands.

Then she knelt in front of him, and a second later her mouth was the only thing in the world. Mal put his hand to her head, threading her glorious hair through his fingers. He'd be lucky if he was still standing at the end of this.

Cara knew exactly what to do to bring Mal so close to coming that he begged her to slow down. She did, and that was even better.

He meant to tell her that was enough, that he wanted to move to the bed, finish this properly. But before he could get the words out, he went completely over the edge. He came hard, and Cara took it, and then he was somehow lying in the bed without remembering how he got there.

"Cara…" he said. Where was she? Didn't she know this was important? That time was running out?

"Just getting a drink of water," she replied, back again. She climbed into the bed, but didn't lie down next to him. She straddled him, giving him a view of her that he'd once pictured, her red hair falling past her shoulders to graze the pink nipples of her incredible, perfect breasts. Her smile, knowing and a little bit shy, even now. Her curves, basically begging him to paw at her, which he did, because even if it was the last time, he wasn't going to miss an opportunity.

Cara laughed softly, then caught his hands and drew them to her breasts. They both moaned, Cara in pleasure, and Mal in half-agony, wanting her and already missing her.

The wanting part of him grew stronger, and it seemed like no time until he was getting hard again. How could he not be, having the most sensuous, redheaded goddess right on top of him?

He put a hand out for the condom, but Cara grabbed it first. She ripped the foil open with her teeth. Yes, please.

And she put it on with her mouth. Yes, *please.*

He had to smother his mouth in the pillow when she guided his cock right into her body. No resistance, no adjustment. Just *yes.*

Was he saying yes? Yes, he was, over and over, half-muffled in the pillow.

"I like being on top," Cara murmured, pulling the pillow away.

"I like it too," he gasped. Cara could do anything to him right now, and he'd like it.

But all she did was ride him, slowly, leisurely, to her own climax. Mal watched her, and ached to think this was the last time. It couldn't be. It wasn't fair to find this woman just before he had to lose her.

Cara moaned a little when she came. He could feel her body tighten and flex around him. Then she leaned forward, letting her hair fall across him. "Your turn," she told him softly.

He took her by the hips and started rocking against her. She opened her mouth in a soundless shock, and then smiled.

"More," she ordered.

Easy. He could do more.

"Don't stop," she said.

He didn't stop. And a moment later, Cara stretched upward, showing off those breasts as she reveled in another climax.

Mal couldn't hold off after that. He finished fast, giving in to the desperation underlying his need.

Afterward, they lay together on the bed, limb stretched over limb. Happy.

For the last time.

Mal was great at breaking things off with women, but only because he'd never wanted to keep them going. And now, all he wanted was to keep this going with Cara. To be the constant man in her life. Not the hookup.

But that wasn't his future, and he had the vision to prove it.

Cara turned her head to kiss him, her lips grazing his cheek. That felt way too good. Too domestic. Too caring.

He had to end this before he got in even deeper.

"How long do you think it will take you to finish the floor?" he asked.

Cara blinked in confusion at the topic, but yawned and said, in a languid, way too sexy voice, "Hmm, not long. If I ever get out of bed. Why?"

"Just thinking about timing. If you finished on the thirtieth, you could be on the road the morning of Halloween. You don't want to be anywhere near here when all this goes down."

She propped her head on her bent arm, frowning at him. "You think I'm just going to zip out right before the main event? What if you need me?"

"What would we need you for?"

Hurt flashed in her eyes, just a brief flash, but he hated it, and he hated himself for causing it.

But then it was gone, and he could see Cara smoothing it over in her own mind, telling herself she'd misunderstood. "Someone ought be on fire extinguisher duty," she said with a little laugh. "The way you guys go through candles! And hey, maybe Marigold might need to hop into me again."

"No. Way." Mal didn't even need to hide the heat in his voice that time. He definitely didn't want a repeat of that.

"Mal, what's up? Why don't you want me there on Halloween?"

"I don't want you here at all."

She froze, unable to recode that into something innocuous. "What?" she asked in a small voice.

"Look, you need to do the floor, and you should do it as fast as possible. And then you should get out. Get on with your life. The faster you're gone from here, the better."

"The better for who?"

"Everyone. You for sure. You don't have any ties here. Your next job could be anywhere."

"I don't have any ties here," she echoed, as if not sure she'd heard him right. "Is that what you're telling me?"

This sucked. Mal wanted to punch himself, but he clenched his jaw and plowed on. "You don't need me to tell you that. You know it. You're your own person. So wind this up and be your own person anywhere you want."

She took a breath, fighting some heavy emotion, then said, "You're veering into dickish territory. Which you told me earlier *today* to keep tabs on."

"I'm just being honest." *Bulllllllshit.* "You can have a life. You should go find it."

Her eyes darkened, and there was a storm brewing there. One that would strike him, and he'd deserve it. She said, "Find what, exactly? You think all women secretly want to get a man and a baby and a picket fence?"

"You don't seem like you'd be satisfied with a picket fence. You'd make a fancy custom fence." *Don't lighten this up. You're hurting her. You're* trying *to hurt her.*

"I would, if I ever wanted one," said Cara. "Which I don't."

"A steady relationship isn't even a little bit interesting?"

"Mal, I don't have a steady life. Neither do you, by the way. You fight demons for a living. How is that stable?"

"All the more reason for you to find someone who's going to take care of you."

"You sound like my mother." Cara sat up and pushed herself off the bed. "I think I should go."

He didn't stop her. He wanted to. He wanted to grab her and pull her back and tell her that the last thing in the world he wanted was for her to go.

You will be the death of her.

Mal closed his eyes. If he tried to keep her, he'd lose her anyway. The vision had been pretty damn clear that his inaction would result in Cara dying in the worst possible way.

Lex once told him to think of someone other than himself for a change. Well, now he was, and he knew why he'd avoided it before. It sucked.

But someone was going to have to sacrifice, and it looked like it was Mal's turn.

* * * *

She got out the house as fast as she could. Three sets of feline eyes tracked her movement, but Cara was too angry to notice. The air had an autumnal bite to it, the sunset just bleeding into its final phase of red and purple.

It was gorgeous, and she didn't even see it.

Cara couldn't believe the crap Mal just laid on her. All that crap about her finding a nice guy and settling down… when had Cara ever put out that vibe? She didn't want a nice guy. She wanted Mal, who she'd actually thought was a nice guy under all his swagger. Until twenty minutes ago.

Turned out, he was as shallow as she initially thought that very first day she met him. And this BS about being concerned for her future. He was just trying to cover up the fact that he'd finally realized that if Cara hung around, he'd eventually be seen with her. And that was extra baggage no guy wanted, no matter how "nice" he was.

I'm an idiot, she thought. *A totally gullible idiot.*

She'd gone along for the ride the Salems offered, accepting the unbelievable stories and the mad logic of their demon-hunting, and why? Because she saw a ghost? Well, one thing could be real without all their demonology being true too. Or maybe it was all because Mal turned her completely around until she didn't know which way was up and couldn't make a decision for herself anymore.

Well, that idiocy was ending right now. Cara was perfectly capable of deciding her fate. And her fate had to be somewhere other than October County, Ohio, with its haunted houses, shifty neighbors, and hot-but-regrettable hookups.

Her feet led her up the hill to Egan House, where she could be alone for half a moment to think things over.

If she didn't finish the floor, then nothing could happen with this magical gate. Right? Nothing good, nothing bad. Cara felt a sting of fear as she contemplated the fallout from upsetting a client. But then again, *she* was the one with skills. She could get other jobs anywhere in the country. Maybe not the jobs she truly wanted, but enough to pay the bills. She had a portfolio, she had a background. Morningside could make a fuss about his contract, but Cara had it up to here with the weirdness surrounding this job.

She stood on the porch, trying to decide whether to go inside or just call for a ride and get out of this town. Impulsively, she took out her phone and called her mom, who answered on the second ring.

"Sweetie? Is something the matter?"

"No, of course not," Cara lied. "I was just thinking I need a little vacation."

"Why not fly home for a week?" her mom suggested instantly. "You can relax and we can do a little shopping and maybe a girls' day out?" The yearning in her tone made Cara realize just how much her mother was suffering too. When her husband went to prison, her whole life had fallen apart. Cara had been able to run away, but her mom didn't have the same options.

"That'd be nice, actually," Cara said. She'd prefer to be anywhere but here. "I'm going to look at flights and then I'll call you back, ok?"

"Sounds perfect, sweetheart. Love you!"

Cara slid the phone back in her pocket. There. See, she'd made a decision. Maybe not a great one, but one that would get her out of the current awkward mess and give her time to decide what to do next.

But first, there were a few things that Cara couldn't leave behind. Her set of tools that her dad had given her, for one. They might be old-school, not the most technologically advanced items in her shop. But they were hers, and she wasn't going to risk them going missing.

She hit the lights on and made her way to the parlor. The equipment was all laid out in the corner of the room, awaiting her. She picked up the chisel first, feeling the familiar weight of it in the palm of her hand. She looked for the duffel bag, thinking she'd pack up the most important items here, grab Pumpkin, and get a ride into town to pick up her own car. Maybe she'd even stay a night at the Calendar Inn before driving to the airport. She needed to look at flights...

"Miss Michaels." Smooth as it was, the voice startled her.

"Wow," she yelped, turning to see Morningside standing there in the doorway. "You scared me!"

"Apologies."

"What are you doing here?" She still held the chisel, and suddenly didn't want to release it.

"I was hoping to get the latest details on your restoration. My client is arriving in town in a few days, and he's most eager to see the results. Looks like you're almost there," he added with a not-quite-sincere smile.

"Yeah, it's close," she said. "But it's funny that you're here, because I was actually going to call you to let you know I need to leave for a while."

The smile evaporated. "Excuse me?"

"Family emergency. Need to be with my mom."

"Surely you can complete the floor first."

"Uh, that's not how emergencies work."

Morningside's expression went frosty. "The contract was quite clear…"

"Shut up about your stupid contract! I need a few days, ok? Is the world going to end if I don't do this by Halloween?"

He held utterly still, and Cara wondered if she'd inadvertently said something revealing by dropping the word *Halloween.*

"Cara Ann Michaels," he said quietly, pointing at her with one long finger. "You will do what I say, and you will never speak back to me or disobey."

She opened her mouth, but didn't reply, because she wasn't an indentured servant, or a robot.

He smiled again, and this time it was nasty. "Now, get to work. The summoning circle must be ready."

"No way."

Morningside's eyes widened at her refusal. "What did you say?"

"I said no. It's the opposite of yes." Did everyone around here need this lesson?

Before she could do anything else, Morningside growled. An actual *growl.*

She blinked and saw that his face was changing. The polished lawyer look faded, and in its place was something more brutal, more feral…more fanged. The air suddenly smelled like smoke.

Not good.

Pure, gut-chilling terror rolled over her body. Cara reached for the chain around her neck. *Please let magic be as real as vampires and ghosts.*

He moved toward her, and even though he got within range for her to smell his breath, she couldn't quite see well any longer. Maybe she was starting to faint.

"You know, my dear, that after I bite you, you'll want to do everything I say. You'll be happy to work through the night, without sleeping, without eating, without any thought at all but pleasing me. And if you're very good and finish what you started, I'll give you a taste of pleasure before the end."

"Ew." *Double ew.*

Morningside grabbed at the chain, but pulled back, repelled by the crucifix. "A worthy spell," he muttered. "Well, there are other ways to control you. I'll keep you in your own little hell until you see reason."

He shoved her down, right into the middle of the unfinished summoning circle. The air was distinctly hazy now, and Cara shook her head to clear her vision before she began to clamber to her feet.

But then Morningside stepped backward and raised both arms. He spoke in a language Cara never heard before and hoped to never hear again. A spitting, slimy set of words all winding around her like snakes.

She caught a few familiar sounds in the tangle: Cara Ann Michaels. Then she felt a slight buzzing in her bones, like someone was holding her tightly, too tightly.

I am sorry, the words floated into her head. *But this is the only way.*

And then Cara was swept into a world of fire.

XXVI

MAL KNEW CARA WAS PISSED. She very likely wasn't going to speak to him ever again. Not after the shit he'd said. But hopefully she'd be pissed enough to leave as soon as the floor was done. And then she'd at least be safe.

Not surprisingly, she didn't return to the Salem house after she took off post-fight. Lex and Dom both asked where she'd gone, and Mal shrugged a response.

"Wow, you truly suck at any relationship longer than a week," Dom said in wonderment. "So Cara was the same as all the others?"

"No. But it doesn't matter anyway." If everything went according to plan, in a couple of days Mal wouldn't be alive enough to care about his past mistakes.

He almost texted Cara about twenty times. But he never knew what to say, so he just deleted each message and sent nothing.

She didn't send anything either. Not a shocker.

The next morning, when he got dressed for work, he mentally prepped himself to get the icy death glare. He'd endure that. He'd really hurt her feelings. Just because it was for a good cause didn't make it not mean.

But he didn't get the death glare, because Cara wasn't on site.

Dan stood on the porch, looking confused. "Did you hear from Cara?" he asked as soon as Mal reached him. "She's always first. And I don't have keys to the house."

"Is there a spare set in the office?" Mal asked.

"Yeah, but the office door is locked too. Natch."

Maybe because Cara was sleeping in there. Mal peered in the windows of the trailer. It was totally empty. He rattled the doorknob. Locked.

He glanced behind him. Dan had wandered back over to his car, not paying attention. Mal took a breath and sidestepped into the otherworlds, just a few feet, and back into the real world, inside the office. He unlocked the door from the inside, and then looked for the spare set of keys.

He found a keyring in the desk drawer. Straightening up, he noticed Cara's sleeping bag, tightly rolled, shoved into a corner. He'd seen her put it there the night he insisted she stay at the Salem house. It didn't look like it had been used since then.

She must have gone back to her room at the Calendar Inn, he reasoned. And she slept in a bit today. That was a perfectly rational explanation.

He returned to the house and unlocked the door.

"How'd you get into the office?" Dan asked, surprised. "It was locked!"

"I managed." He handed the keys to Dan. "You're in charge, man. At least till the boss shows up."

"Five minutes," Dan guessed. "She's never late."

But she was. Even after all the rest of the crew showed, Cara was still missing. Looking uneasy, Dan assigned everyone to tasks, and they went to work like it was an ordinary day.

The mood was off for everyone. Mal saw Dan fiddling with his phone more than once, and he guessed that Cara wasn't responding to Dan's texts, which was more concerning than her just ignoring Mal.

Hoping to get some sort of idea about Cara's plans, Mal entered the parlor room, checking out the floor. It looked a little more done, though he couldn't remember precisely how far along it was last week. Cara must have come after their fight to work on it.

But there was no sign of her now.

He spotted a duffel bag near Cara's craft table. Had she already started packing to leave? He opened the bag and saw the old-school tools she used for her detail work, the ones she'd said once belonged to her dad. They were thrust haphazardly into the bag, as if she'd been in a hurry. But then why were they still here? And where did Cara get to?

He called Thalia at the Calendar Inn.

"Hey there, Mal," Thalia chirped. "What's up?"

"Thalia, I need to talk with Cara Michaels. Can you call her room and ask her?"

The other end went silent for a moment. "I, uh, can't do that."

"Look, I know that you can. She's not answering my calls, and it's actually really important. It's about her job site, ok?"

"No, I mean I can't do that because she's not here. I haven't seen her since the night you came by."

"You mean she just packed up and left?"

"Well, no," Thalia said, sounding more distressed now. "Her car is still parked out front, and she didn't check out. But she's not here. I knocked this morning because I wanted to be sure she was all right, and there was no answer. I finally used the master key to open the door—like what if she was sick or something? But the room was empty, except that her stuff is all still there."

"That's not good," said Mal.

"I thought she was staying with you," Thalia said almost accusingly.

"She was, but she's not now. Give me a call if she shows up, ok?"

"That's not exactly kosher, Mal. Like what if you're a stalker?"

"If I were a stalker, I'd freaking know where she was, wouldn't I?" he snapped. "Instead, I'm calling around every place in town to find her, and it's not looking good."

"Ok, ok, I'll text you if I see her."

"Thanks."

"I hope everything's ok," Thalia said quietly.

"Me too." But he wasn't optimistic.

He found Dan not long after. "No word from Cara?" he asked, no longer bothering to pretend like he didn't have a personal interest in this.

"Nothing," Dan said with a frown. "I even called Morningside—found his number in the office. He was busy, but the secretary said everything's still on schedule."

"How can we be on schedule if Cara's not here? She's the only person who can finish up the floor, and all the detail work."

"Well, maybe it's just a blip," Dan said. "She could be back tomorrow and we're all worrying for nothing."

When he got home that afternoon, Pumpkin mewed at him. Mal picked the kitten up. "Did Cara leave you behind?"

The kitten didn't answer, but Behemoth did.

I find it difficult to believe she would abandon the little one.

Mal did too. "But then where is she?"

He told his brothers the news. "No one has seen Cara since she left here. None of the work crew got any message, not even Dan, who's basically second in charge. She never went back to the inn, and her car is still there, so she didn't leave town either. Her cat is still here, her tools are still here, but she's not."

Mal took a breath before saying what was now completely obvious: "She's not anywhere."

* * * *

Cara was definitely somewhere, she just wasn't sure exactly what was going on. She must have fallen asleep, because she woke up from a horrible nightmare of a massive wall of flames and smoke engulfing her. She found herself lying on the floor of the parlor room where she'd been when Morningside surprised her.

She shivered, thinking of her dream again. She'd seen Morningside turn into a monster—a vampire complete with fangs. And she dreamed he cast a spell on her, which…vampires didn't do that sort of thing, right? They just bit people. But Morningside didn't bite Cara. He said he was going to hide her. Or something.

He thinks he's got a use for me.

Or she hallucinated it all. Cara looked around the parlor room, wondering just how long it had been since she lost consciousness. Where was Morningside? Surely he wouldn't have just left her there, evil or not. And why would she have fallen asleep right here? Or did she hit her head?

The room was even more shadowy than usual, meaning it must be nighttime still…or again? How long *had* she been out?

She pulled out her phone and found that it wouldn't even turn on. The battery must be completely dead.

Luckily, there was a charging cord near her supplies. Cara crawled over to the wall outlet, her head pounding—lord, she needed either coffee or a solid night's rest—and plugged the phone in.

Nothing. Not even a blink.

Frowning, she flipped the switch on a nearby work light, hoping to illuminate the space.

Nothing.

"The power went out *again*?" she muttered.

If there was no power, where was the light coming from? Cara looked up and noticed the room had a strange glow, like the air itself was luminescent. Weird.

She went back to the craft table, hoping to find a flashlight or something else useful. Her hand rested on the electric drill for a moment. She lifted it, slid the battery pack in, and hit the switch.

Nothing.

Well, this was wrong. The battery pack was fully charged, and the drill should work. Then Cara squinted at the label on the drill. It was Milwaukee brand, but the word emblazoned in red on the side of the drill was backward.

Why was the text *backward*?

This was either an epic-level prank, or something was much more wrong than she thought.

"Do I have a concussion?" she asked out loud.

"What's a concussion?"

At the sound of the voice, Cara spun around, holding the drill like a gun.

Marigold stood there, looking extremely serious, and also extremely solid. More like a real person than a ghost.

"What's happening?" Cara demanded. "Why do things look weird and the power doesn't work?"

"You're not where you were," Marigold said. "I'm sorry, but I had to do it, or else Morningside would have completed his spell and that would have been very bad for you."

"He really did cast a spell? I thought that was a nightmare."

"Oh, yes. He used your true name and everything. Don't you remember?"

"He doesn't know my true name," Cara said absently. "He's using a fake name I gave him."

Marigold's eyes widened. "Really? You're so smart!"

No, she was not. If Cara were smart, she'd be a thousand miles away from this nonsense.

"That must be why his spells didn't take hold of you. I thought it was just the protection you wear."

"Protection?"

Marigold pointed to Mal's necklace. "That. I can feel the power in it. Not enough to keep a monster like Morningside away, but a worthy charm all the same."

"What did happen? Because he was yelling, and then things went dark, but then there was fire…"

"Yes. He was trying to imprison you, and I didn't want that. I stepped in between and pushed you into my prison instead."

"Uh, is that a good thing?"

"Well, he doesn't know you're here. In fact, I don't think he knows my prison exists at all. He's quite single-minded. Every time he's come here, he looks only for the gate."

"Wait, how many times has he come here?"

"Dozens, over the past several decades. Sometimes alone, sometimes with others like him. Always trying to clear the gate and open it up."

"Dozens?" Cara echoed. "Why did he wait so long to hire someone like me to fix the floor then?"

"From what I gather, he didn't know what was required before. But now he does, and I'm afraid it's quite dire for us all."

"Ok, then let me out of this place and I'll go talk to the Salems and they'll fix it."

"I'm not sure I can, and anyway, the fire will be coming soon."

"But we just saw a fire! Didn't it already happen?"

"Yes. And no. In fact, it never stops happening. Oh, there's the smoke. It's beginning."

Marigold looked around worriedly. And yes, there was the first hint of smoke, and a faint crackle from beyond.

"We need to get away from here," Cara said. "Now."

"Yes. You must try to stay with me, Miss Cara. This place is very confusing, and things move around. You must not get lost."

But the smoke was thickening, and when Cara went to grab Marigold's outthrust hand, she missed, and she heard screaming, and then she was swept into fire…

XXVII

MAL WAS SLOWLY LOSING HIS mind. Cara continued to be missing, Halloween continued to creep closer hour by hour, Egan House continued to be on a hellhole, and everything continued to go to shit.

Both cats kept constant watch on the house, giving up any pretense of needing to sleep twenty-three hours a day.

The vampires are there again, Behemoth told the brothers the night of the thirtieth.

"Then we'll go and kill them," Dom said. He was more than ready, having prepared a little anti-vamp kit by the door.

They're just going to flee, like before.

Since the one night they'd caught a vampire on the Egan property, the brothers hadn't been able to actually engage with another one. They ran away at any hint of movement. Normally, Mal would be pleased that some monsters knew enough about the Salems to steer clear. But this wasn't normal. He wanted to dust these things, and they weren't obliging.

"What do they look like?" he asked Behemoth anxiously.

All male. The cat was aware of Mal's fear—that Cara's vanishing act was the result of being turned. *I still have not seen her, alive or otherwise.*

"She's got to be somewhere!" he snarled, wanting to lash out.

"Go practice," Lily told him quietly, looking up from the Magic 8-Ball she was holding. "You're no good to anyone like this."

His mood was crap, and he took it out on her. "Oh, really? Is that what your plastic non-crystal ball advises?"

"Oracles don't offer advice," she said with admirable patience. "They don't tell you what you should do or shouldn't do. They tell you what will occur on a certain timeline if things remain unchanged."

"And on this timeline I'm going to go into the basement and kick a heavy bag for a while?"

She tipped the Magic 8-Ball over. "Signs point to yes."

"I hate you." But he headed for the basement.

"Love you, asshat!" Lily called after him.

Practice wore him down, which was good. Mal needed focus, and fighting always helped him focus. *Think of how to help during the spell. Think of closing the hellhole. Think of doing something for others this time.*

Don't think of dying. Don't think of not dying, and just being trapped for all eternity.

Mal still thought of dying. He wasn't scared of death, not exactly. He could see the upside. Being reunited with his parents and all his family gone before. Not worrying about the mundane crap of life. Never being left behind again.

Still, he was afraid of dying. The actual, painful *your heart just stopped* bit. And if he was really trapped, the painful part might go on forever. Which would suck.

"Better me than them," he muttered, delivering a vicious kick to the practice dummy.

His brothers had lives to live. And so did Cara, if his vision could be trusted.

No one knew where Cara was. But strangely, the floor of the parlor was changing. Mal saw the differences that morning. More of the wooden bits of the summoning circle were complete, more of the floor was ready to go.

It made no sense. The vampires couldn't be doing it, since they were lurking outside. Cara couldn't be doing it, since she was missing.

No one was doing it. Mal even peeked at the camera feed Cara set up. There was no movement at all. Just a few little blips marred the feed, which he assumed was Marigold passing by on her ghostly little way.

He kept going back to the parlor, feeling like Cara was somehow there still. So much of her attention had gone into the floor, into creating this work of art.

How was it possible that she could be missing?

The next day, Halloween came, ready or not.

The Salems were ready. They'd hashed out a plan, sort of. They'd get to the house before sundown to beat Morningside and his vampires to the site. They'd set up their own spellworking apparatus in the parlor room, and Dom would do the actual casting. Having Dom was a huge advantage, since he excelled at magic and could cast spells much more quickly and flexibly than anyone else.

Dom's idea was that they'd only try to interrupt Morningside's own ritual. By killing the vampires and physically disrupting the summoning circle, they could gain a little time to figure out how to close down the hellhole itself without losing a life.

But Mal also intended to be close by, because he was certain that a sacrifice would be needed after all.

Dom was casting. That left Lily, Lex, and Mal to be the anti-vamp squad. They each had stakes, holy water, and a container of lighter fluid and matches. Mal would take point on fighting, with Lex and Lily providing support.

Mal had rifled through the family collection of saints' medals, all gifts from his mom's relatives, who took a distinctly religious approach to demon-slaying. He pulled out the medals for Nicholas, for Gertrude, for Michael. Basically he wasn't being picky. The medals held both the standard blessing, as well as an extra layer of magical protection courtesy of the de Silvas.

Behemoth informed them that he would help as well, but he didn't say what that meant. He sharpened his claws a lot that day, though.

Mal spent a rough couple hours locked in his room, writing. He wrote a letter to his brothers, and one for his abuela and his grandparents. One that would have to serve as a will, not that he possessed anything worth willing. He put them all into envelopes and labeled them, then left them on his desk.

A furious Vinny was the designated survivor, staying at the Salem house with Piewicket and Pumpkin. She didn't like it at all. However, if everything went horribly wrong, someone had to notify the family and feed the cats.

"This is not cool," Vinny growled.

Dom finally talked her into it by pointing out that the only way he'd be able to cast anything was if he knew Vinny was safe.

"Have fun," she said from the porch, looking more punk rock than ever. "I'm going to have Mal give me ass-kicking lessons after this just so I can punch you."

Mal laughed weakly. He wouldn't be coming back.

Vinny kissed Dom hard, and then stomped back into the house.

They walked up the hill. The workers were long gone, most of them having families and lives to get to on Halloween.

So no one was there to stop Mal from opening the door in his own otherworld-y way. He let the others in.

"Remember," Dom said. "No one invite any strangers in the house, even if they look like cops or EMTs or whatever."

"Not our first rodeo, dude," Lex said.

"Yee-haw," Lily added.

They got set up in the parlor room, distributing needed items like candles and crumbled sage. Sundown would occur within minutes.

Mal kept an eye out for Marigold. He didn't see her, but he kept getting hit with waves of anger and sadness.

Which might just be because he was still planning on sacrificing himself in a couple hours.

They're here, Behemoth announced, hissing.

And yes, there they were. Morningside walked into the room, flanked by three more vampires, including…

"Barry," Mal said, smiling at last. At least he could finally kick the shit out of this guy.

Barry grinned back, his teeth sharp and white in a pale face.

There was also a total stranger. Mal asked, "How did you get in here? No one invited you."

"I don't have to be invited into my own home," the new vampire said. "I'm Karl Egan. This is my house."

"You're the client!"

Egan nodded, evidently pleased to be recognized.

"Karl. Didn't he die in the war?" Lily asked.

"I died and was reborn," Egan replied proudly. "And I knew that my father's work could still be completed, even if it took far longer than expected. But then, my father was a rather naive man. He never knew what opening the gate would really mean for the world. For many worlds."

"But Morningside does, because he was probably around in your father's day. It was probably him who put the idea in your father's head in the first place," Mal said.

"And to think you're the dumb one," Morningside told him with a cold smile.

Barry pointed to Mal. "I get to eat him."

Morningside shrugged, barely paying attention. "Feed yourself however you like." He gazed at the humans. "Ah. Introductions are in order. Now, what is your little group exactly? A coven? A cabal?"

"It's technically a limited liability company," Mal said. "Demon-hunting, exorcisms, vampire staking, whatever."

"A family business, I see," Morningside said. "Dominic Salem, Malachy Salem—not East! This must be Alexander Salem. And the young lady?"

"Lily," said Lily coolly. "No relation."

"Hmm." Morningside's eyes gleamed as he looked Lex over. "That means you're the youngest of the family. How interesting. I'd like to know more about you."

Lex lifted up the stake in his hand. "Come closer and find out."

Don't be tough, Lex, Mal thought frantically.

Before he could react, Behemoth jumped into the space between Morningside and Lex.

Morningside looked surprised, and actually gave a small bow to the cat.

"My lord, it is an honor."

I know, Behemoth responded haughtily. *And if you are half as intelligent as you are honored, you'll leave this place immediately. For I claim it.*

"Ah, I can't do that, my lord. I have claimed it first. You see, I've already bound a woman's soul into this circle, just as she put her whole heart into the physical creation of it. It seems such a shame to waste our efforts."

"Cara," Mal said, his heart freezing up. "Where is she?"

"Oh, I put her somewhere safe. A special spot in the otherworlds just large enough to accommodate her. I'll pull her out when I need her body for my ritual. Her blood will be the final binding to the circle her skill made. Thus the spheres align, and thus her sacrifice will glorify Netjerunakht."

"What's the deal?" Lex asked. "Prince Networknews gets the profits on the Riimaran side and you get them on this side? Is that like a fifty-fifty split?"

Morningside's face went stony. "Do not mock the Prince of Riimara, for his subjects will soon be here."

How boring. Behemoth punctuated his opinion by flicking his tail and spraying pungent urine over the gorgeous, shining floor.

"What are you doing?" Morningside yelled. He grabbed Barry by the arm. "Clean that up!"

"I'm not a damn janitor."

"You exist because it amused me to turn you," Morningside snarled. "Now clean the circle. It must be pure for the ritual."

Barry took one step forward, which was as far as Mal was willing to let him go. He sidestepped into the otherworlds just far enough to catch Barry by surprise—

—and saw Marigold standing in the doorway—

—and Mal popped back into the real world right in front of Barry, surprising the newbie vamp. The fight was short and brutal, and not really fair. Mal had far more training and more experience than Barry, who was a bit clumsy, even with the preternatural gifts of being a vampire.

Mal staked him seconds later, and Barry looked aghast, right before he started to disintegrate.

Morningside didn't blink at the loss of one soldier. He ordered Egan to take care of the annoying humans, since Lex and Lily were already advancing with holy water at the ready. Morningside then went for Dom himself.

Mal rushed to block the vampire's path to his brother, slipping into the otherworlds again with the intention of confusing Morningside or at least getting him into a weak position between him and Dom.

But the moment he slid into the shadowy, nearby otherworld, a small hand slipped into his.

Marigold.

"Malachy," she said urgently. "Please listen. Your Cara is lost in the bad part of the house."

At the word *Cara,* his plan for fighting went poof.

"Can you show me how to get there?" he asked the ghost.

"Come with me! It's easier my way, especially now that the gate is so…busy." She gestured to the indistinct shapes of the humans and vampires engaged in separate fights in the room. Mal watched the figures as if in a fog —Lex and Lily had advantage of numbers, but Egan was way older and more wily than Barry had been. And Morningside was more than a match for Dom.

Then two green eyes gleamed right through the fog. *Go find her.*

Mal nodded to Behemoth, then let Marigold lead him into a weird, twisted version of Egan House, almost the same as the real world one, but not quite. This one showed flashes of pictures on the walls, and furniture that appeared to be solid until Mal looked directly at a piece. Then it would blink out. Were they just Marigold's memories manifesting? Or was time bending more than usual this close to the hellhole?

They climbed insubstantial stairs, and Mal reached the room where they'd first seen Marigold. He walked to the ornate carved door with the mirror set into it.

"Open it," Marigold said.

"This doesn't go anywhere." But he turned the knob anyway. He'd see a brick wall, nothing else.

Beyond, he saw no bricks, only smoke and flame. "*Madre…*" he muttered. When he'd first seen this door in the real world, he wondered why they kept it. Now he knew that it was probably bound into the house by a lot more than nails and caulk. This door, with its carvings and the mirrored inset, existed on multiple planes, a doorway in more ways than one.

For example, right now, it appeared to lead to yet more house…even though no such house existed in the world Mal called home.

"How is this…there's nothing on the other side of this door. It's outside! It's empty air," he said. But there was house there now, a burning house.

"I told you it was the bad part." Marigold faced the inferno, her black eyes reflecting the flames beyond.

"How is that possible? It's not even there, but it's there, and it's still on fire?"

"It's always right now," Marigold said, emphasizing each word. "Here, in this place, it is always the moment I die."

XXVIII

MAL WATCHED THE SMOKE AND flames, his heartbeat already spiking as panic took hold. The scene was so similar to his vision that he checked his clothes for errant sparks and ash.

"And that's where Cara is?" he asked, really hoping it was not.

The ghost nodded gravely. "She's lost in there. I hate this part. Every time."

"I can see why." On a sudden impulse, Mal slipped off one of the bracelets he'd shoved on. He gave it to Marigold, who now seemed as solid and as real as any human. "Here. It's St. Nicholas."

"Santa?" she asked, putting the bracelet on and tightening the cord around her tiny wrist.

"That's one of his jobs, yeah. But he's also a patron of children."

"I can feel the blessing in it." Marigold smiled, trying to be brave. "We should go. I can help lead you, but Cara is lost, and the house doesn't always stay the same. The mirrors are especially bad."

Marigold wasn't kidding. This mirror world was a labyrinth, with a hundred doors and strange rooms and the constant cloud of thick smoke obscuring his line of sight, making it impossible to get a handle on the layout of this sick carnival funhouse.

The little ghost did her best, calling out to Cara and shutting doors that led the wrong way. "This isn't it," she said at one door. "This is just another trick. I remember this room from Mother's stories."

"Is that what this place is? Memories?"

"Memories and dreams," Marigold replied. "It's hard to know which sometimes. I think the gate being here makes them all collect and linger. Like a magnet."

And she'd been stuck here too, a little piece of iron with no choice but to hang around.

"I pulled Cara away from Morningside when he tried to trap her, but I only had my own hell to pull her *to*. And then she got upset and ran, and got lost. I think Morningside's spells still have some hold on her. He's a very powerful caster. If he gets to her before we do…"

"I'll find Cara first," Mal promised.

All his noble intentions of being a willing sacrifice fell away. Mal had one goal, and it was to find Cara and keep her safe and alive and healthy for the next eighty years.

Because he loved her.

Mal always sort of assumed that falling in love was a grown-up thing that would involve some choice. See a woman, assess, and decide which way to swipe. But with Cara, there was no conscious decision at all, and there never had been. He never got to choose loving her. He just did. And even though it all happened fast, it still took him a while to understand what had happened. He loved Cara. He couldn't unlove her if he tried. He needed her in his life. Every part of her. Her front side. Her back side. Her no-nonsense, workaholic side. Her drop-it-all-to-rescue-a-kitten side. Her weird, sweet side. The side of her face with the dimple that appeared when she laughed. He definitely needed that side in his life.

And he'd go into literal hellfire to get her. He didn't stop being terrified of the flames, but every time he started to go into flight mode, he thought of Cara, took a breath, and went on.

* * * *

Cara kept bumping into herself. Literally. She'd run down one corridor, evading the smoke and flames on her trail, only to hit a mirrored wall that appeared from nowhere, stopping her in her tracks and usually making her fall to the floor.

Worse, the mirrors were always distorted and discolored, making Cara's reflection into a monster. She screamed at blobby creatures, at faces melting into Dali-like horrors, at long dangling arms and short stubby legs, only to realize they were all just her.

Eventually, her throat went raw and her eyes dried out. The screaming and crying stopped as her terror drained into exhaustion.

She hadn't had a sip of water in days. Nor a clear breath.

She was dying.

She had to be dying.

Why else was she lost in this broken world, her vision fracturing and her memories fading? Cara's feet keep circling through endless corridors and rooms, and her mind kept circling back to the floor of the parlor. Even within this nightmare, she dreamed of working, patiently assembling the wooden pieces and sanding and polishing the design until it was there, complete and shining and reflecting her face in the wood grain.

As if she put her whole soul into it, and there was nothing left for her body.

Cara knew she was slowing down, weakening. Sometimes she just stood at an intersection of the house, frozen, not knowing where to go. She'd pick a direction at random, but nothing ever changed. There was always fire crackling, ready to consume her if she stopped to rest.

She hung her head, her dirty hair falling in front of her face. What was she even fighting for? She had no reason to live. No one who cared about her. No one who would even try to get her out of this hell.

"Cara!"

Confused, she looked up.

And saw Mal.

Before Cara could take another ragged breath, she was in Mal's arms, being lifted until her feet dangled above the burning floor.

"*Madre de Dios*, I found you," he said, his voice rough. "No one knew where you were. We thought you took off. But then Marigold…"

Cara smiled at the little girl. "She dragged you along too?"

"To find you and bring you out of here, yeah. And we have to hurry. I don't know how much time we've spent in this little hell pocket, but everyone is downstairs now, and we've got to get there before the wrong spell gets cast."

"I'm not sure I can get out the way you came in," Cara said. She winced as she felt something pulling on her, like a magnet, but for her very being.

"What's wrong?"

"I can feel some sort of…connection, like a rope or a chain that's yanking on me. I think it's Morningside."

"Undoubtedly," Marigold said. "That's why he tried to imprison you in the first place, to have you at hand tonight. He's calling you back. Even though I was able to divert your path to here, the connection must be very strong."

Mal looked grim. "Then we keep Cara way from him, whatever it takes."

Ignoring Mal's pronouncement, Marigold stepped to Cara, who knelt down to be on the same level as the ghost.

"Miss Cara, I once possessed you when my presence was summoned. This time, it is your presence that is being summoned. Will you let me possess you once more? It may be our only chance."

"Do you think it will confuse Morningside's spell?" Cara asked, puzzled.

"Allow me to merge with you, and all will become clear."

"Ok," Cara said. "Let's try."

"Say my name," Marigold told her.

"Marigold Edith Egan," Cara said formally, "I give you permission to possess me."

The little girl's form wavered, becoming much less substantial. She took a step forward, as if she intended to walk right into Cara.

And then she *did* walk right into Cara, their forms blending. Cara felt a shiver as Marigold's spirit settled over her own.

"You ok?" Mal asked nervously.

Cara didn't respond, too focused on the inward conversation with Marigold, a melding of minds.

And yes, everything became clear.

"Cara? Are you all right?" Mal put out his hands, helping her to her feet.

She nodded, feeling a new resolve. "Yes, I understand what needs to happen now."

"Which is what? Let's get out of this place and you can explain."

Cara felt the pull again. She said, "Morningside is still trying to call me back to him. He's at the point in his spell where he needs my presence, and my soul."

Mal's hands tightened around her shoulders. "It's ok. Just resist it, and I'll help you."

She smiled at Mal, standing up on her toes to give him a kiss. "That's the catch, Malachy Salem. I don't want to resist."

XXIX

Even while Mal had Cara literally in his hands, she seemed to fade, and then was pulled backward rapidly into…nothing. He grabbed for her but was too slow. Like his vision, but worse because it was real.

He stood alone in a hell of smoke and flickering red fire, and everything he tried to do right had gone wrong.

He had lost Cara.

Mal hated losing people he loved.

His howl echoed through more worlds than he knew about, but afterward he was still alone.

Cara was gone, Marigold was gone. It was just him.

"Morningside," Mal growled.

Cara said the vampire was calling to her.

Which meant that she was going to join him.

Mal turned around, ready to race to the door that Marigold originally led him to. But that was ages ago, after a thousand twists and turns in this mirror world where nothing made sense.

If only he could just sidestep into the real world, like he…wait, what if he could?

Mal concentrated and slid into the amorphous in-between, the thin barrier that separated one world from the next. And this time he stayed there for a moment, searching.

He sensed the hellhole almost immediately. It was so powerful that it practically had its own gravitational pull, no matter which world you were in.

Mal moved toward the hellhole, reasoning that if he stepped out into the real world just at the boundary of it, he'd find the summoning circle Morningside was desperate to activate.

The hellhole seemed to rumble and glow as he approached it, like a volcano ready to erupt.

Then Mal felt something else, little lines pulling him toward other sparks of light. With a shock, he recognized the connections with his own brothers. And a little thinner, to Lily. A black metal chain to Behemoth, punctuated with locks.

And finally, new but blazing, to Cara.

Like a predator tracking prey, Mal stepped out into the real world.

Right next to the summoning circle.

He had no idea how long he'd been gone. Lex and Lily had been fighting the vampire Karl Egan, but now there was just ash near their feet, and both of them stood looking wiped out but still wary.

Lex's eyes widened on seeing Mal emerge from nowhere, but he gestured for Mal to get out of the way. Good advice, since Dom and Morningside were engaged in some sort of mental battle. They stood on opposite sides of the marquetry floor, their attention locked on each other and no one else. Behemoth prowled the circumference of the circle, hissing and yowling.

Where is she? the cat demanded when Mal appeared.

"I don't know! She got sucked out of wherever we were because she said Morning—"

Then Cara flickered into sight, exactly between the two casters.

"Cara!" Mal screamed.

She didn't react to that, even to turn her head and look at him.

Mal tensed, ready to jump into the circle and grab her out of there.

Hold still.

Mal glared at the cat. "Cara needs help."

You need to let her act as she wishes.

Before Mal could respond, the vampire raised its arms above its head. "There she is. My darling girl who's going to put her heart and soul into this gate. Come here," he ordered Cara.

She swiveled her head partway, giving a disdainful glance to Morningside. "If you're going to break a girl's heart and soul, you should at least know her name."

"Cara Ann Michaels!" he shouted.

She laughed and shook her head.

Now, Behemoth ordered. *Distract him.*

Mal was moving before the cat finished. Morningside, focused on why Cara was eluding him, reacted a little too late when Mal attacked.

The two of them ended up in a tangle, wrestling for some advantage on the other. A candle was knocked over, then another. The flames suddenly brightened.

Mal pulled out the stake he'd stashed away, but Morningside anticipated that and knocked it away. The vampire was by far the toughest Mal had ever faced. Older, smarter, stronger.

Lex rushed up, throwing something toward them. A second later, Morningside let out an earsplitting shriek as holy water rained down, scorching the vampire's flesh.

Mal took a breath during that moment of respite.

Cara still stood directly in the center of the ornate circle.

"Dominic Salem," she said, her voice clear and remarkably stable. "You know what spell you need to cast. To close the portal requires a sacrifice, and I am that sacrifice. I was afraid before, but now I am willing to face my fate. Now I understand what my sacrifice means."

Dom looked once at Mal, his expression haunted, then refocused on Cara. "I will. Be ready when the portal opens. If you hesitate, a lot of bad could come pouring out."

"Have faith," Cara said, pulling on a chain around her neck, then touching a silk cord bracelet on her wrist.

Mal wanted to stop her, convince her there was another way. This was supposed to be *his* big surprise, damn it.

Then Morningside sunk fangs into Mal's arm and he nearly passed out.

He saw a streak of blackness rush toward him.

Behemoth.

The cat's claws shredded half of the vampire's face, and the fangs retracted.

Mal summoned every ounce of survival instinct and lashed out hard at Morningside, knocking the vampire to the floor, just outside the border of the circle.

Lily called out, and Mal caught what she threw to him —a silver cross. He pressed it into Morningside's chest, and the creature's flesh started smoking.

Dom was speaking, his voice unnaturally loud. Mal looked over in horror when the marked boundary of the circle erupted into a wall of thin green flames. Dom wasn't inside it anymore, but Cara was.

No.

Mal tried to stand. He'd get to her, he'd pull her to safety.

The vampire dragged him down, still as tough as when this started. Mal struggled, even as his spine tingled and his skin prickled. Like a lightning storm was coming.

Dom's ritual hit the crucial point, and even Mal felt the energy level spike as the long-suppressed gate was wrenched open with the magic of Dom's spell.

Cara put her hands into the vortex that opened in the center of the circle.

And then she stepped into it.

Mal was sure his heart stopped.

Behemoth raced toward Dom, who spoke a final phrase just as the cat raked his claws across the border of the circle, disrupting the flow of magic. The green flames flickered and died as the energy dissipated into the atmosphere with a loud boom.

Lily screamed as the wax of several candles ignited at once, little supernovas all around the circle. Morningside also reacted to the presence of living, licking flames, letting go of Mal and looking around for a place to flee.

The vortex pulsed once, and Mal tensed, fearing what might come out of it.

He saw Cara, her red hair swirling around her head like a halo of fire. Her eyes were closed.

She returns, Behemoth called exultantly. *Reach for her!*

Mal reached out, taking hold of Cara, pulling her from the closing portal into the world where she should be.

They crashed backward onto the wooden surface of the parlor floor. Mal kept his arms around her to cushion the impact. "Cara, I've got you. It's ok."

He looked up and saw that where the portal had been, there was only a dwindling spot, like everlasting night being compressed to a pinprick…and then nothing.

"It's over," he said. "Cara, it's ok."

She lay there, unresponsive. Not even breathing.

"Cara!" Mal shoved aside the terror that wound up his spine and bent over Cara, ripping her shirt aside to expose her skin.

Mal's physical training included CPR, and he knew that he needed to be her lungs and her heart, counting until her body caught the rhythm and could work on its own again.

Two breaths. A sharp hit to her chest, pushing down to jumpstart her system.

He waited. Nothing. Repeat. He'd do this forever, until he had no more breath to give.

Then Cara coughed, smoke curling past her lips as she took a rattling inhalation.

Relief flooded through Mal. "Cara, you're breathing."

He stared at her chest, now rising and falling. He saw that a faint bruise was spreading over the spot where he'd jammed his palms on her ribs.

She took a few more ragged, rough breaths, and none of them had any more smoke in them.

"Mal," Cara whispered, her eyes fluttering open. "You're supposed to ask before you kiss someone. You trilobite."

XXX

EGAN HOUSE WAS BURNING AGAIN, and this time no one would be able to save it.

Cara's impressions of those last few moments were hazy. Mal picked her up and got her out of the house, the others close behind.

Smoke nearly suffocated them by the time they reached the door and got out to the lawn.

"Back home," Dom ordered, his face streaked with soot and his voice scratchy. "We need to get behind our wards. I think Morningside is still out there."

Cara wanted to protest that she could walk, but by the time she got the words out, Mal was setting her down onto the green lawn, wet with cold dew. She lay back, soaking up the moisture from the ground and the starlight from the clear sky. She inhaled, so happy to have lungs. Lungs were great.

Soft fur brushed the side of her face. Mr. B nudged her insistently.

"I'm fine, I'm fine," she told the cat. "Glad to see you."

Vinny rushed out of the house, Piewicket and Pumpkin on her heels. "I called 911 when I saw the fire. What happened?" She launched herself at Dom, demanding to know if he was ok.

"We're all ok. Ish. The gate is closed. We killed a couple vamps. Did anyone stake Morningside?" he asked, looking around.

Everyone exchanged glances and shook their heads. Mal asked, "Maybe he got torched?"

"He must have got away," Dom said. "We have to assume he did."

Lily raised a hand. "Also, did that dude seem unhealthily interested in Lex?"

"Ugh, yeah." Lex shivered. "What a creeper. It'd be creepy even if he wasn't a vampire, but now it's extra creepy."

"Even if he's still around, he can't get to you," Dom said. "Not through our wards. And we'll—"

The howl of sirens interrupted them. Two firetrucks raced up the hill, and an ambulance and cop car stopped in front of the Salem house.

"There's no one alive up there!" Vinny shouted, delivering the most urgent fact to the EMT in the driver's seat. "We all made it out."

Cara looked the worst of them all, so the EMTs treated her first, cleaning a burn and wrapping up several scrapes she didn't even remember getting.

Hallihan took a statement from Mal. She clearly did not believe one word of Mal's story about some persons unknown starting a fire in a haunted house on Halloween night, but let it go because, in her words, "What else can I do about this mess?"

"You could have a beer," Mal said. "I know I need one."

"I'm on duty, and you all look like you're about to collapse in three minutes." Hal looked to Cara. "You ok?"

Cara nodded. "Yeah. I think I finally am."

The cop regarded her quizzically for a moment, then nodded. "All right then. Do me a solid and everyone stay out of trouble until at least New Year's."

"Yes, ma'am," Mal said with a grin.

The cops and the EMTs left. Cara sat on the lawn again, Pumpkin in her lap, mewing and pushing his fuzzy head into her belly. She watched the haunted house go up in flames. Mal sat right behind her and put his arms around her.

Lily sat down not far away, and Piewicket jumped in her lap. "We should get marshmallows," she said.

"No roasting marshmallows over hellholes," Dom said. "That's the first rule of hellholes."

"Yeah, but it's closed now."

Dom shook his head. "The gate Egan tried to build is closed. But the hellhole—the actual locus of power—is still there."

"Sounds like we'll have to stick around then," Mal said with a yawn.

"I hope Marigold isn't suffering." Cara didn't like that idea at all.

Mal tightened his arms around her. "If everything went right with Dom's spell, she's not. And I gave her a medal of St. Nicholas, one of the spelled ones. Who knows? It might help."

She plucked at the few bracelets still on his wrist. "You had two?"

"What?"

Cara tapped one of the medals, hanging from a red cord. "St. Nick. Right here."

"Oh. That means I actually gave her…" He flipped quickly through the remaining ones. "Gertrude. Huh."

"Who's Gertrude?"

"Patron saint of cats."

"That should help a lot," Lex noted dryly.

Piewicket mewed, and Mal said, "Good point. Protection can take forms you don't expect."

Cara was still focused on the display at the top of the hill, picturing the destruction it would leave in the morning, the charred remains of the house.

Mal bent his head to her ear. He said quietly, "I'm sorry the fire burned everything. All your work. Your dad's tools."

"I'll miss the tools. On the other hand, I do still have my dad. Or I will pretty soon, with good behavior." Cara bit her lip. "There was a lot about that house that was beautiful." The paneling, the carvings, the glorious parlor floor. "Unique. I'll never get to be in a place like that again."

"Sorry."

"It's ok. I don't want to be in a place like that again. It was pure evil. It tried to eat my soul. I like my job, but not *that* much."

"What are you going to do now?"

"I'm not sure."

"I got an idea."

He stood up, pulling her up with him. He told the others that he and Cara had some important something or other to discuss—he didn't even bother to make it sound plausible. Then he took her inside the house and upstairs.

"I think you're overestimating my energy level," she said when he started taking off her shirt.

"No, I'm correctly estimating it. We smell like smoke and we both need a shower, and that's all I'm after."

"Oh, that's all?"

"For now."

That was in fact all he did want, and a little while later, they lay on his bed, naked, clean, and lazy.

"This is nice," Cara said sleepily.

"What is? Lying around? Getting pawed at by me?"

"You're not pawing at me."

"Crap. Oversight." He started pawing at her, making her giggle.

Mal kissed her. "You should stay here."

"Tonight? You bet. I can't muster up the energy to move."

"Not just tonight. I mean stay here. With me." He propped himself up, gazing at her seriously. "And then Pumpkin gets a solid kittenhood with good role models and stuff."

"You're bringing the cat into this?"

"I'm going to bring everything into this if it'll convince you. Would seduction work?"

She smiled, but pushed against his chest to forestall any seduction. "Mal, what are you suggesting? I can't be like Vinny, learning magic to fight vampires and demons. Or like you, kicking ass and taking names. I'm a carpenter. I'm good at what I do, which is not demon-hunting."

"Hey, hey. Slow down there, girl. I'm not saying change jobs. I don't want you to do anything you don't want. But can't we try this? I really like you, Cara."

"Are you serious about this?"

"Yes. For once, I'm serious. Long-distance relationships have been known to work. You could stay here when you're not on a job. And when you are on a job, just expect a lot of sexting."

"Mal!"

"Look, before, when I said I really like you. It's not true."

Her stomach clenched. She knew things were too good to be true. "What?"

"I don't like you. I love you, Cara. It took a while for me to figure it out because I'm a dumbass, but it's true. I love you."

"You're not a dumbass. You're just a trilobite, sometimes."

"I don't have a good track record with relationships," he warned her. "I thought that if I never needed anyone, I couldn't lose them. But I did nearly lose you, and that was way worse than never having you. So let me try."

"I'll let you try," she said, "but only because I'm pretty sure I'm in love with you too."

He kissed her nose. "As long as we're both in love with each other, I think we can work out the rest of the details."

Her heart beat a little faster, fluttering in a new and unfamiliar way. What was she feeling?

Oh, yeah. Hope.

Epilogue

A LIGHT LAYER OF SNOW had fallen during the night. Cara peered out onto the porch. A track of cat paws was the only thing interrupting the veil of white.

She looked up to the hill across the street. The snow-fall had covered the worst of the devastation. The house had collapsed into itself, crushed under its own weight, filling up the basement. Now there was just a mound of charred rubble, obscured by snow.

It was the first week of December, and things had been blissfully calm ever since Halloween. No more vampires, no more ghosts, no more dire predictions from cats about impending doom. Cara had been living at the Salem house ever since Halloween, with the exception of a week to visit her mom.

Things were all going shockingly well. She had two more jobs lined up, beginning after the holidays. Until then, she could focus on the house she was in.

Cara moved to the kitchen, starting a pot of coffee. She had a full day ahead of her.

Pumpkin leapt up onto the kitchen island. The orange cat had grown a lot over the weeks, well-fed and spoiled rotten. Cara kissed the top of his head. "Morning, sweet-heart. You're so cute."

"Thanks." Mal's voice caught her by surprise, and she turned around just in time to get soundly kissed on the mouth.

"Not you, trilobite," she said with a laugh.

"What's happening today? You finished the floor." Mal gestured to the sunlight slanting across the wooden floorboards. The morning glow turned the hues of the woodgrain to amber and honey, warm and homey. Cara had made everyone help her move the furniture last week so she could "tidy up a bit," which meant replacing a dozen broken boards and then sanding and refinishing the whole surface of the first floor.

The smell of orange was in the air, thanks to the oil she used to seal the wood before she waxed it to the soft sheen it had now. She stayed up until one in the morning for five nights in a row, utterly uninterested in lazing around until her latest project was done.

"Pretty nice, huh?" she said, giving the floor a professional once-over.

"Very nice." Mal wasn't looking at the floor as he spoke.

It took Cara a moment to register it—he leered just a bit so she got the hint—and then she laughed. "You doofus. What's for breakfast?"

"I was thinking of making pancakes."

"Mmm, perfect. And then I can get to work on the side of the house. We need to get that done before the real cold sets in."

The fire had completely consumed Egan House, but it hadn't leapt to the supply of new lumber that the workers stored in the shed. After the conflagration, Cara liberated the supplies and even hired Jalen and Reyes to help cart the lumber across the street to the Salem house. No sense in wasting materials, and it seemed unlikely Morningside would ever cut her final check.

An hour later, Cara was up on the scaffolding, hammering at the edging of the window. She was delighted to be working again, to be improving a home with her own hands and her own tools. She especially loved solving a problem.

"Oh, that's what happened. Some idiot put up the waterproofing layer wrong!" she yelled down to Mal, who was assisting. "That's why you kept getting mold in this room, and why all the wood's rotted."

"How can we fix it?" he asked, tipping his head up. Pumpkin mewed in agreement, also looking up. The kitten generally wanted to be in sight of Cara, whether she was in the house or out of it.

"Easy peasy. I'm just going to ditch the old siding, and then we rip off the bad paper and put up a new layer the correct way." She paused. "Might need to reframe under the window. Depends on whether the supports got too much moisture. In fact, I'll reframe anyway, because the new wood is treated to be termite resistant."

"What about that is easy? Or peasy?"

Cara smiled down at him. "Cheer up, Mal. We can get this done in a week!"

Catching movement in the corner of her eye, she looked up at the hill. For as long as she stayed here, a part of her would always be drawn to where Egan House once stood.

Against the white snow-covered hill, a black shape was descending.

"Is that Mr. B?" she asked, pointing.

Mal shielded his eyes with his hand. "Looks like. But he's not alone."

Indeed, the massive black cat was going slowly, accompanied by a small creature with a bright gold coat, like if a palomino decided to turn into a feline.

Cara scrambled down the ladder, curiosity overtaking her.

"Who's our new friend?" Cara asked when they reached the house.

Pumpkin mewed excitedly, giving the new kitten a sniff and then head-bopping it. The newcomer responded enthusiastically, and Mr. B looked on like a proud parent. Pumpkin looked from Cara to the new kitten and back again, virtually demanding that she introduce herself.

She bent down to get a closer look at the little kitten. She was surprised to see that it wore a collar. No, not a collar. Just a silk cord, from which a little enameled decoration was hanging. She lifted it and saw the outline of a saint, with *Gertrude* written underneath.

Cara's jaw dropped.

The kitten mewed and bumped into her hand.

"It's Marigold," Mal said stunned. "But Behemoth says we should call her Goldie."

She picked up the little cat. It looked like a cat, felt like a cat, and purred like a cat. "Well," Cara said, "it's not the weirdest thing I've encountered lately."

"Oh, stick around." Mal smiled. "Things will get so much weirder."

"You promise?"

He gave her a kiss. "Cross my heart."

* * * *

ABOUT THE AUTHOR

Elizabeth Cole is a romance writer with a penchant for history. Her stories draw upon her deep affection for the British Isles, action movies, medieval fantasies, and even science fiction. She now lives in a small house in a big city with a cat, a snake, and a rather charming gentleman. When not writing, she is usually curled in a corner reading...or watching costume dramas or things that explode. And yes, she believes in love at first sight.